AF413503

WEDDED TO HER ENEMY KNIGHT

LISSA MORGAN

Harlequin

HISTORICAL

If you purchased this book without a cover you should be aware that this book is stolen property. It was reported as "unsold and destroyed" to the publisher, and neither the author nor the publisher has received any payment for this "stripped book."

Harlequin® HISTORICAL

ISBN-13: 978-1-335-98375-6

Wedded to Her Enemy Knight

Copyright © 2026 by Lissa Morgan

Recycling programs for this product may not exist in your area.

All rights reserved. No part of this book may be used or reproduced in any manner whatsoever without written permission.

Without limiting the exclusive rights of any author, contributor or the publisher of this publication, any unauthorized use of this publication to train generative artificial intelligence (AI) technologies is expressly prohibited. Harlequin also exercises their rights under Article 4(3) of the Digital Single Market Directive 2019/790 and expressly reserves this publication from the text and data mining exception.

This is a work of fiction. Names, characters, places and incidents are either the product of the author's imagination or are used fictitiously. Any resemblance to actual persons, living or dead, businesses, companies, events or locales is entirely coincidental.

For questions and comments about the quality of this book, please contact us at CustomerService@Harlequin.com.

TM and ® are trademarks of Harlequin Enterprises ULC.

 Harlequin Enterprises ULC
22 Adelaide St. West, 41st Floor
Toronto, Ontario M5H 4E3, Canada
www.Harlequin.com

HarperCollins Publishers
Macken House, 39/40 Mayor Street Upper,
Dublin 1, D01 C9W8, Ireland
www.HarperCollins.com

Printed in U.S.A.

1 2 3 4 5 6 7 8 9 10 HDC 28 27 26 25

"If we were to marry...it wouldn't be for love, naturally. It would be a mutual union, a practical arrangement, of advantage to us both."

Isobel was speaking again, deliberately, yet carefully, as if her thoughts were forming only an instant before the words. "I would keep Mistlecote and you...you would have a wife who would give you heirs...sons... I presume you want them?"

Edmund lifted his gaze to meet hers. "Yes, someday I will require heirs."

"Then why should I not be the one to give you them? I think..." A flush mounted her cheek. "I believe that you feel some sort of...desire toward me...do you not? Why else would you have kissed me...like you did last night?"

"Why indeed!" The bitter inflection was out before Edmund could stop it. He didn't want to desire Isobel. He didn't want to desire anyone. For in the wake of desire, who could tell what might come next? But he would not lie to her, nor to himself. "Yes, I cannot deny that."

Author Note

In my last book, *Alliance with her Renegade Knight*—also set during the Wars of the Roses—I explored the way life went on much the same as usual for ordinary people as they faced social injustice and abuse of their common rights. My hero and heroine's story fitted neatly into that setting as they, too, were of humble birth. In this current book, the tribulations of those higher born provided me with an equally compelling backdrop. Noblemen had to choose sides, and often change sides, resulting in kin fighting kin as well as the enemy, frequently settling old scores and furthering ambitions in the process. Noblewomen were forced, or entered willingly, into political and strategic marriages, while the Lancastrian Queen, Margaret of Anjou, proved far more belligerent than her fragile and pious husband, King Henry VI. The ravages of war, in any period, impact on participants and bystanders alike, and the Wars of the Roses was both long and brutal in this respect. It is within this turbulent arena that the fates of Isobel and Edmund—and their horoscopes too!—become inextricably entwined.

Lissa Morgan hails from Wales but has traveled far and wide over the years, usually in search of the next new job, and always pursuing her love of the past along the way. A history graduate and former archivist, she now works in website design and academia. Lissa lives between the mountains and the sea in rugged North West Wales, surrounded by medieval castles that provide the perfect inspiration for her writing—the best job of all! Visit her at lissamorgan.com, Facebook.com/lissamorganhistoricalromance and X @lissamorganauth.

Books by Lissa Morgan

Harlequin Historical

Alliance with Her Renegade Knight
An Alliance with His Enemy Princess
The Welsh Lord's Convenient Bride

The Warriors of Wales

The Warrior's Reluctant Wife
The Warrior's Forbidden Maiden

Visit the Author Profile page at Harlequin.com.

For Marie

Prologue

June 1460

Edmund Deverell leaned on the rail and watched the town of Calais, with its isolated but stubbornly entrenched population of English colonists, slowly recede into the morning sea mist. The cog he'd boarded half an hour earlier belonged to the Earl of Warwick, Captain of Calais, who was standing now in the forecastle, his eyes fixed seaward. With the Earl sailed his father, the Earl of Salisbury, and Edward of March, eldest son of the Duke of York.

Edmund was in illustrious, if attainted company. Richard of York had been declared a traitor after the rout at Ludlow nine months ago and had been in exile in Ireland ever since. His sons too had fled the realm but now the time was ripe to return to England and seize the throne from the weak King Henry of Lancaster. Behind their vessel sailed two more cogs filled with soldiers, warhorses and weapons to aid York in his bid for the throne of England.

Like his exalted fellow sailors, Edmund was returning to England to claim something. Not a throne but his home, his lands and his inheritance, and the powerful Earl of Warwick, who had become his friend as well as his lord, had pledged to help him.

Anticipation sent a thrill down Edmund's spine. Before noonday, he'd be stepping onto English soil for the first time in ten years, apart from that one sad and secret journey home after the battle of Castillon to tell his mother of Hugh's death.

The loss of his brother had been hard but Edmund couldn't deny he himself had done well out of war. It was surprising how quickly a mercenary could amass money if he had nothing to spend it on, apart from the food to keep himself and his horse alive. And how easy if he had no conscience to fight for France—the enemy of England—to kill one's countrymen, to oppose one's king. But then, why should he be loyal to a country that had disowned him? To a king who had destroyed his family?

He *had* minded the killing of Englishmen in the beginning, but after Hugh's death he'd fought his foes all the harder, and among the French had earned the nickname *L'Invincible*. But then when Mariette had broken both his heart and his pride, he'd learned that love was not invincible any more than he was, that it could destroy a man where weapons of steel could not.

As the sea lapped quietly and time washed backwards, Edmund asked himself what he'd asked a thousand times already. Had it all been his fault? Had he failed his wife somehow? He'd never know now she was dead, killed by the sordid life she'd chosen instead of the better one he'd tried to make for her, for them both. He hadn't understood it then and he understood it even less now.

The sound of footsteps, firm and sure, came to his ears and, turning, he saw Warwick walking towards him.

'Not long now, Edmund.'

Edmund shook his head, blinking salty sea spray from his eyes. It had been four years since Mariette's death, seven since Hugh had been killed. Why now, when he was finally leaving, did France reach out to him and bury her claws in his soul, as if to hold him forever in his sorrow?

'No, my lord,' he replied. 'Not long.'

The wind picked up suddenly, the boats that had rowed them out loosed their tug ropes, and the French coast gradually disappeared from sight. Edmund shivered, drew his cloak tighter around him, and went to the forecastle to look towards England. Just twenty or so miles, a few short hours if the weather stayed fair, the wind held its course, and the sea remained calm. The sun rising in the east behind their fleet cast a golden rippling path across the grey waters ahead.

It was an omen, surely, lighting their way to glory. France was lost to England forever and the English king, stricken by its loss, was reputed to have lost his wits too. York was in the ascent, Lancaster was in disarray, and England was embroiled in civil war—a war that would provide the opportunity to take revenge on his enemy at last.

The French had a saying: *Tout vient à point à qui sait attendre.* All things come to he who waits. Well, he'd waited long enough. Vengeance was sweet, they said, and God willing he'd soon savour its taste.

Chapter One

The twenty-fifth day of October 1460

'But…surely this cannot be!'

Isobel Calvert stared at the letter in her hand, outrage flooding her heart. 'I will never relinquish our manor to this Yorkist! Now my father is dead…' Her voice threatened to break. 'My brother is lord of Mistlecote, not this cur Deverell, whoever he be.'

The messenger enlightened her. 'Sir Edmund is a knight in the service of the Earl of Warwick, newly come from Calais.'

She looked up at him. 'Then he can go back there! I refuse, absolutely, to leave my home, not now, not ever.'

His face remained impassive as he replied. 'It matters not what you wish, Mistress Calvert. This is a command, signed and sealed by the Earl of March himself, heir to the Duke of York.'

Isobel recognised the seal, of course. Richard of York had been overlord of these parts until he was declared traitor and all his possessions in England forfeit after he fled the King's army at Ludford Bridge last year. Now they were returning to regain all that they'd lost, Edward of March and Warwick here already, laying the path that would lead England once more into war with itself.

'Is it lawful to seize the lands of a loyal subject, one who fights for his rightful king?' she said, giving the messenger a venomous glare. 'Edward of March and his father are traitors, since they fight not for but *against* our anointed sovereign!'

She looked down at the parchment again, the name Edmund Deverell swimming in and out of focus. Deverell… Deverell. She knew the name, surely?

'Henry of Lancaster is captive of the Earl of Warwick, mistress.' The man's tone was shockingly irreverent. 'His wife and son fled for their lives to Wales.'

'Is Warwick so powerful then that he dares to depose the King? Is that what he intends to do? Unseat King Henry and put Richard on the throne?'

The messenger glanced towards the door, clearly eager to be away. 'As to that, I know not. I have merely been charged to inform you that Sir Edmund Deverell is on his way here to take possession of this manor and hold it in fee of the Lord Edward.'

Crushing the parchment into a ball, Isobel threw it at the man's feet. 'You can take this abomination back from whence it came and inform Sir Edmund that my gates are closed to him—indefinitely!'

The man shrugged, left the parchment where it was, and took his leave. Isobel sank into a chair at the table, fury burning behind her eyes and a sense of helplessness closing around her heart. If only her brother were here…

At first, when the news of the defeat at Northampton had come three months ago, she'd refused to believe her brother had been slain by the Yorkists, just as her father had been a year ago at Blore Heath. Thousands of Lancastrians had died at Northampton, it was said, and many more were drowned in the River Nene as they fled the carnage of the battlefield.

Even so, Isobel had told herself Tom was simply missing, and making his slow way home, or at worst a prisoner. But the months had passed, and he hadn't come, and now with this latest blow hope began to desert her. If her brother still lived, she would have heard *something* from him, surely, after all this time?

Rising to her feet, she flung the door open and called for the steward. He came so quickly that he must already have been on his way to her chamber after seeing their unwelcome visitor off.

'Has he gone?'

Ned had been steward of Mistlecote for nearly forty years and suddenly, as he replied with a grim face, he looked his age. 'For now anyway.'

Isobel picked up the parchment from the floor and smoothed it out. 'Do you know a man called Edmund Deverell, Ned?'

'He is the son of Roger Deverell, the man your father fought a trial by battle with over this manor.'

'Of course! I knew the name was familiar. I remember the incident but have forgotten the exact cause…'

Ned, despite his advanced age, had a better memory. 'Mistlecote was originally the Deverells' estate, gifted to them by William the Bastard in return for helping him conquer England four hundred years ago.'

'But they lost it to us?'

Her steward nodded. 'More than half a century ago, when King Richard was deposed and your grandfather supported the claim of Henry Bolingbroke to the throne.'

Isobel cast her mind back to the trial by combat, ten

years ago. She'd not been present, of course, being but a girl of fourteen, and besides it had been played out at Windsor. 'And my father killed Roger Deverell. What happened to his family?'

'The two sons were banished from the realm and Lady Deverell retired to a nunnery—the White Ladies at Brewood, I believe. I know not if she is still there, or even if she is still living.'

Isobel nodded. 'Poor lady,' she said, but didn't linger there. After all, she didn't know the unfortunate woman or her family, come to that. In fact, she'd forgotten all about them when her father had returned victorious from Windsor with the matter decided once and for all. They'd disappeared, never to return as far as she knew.

But now, one of them at least was back!

She handed the parchment to Ned. 'This is a command from Edward of March to hand Mistlecote over to one of those Deverell sons, who it seems is banished no more.'

The steward read it and his face blanched. 'Master Tom has been disinherited?'

'It seems so, doubtless for being a loyal Lancastrian!' Isobel sank down into her chair once more. 'But the knave will never get his hands on Mistlecote. When he comes, we'll bar the gates to him and hold until Tom returns.'

'Hold with what?' Ned frowned. 'Most of the men went to Northampton with your brother—' he crossed himself '—and as yet not a single man has returned.'

'They can't all have been killed, surely?'

'I suspect those of the common soldiery have gone back to their villages, believing the Lancastrian cause lost with the King. The men of this manor…' Ned paused, then continued gravely. 'They would have been fighting at Master

Tom's side, and many might well have died or else been taken prisoner.'

Isobel closed her eyes for a moment, the grief in the steward's voice as he reverted to the childhood term for her brother—now Lord Calvert and not Master Tom at all—wrenching her heart. But she too must face reality, no matter how bitter it was.

'Exactly how many men do we have left, Ned?'

'Eleven, and that's mainly the grooms and servants, not trained soldiers, and none of them fit to withstand a siege, for that is what it will be if you close the gates to Deverell.'

A siege! But Ned was right. They had no fighting men to repulse an attack. They might hold for a while, but what would happen when the food ran out? Clasping her hands together, Isobel felt her whole world begin to topple, even as Mistlecote's walls might topple very soon.

Mistlecote. Her home. Her haven. From the age of twelve, she had taken her mother's place as mistress here, looking after her father and her younger brother. That was all she'd ever wanted to do, all she knew how to do, a role that had become as familiar as it was comfortable.

Now it seemed all that was about to change and her life would never be the same again. If Tom truly was dead, she was the only Calvert left, and for that reason alone she would not give Mistlecote up without a fight. She'd keep Edmund Deverell out even if she died in the attempt.

'Nevertheless, close the gates we will.' Isobel nodded, her mind made up. 'God willing Tom is alive…and if… *when* he returns home he will find us still here to welcome him.'

The steward looked at her doubtfully but he nodded too, albeit with misgiving writ clearly on his face. 'As you wish, mistress. With luck, and if we prepare adequately, we might just hold out long enough…'

That 'might' sent a shiver down Isobel's spine. If the flower of the Lancastrian army was slain, many of the great lords of the land with them, the King himself a captive and the Queen and their only son fled to Wales, what hope was there that Tom would return, in truth? And what hope had *she* to withstand what was coming?

Ned bowed and, placing the parchment on the table, left her alone. Silence filled the chamber, broken from sounds down below. Ominous sounds of the gates being barred, Ned's voice issuing her orders, the excited and fearful chatter of those ill-suited to face a siege, however short it might prove to be.

The manor wasn't a castle, for all its crenellated towers, high walls and gates of studded oak. The valley it sat in was flat and lush, no high mountains or thick forests to deter or confuse an enemy. The river that curved around three sides of it was narrow and shallow, hardly deep or wide enough to stop a man on a tall horse.

And she'd just bet that this Edmund Deverell rode a tall horse. Just as all the Yorkists rode tall and arrogant in their saddles now that their star was in the ascent. She tried to picture him but her mind conjured up only a faceless monster bent on stealing her home, perhaps her life too.

Well, she'd made her choice. She would stand tall too, for as long as she could, on her own two feet, with her handful of house servants at her back. And pray that determination alone would be sufficient. If it proved otherwise…well, she would face that too with all the courage she possessed.

Edmund reined in his horse on the crest of the hill and looked down at the valley stretching before him. The river ran through it like a silver thread and oak trees climbed the valley sides, their leaves already turned from green to red-gold. On the low ground, stubble indicated the late harvest of corn and barley, and lazy smoke drifted skywards from chimneys, marking out the farmsteads dotted here and there. In the distance, a bull bellowed, the sound carrying on the light breeze.

But it was the house in the distance that held his attention. Built on the site of an old Saxon court, its golden walls gleamed and its great tower stood proud at the northern corner. Behind the ramparts, against the south wall, the manor house itself, the sun catching its mullioned windows and tiled roofs.

A lump rose into Edmund's throat. He'd never seen Mistlecote but he had pictured its beauty many times in his mind. Now, on this first day of November in which a mellow autumn still lingered, it shimmered like a fairytale palace, surpassing even his dreams. France was beautiful, of course, but because he'd been in constant battle there, he'd soon ceased to notice anything of beauty at all—until Mariette had come into his life.

But her beauty had been all on the surface. Underneath had lurked a woman who had shamed him and betrayed him, a woman he'd never really known. Then beauty had ceased to exist for him, but now he discovered that there *was* still beauty in the world. The beauty of England and the beauty of Mistlecote—more glorious perhaps because he had not once stepped inside its gates.

Just then his sergeant rode up beside him, his voice with its thick Bordeaux accent breaking the stillness. 'The bridge over the river is unmanned, Edmund, but the gates beyond are closed. Think you they mean to bar us entry?'

Alain Vachier had been with him since he'd left Bordeaux, first as his squire, now as his second in command, both of them finding a place with the Earl of Warwick's garrison at Calais.

'I am certain of it.' Edmund squinted against the sun. 'This is a Lancastrian house, after all,' he added, 'or rather it was.'

With the death of John Calvert at Blore Heath last September, and now the probable death of his heir, Mistlecote would become a Yorkist house, regardless of what its current occupants thought. The woman of the house, Blanche Calvert, had died long ago but there was a daughter, and about her something would have to be done.

He had no quarrel with Isobel Calvert, who he knew to be unmarried, though well past marrying age, being a full four and twenty. If she were pious, he would suggest she enter some convent, provide her with a dowry even, perhaps speak to his mother, who was Prioress of the White Ladies at Brewood, and secure a place for her there.

The recent visit he'd paid his mother, en route here, had been almost more painful than the previous one, when he'd gone to tell her of Hugh's death. Then she'd been beside herself with grief but she'd still been herself. The woman he'd left a few days earlier had not been his mother at all.

Constance Deverell had greeted him politely, wished him well, and then vanished, serenely enough, into another world, her life devoted wholly to God, her former life forgotten. Or perhaps she'd chosen not to remember it, because it was easier that way to bear the losses of her husband and her youngest son. Easier not to contemplate the death too of her eldest son, which might come one day, if this war continued.

Gathering his reins, Edmund touched his heels to his courser's sides. As painful as it was, he had to accept that his mother had retreated to place where he could no longer reach her. *'Allons-y!'* he said to Alain. 'Let us find out just how firmly those gates are barred.'

As they rode along the valley floor, alongside the river, a hawk hovered over a mown cornfield, keenly eying some rodent that hoped to hide in the stubble. Suddenly, it dived and captured its prey just as he would soon capture Mistlecote.

Edmund watched the bird soar high into the sky again, its prize clutched tightly in its talons, and considered *his* prey—the current mistress of the manor. Would she be as helpless as that poor shrew? Would she submit demurely to her fate? Or would she resist?

They forded the river easily, since the water was barely up to their horses' knees, and halted at the gates. They were indeed barred and no sound at all came from within. The place might have been completely empty, though he knew it was not.

'Ho!' he called, looking up to the walled parapet above the arched gateway. 'I am Edmund Deverell and I demand admittance to my manor house.'

There was no response, although he sensed eyes watching him from above. He could almost hear the owners of those eyes breathing, see the look of apprehension on the faces, feel the tension in the bodies. He scanned the walls and saw one…two…three pike heads above the parapet, and a pitchfork.

Not a large defensive force, but then he hadn't expected one, since most of Mistlecote's men had perished at Northampton. A few survivors had fled but two rode with him, having wisely changed sides to save their lives.

Suddenly a flash of blue showed above and a face appeared. Not the face of a soldier, or even of a man, but a woman's face, pale and framed by wisps of dark hair. He'd never seen Isobel Calvert but he knew instinctively that it was she.

'I am waiting, Mistress Calvert,' he called, but the face promptly disappeared from sight. Edmund looked at the oaken gates, assessed quickly and accurately how long they'd hold. Too long and he'd done enough waiting already. Beckoning the two former Lancastrians forward, he ordered them to dismount, which they did, warily, obviously wondering what he was up to.

'Turn towards the house and let them see you clearly,' he commanded.

Reluctantly, and sheepishly as well they might, the two men obeyed. Edmund waited a few moments, letting those inside the walls recognise their former comrades, then he rode forward a few paces.

'Doubtless you know these men? They are my prisoners, captured at Northampton, where I spared their lives. Unless you open these gates immediately, they will hang from the nearest tree.'

There was a silence that seemed to make the air crackle, though he knew they'd heard and understood his words. Would they open up—or let the two hapless men suffer for their stubbornness? After all, they had no idea of their comrades' change of heart, nor that he had no intention of hanging the men, but it would be irksome to lose face at the moment of his arrival.

'How many more deaths do you want on your hands, Mistress Calvert?' Edmund called again, louder this time. 'There has already been bloodshed enough. Would you add to that toll?'

Another silence and then a flurry of activity erupted on the parapet. The sound of bars being drawn back was heard, the gates swung slowly and heavily open, and a figure emerged and strode towards him. A tall, slender young woman, dressed in a light blue gown, her hair dark, her head bare of veil or coif. On her heels came two lean greyhounds and, with a hand on each of their collars, a man, old and grizzled, with the stamp of a steward upon him.

She halted before Edmund and he looked down into eyes that were green and compelling. Her face was perfectly formed, with a straight nose and a wide mouth of dusky pink. Beneath her gown, her breasts were small and high, and they rose and fell furiously as, with a reckless disregard for caution, she addressed him in a torrent of hostility.

'How dare you demand entrance here? How dare you threaten to kill my men? You will release them to me at once and then go away!'

Isobel Calvert was nothing like he'd imagined and, as he stared, the wild beauty of her stirred something within him that had not been stirred for a long time.

'I had no intention of killing your men,' he replied. 'I merely said they would hang from the nearest tree.'

'Then you have a lying tongue, like all your kind.'

'And who *are* my kind, mistress?'

'Yorkists!' The word was spat out with venom. 'Traitors all.'

Edmund dismounted and handed his reins to Alain. 'You know why I am here?'

Her hands were on her hips now, her feet planted firmly on the ground, as if daring him to pass at his peril. 'Word of your coming was sent me, yes; however, I ignored it.'

'Ignore it if you like but Mistlecote is mine as of today.'

'You have no place and no right.' Her chin lifted and she drew herself taller. 'Mistlecote belongs to my brother.'

'Your brother is likely dead, mistress, and disinherited,

in any case. Even if by some miracle he still lives, he forfeited the title to these lands when he fought on the wrong side at Northampton.'

Her face paled and Edmund steeled himself to not pity her. Such was the way of war. 'I fought on the right side,' he went on, 'and have been granted this manor as a reward.'

'You?' The scorn dripped from her lips. 'A mere knight, like your father before you, and a tainted one at that!'

Edmund felt his shirt cling to his back as the sun beat down from on high. Here and now was not the time to tell her that his family was noble, with a lineage that went back centuries. That the Deverells' title of lord had been extinguished with the execution of his grandfather, their family attainted for the crime of loyalty to the true king, poor murdered Richard.

'I have more claim than you know,' he said, 'but I suggest we go within now and get out of the sun. My men and I have ridden far today.'

Her lips parted, doubtless to aim more curses at him, but Edmund didn't give her the opportunity. She would have plenty of time to rail at him in the days to come, until he could find some way to be rid of her.

'We *will* enter, whether behind you or in front of you. It is your choice, mistress.'

Chapter Two

Isobel glared up at Edmund Deverell. He'd sat his tall, grey horse as she'd known he would, proud and arrogant, and he stood now with the same stance, waiting for her compliance. Orion and Sirius were growling and straining to break free of Ned's hold and the urge to tell her steward to release them and let them bring Deverell down burned like quicksilver on her tongue.

But she'd counted the number of men that accompanied him, thirty at least and all of them soldiers, with the mark of battle experience on every one of them. Her motley band of grooms and servants wouldn't stand a chance, not now the gates were open. And how could she have kept them closed with the Yorkist's noose around the necks of those two men—*her* men?

She saw the same battle experience on Deverell's face too, the features set stern and hard as granite. There was a thin scar on the line of his right jaw, where the edge of a sword perhaps had just split the skin. He wore no helmet and his hair, blowing in the breeze, was fair, like flax. His eyes were blue-grey, like steel, and his well-shaped mouth she imagined could change swiftly from a smile to a snarl, from kindness to cruelty.

Isobel steadied her breath and tried to calm the knocking

of her heart against her ribs, as she found herself confronted with a male presence unlike any she'd ever encountered before. A cool, calm yet irresistible intent that threatened to disarm her without resort to weapons of any kind. She'd not gauged his intelligence yet, only that he was arrogant—and startlingly handsome, not that that mattered. But every suit of armour had a weak and penetrable spot. She just needed to find it.

'Since I have no alternative but to admit you—for now at least—then you may follow me.'

Turning on her heel, her soul screaming silent resistance but her thoughts scattered in all directions, Isobel walked in through the gates, the Yorkists at her back. Inside the outer courtyard, the household had gathered to survey the invaders with curious and fearful eyes. The soldiers dismounted and their horses were led to the stables, almost empty now as most of *their* horses had gone to Northampton, and like their riders, not returned.

After a keen glance around him, Deverell assessed her household as of neither threat nor consequence. Then he spoke in French to a soldier that she guessed was his second in command, before turning to her but pointing at Ned.

'This man is steward here?'

Isobel nodded. 'My father's steward and now my brother's.'

Her barb went ignored and he beckoned Ned to him. 'See to quarters for my men, if you please, and storage for our gear and arms. And then make ready chambers in the house for myself and my sergeant.'

Ned turned enquiringly to her and, fury twisting in her stomach, Isobel nodded. As her steward went to do Deverell's bidding, she called her hounds to her and addressed the Yorkist with as much authority as she could summon.

'But I would prefer it if you both slept in the outbuildings, with the rest of your men.'

Deverell tilted his head, looked at her speculatively, then dismissed her preference as he would a hornet buzzing around his face. 'I will sleep in the house, since it is mine, and so will Alain. You, Mistress Calvert, will retain your room—for now.'

She glared at him. 'Do you expect my thanks for that?'

A ghost of a smile touched his mouth. 'I expect nothing.' He ran a hand through his hair, and down the back of his neck, flexing broad shoulders. 'I am travel weary, so first I will bathe, then sup, and then you and I will have a little talk.'

Isobel bit her tongue. She could tell him here and now that she had nothing to say to him. But in her anger it would all come out rashly, with feelings that she needed to check if she was to outsmart this Yorkist usurper. Feelings that, like her thoughts, were scattered too and not quite under her usual control.

'How many servants are there here?' he asked as they ascended the stone step to the hall, he just behind her, his presence like a menacing shadow. 'And have any of your soldiery returned from Northampton?'

'You have seen the extent of this household already,' she said, curtly, over her shoulder, and quickened her pace slightly to distance herself from that looming and over-powering presence. 'None of those who went to Northampton have returned—as yet—apart from the two you took prisoner.'

They'd entered the hall, the Frenchman he'd called Alain behind them, before he spoke again. 'Concerning that, I have a confession to make.'

'A confession?'

'Those men…they would not have been hanged, in sham or otherwise, since they now march on the side of York.'

Isobel gasped, her mind sharpening at last. 'They have changed their allegiance?'

His shoulders lifted then dropped. He was dressed, plainly enough, in a dark woollen doublet and hose, with a grey surcoat over, though his cloak of russet was finely embroidered at the edges with gold thread. 'It is common enough in times of war,' he said, removing that cloak now and tossing it over a chair. 'Men are swayed very easily when one side is so favourably starred against another.'

As he turned back to face her, the sun came in through the window and fell full on his face. He was younger than she'd first thought, not above thirty certainly, and his features were strong, resolute. His gaze was steadfast, as if he doubted nothing, least of all himself. And, as she stared at him, Isobel suddenly found herself lost for words, not just at a personality that she sensed was as determined as that firm, square chin suggested, but at an explicable inability to tear her eyes away.

'I would never have believed it of *any* man of Mistlecote!' Outrage—and something else that she couldn't define—shook her voice as he dropped with an easy grace into the same chair, stretching long legs out before him. 'Doubtless you persuaded them on point of death, or did you cross their palms with silver?'

'A little of both, as is customary.' He looked around the room, as if surveying his new kingdom, but when his eyes came back to hers, there was a frown on his brow. 'You have no women here, only men?'

'When I heard you Yorkists were coming, I sent the women away to safety.'

'And your own maidservant?'

'I have sent her away too. I can attend to my own needs.'

As he stared at her, suddenly Isobel felt uncomfortable, and acutely conscious of herself in a way she'd never been before. Worse, she felt naked, as if he could see the skin below her clothes, the tangles in her plait where she'd tied it too hastily that morning, the scuffed boots on her feet, and the faded kirtle that any other woman would have discarded by now but that she'd kept because it was simple and concealing.

She had a wardrobe full of such gowns aloft, nearly all of which had belonged to her mother, most of them dating from the time when women dressed more modestly, not like the low-bosomed, high-waisted gowns that women wore these days.

His gaze held far longer than was decent and heat rose into her cheeks. Men had looked at her like that before this, but she'd paid none of them any heed, and neither had their eyes troubled her. But this man's eyes were not like any others. They reminded her of a stormy sky, more grey now than blue, and their candid hold seemed to see far more than eyes ought to see.

Boldly lifting her chin, Isobel matched that stare, damning him to look his full, willing him to see her hatred, even as an awareness of him as a man stirred inside her.

She'd had suitors aplenty as she'd grown to womanhood but had rejected them all, not only because her father allowed her to remain at home and run the manor but because she'd never felt any inclination to marry any of them, less still felt any attraction towards them.

Now…surely she wasn't feeling attraction for *this* man of all men!

'I will, of course, recall my maid, and the other women

too,' she said, shaking that impossible notion firmly away, 'once you and all your men ride back from whence you came!'

Edmund didn't take up the challenge, tempting though it was. Instead, letting her fume like a ruffled hen, he got to his feet and strolled around the sumptuous hall he'd only dreamed about—until now. The oak-panelled walls were richly dark, embellished at regular intervals with swirling leaf and knot designs. The hammerbeam ceiling was the same one his ancestor, Sir Guy D'Aueville, must have looked up at, the bosses and paint put there at his wishes, as he'd decorated and enlarged the old Saxon building in the Norman style all those centuries ago.

The Deverells—for the name had long been Anglicised from its French form—had called this manor home until it had been stolen from them by this woman's grandfather. *His* grandfather had been executed for the crime of loyalty to a rightful king—Richard, the second of that name—and his father disinherited and disentitled.

Roger Deverell had vowed to reclaim their manor one day and had perished in the attempt, leaving his sons to keep that vow and put those wrongs right again. Hugh had perished too, before he could return to England, but now, at last, Mistlecote was theirs once more.

'Surveying your conquest, Edmund Deverell?' Isobel Calvert seemed to read his thoughts. 'Look your fill, so that you remember it well after Lancaster drives you out again!'

She stood with her body erect, her chin haughty, every inch the lady of the manor, yet still with that essence of something untamed about her. Edmund smiled to himself. Taunt him all she liked, now he was here, his long-lost inheritance finally in his hands, he was going nowhere.

The steward entered the hall then and informed him his men had all been billeted. Edmund nodded and handed him his discarded cloak. 'You need not wait for me but go ahead and prepare my bath.'

The man hesitated then, with a bow that was more hostile than reverent, disappeared into the solar. Alain had been standing before the fire all this time and now Edmund jerked his head, indicating to his sergeant to leave too.

When they were alone, he stepped towards Isobel, noting the widening of her eyes, the intake of breath, the stiffening of that slender body of hers. But she wasn't afraid of him, he knew that much, and her courage stirred him to a grudging admiration even as her beauty struck him anew.

'Now we can speak privately, let us have something clear right from the start, Mistress Calvert. Mistlecote is mine by right, and now that I have it back I will not relinquish it ever again. Do you understand me?'

If he'd expected her to wilt before his words, he was wrong. She straightened, although she'd been as straight as a spear shaft already, and looked him directly in the eye.

'Then it seems we are in an intractable situation, does it not? For neither will I relinquish this house, to you or to anyone else. Once King Henry is free again—'

'He will never be free, mistress.' Edmund cut her words short. 'Even if he were, his wits are addled, and the people of England have lost their faith in his government.'

'That is a lie!'

'It is the truth. England will welcome Richard of York because he will lead the people out of their muddle to better times.'

'There was peace in England before York made war!'

She was shaking with fury, her hands fisted at her sides, as if she was longing to fly at him and pound him to dust.

The hounds, which had settled at her feet, watched him intently, doubtless ready to attack too at her word.

And, with a sinking heart, Edmund realised they were indeed at an intractable impasse, one that perhaps he should have expected and prepared for. After all, Isobel was alone, her parents dead, her brother too, mayhap, leaving her with only an elderly steward and a handful of minions to protect her.

It crossed his mind to wonder why, at the age of twenty-four, she was still unwed, which was even more unusual for a woman of her standing and beauty. Was it her lonely and defenceless predicament that roused pity in him? Or did her beauty, as well as her courage, touch him deeper than he liked to admit?

'And there will be peace again when York finally sits on the throne,' Edmund went on, clearing his throat as desire stirred, stronger than pity. 'As regards our concerns, there are options available to you, naturally, and I will do my best to see you settled to your contentment.'

'Contentment!' Her face paled. 'How could *you* know what would content me?'

'Then tell me.'

'I wish to remain here and remain I will, no matter what you say. You cannot force me to go!'

Edmund cursed both pity and desire, neither of which he should be feeling in any case, and shook his head. 'It is impossible for you to stay. You are alone here, a maid, without protection of a husband, or lord.'

'I need no one's protection!'

'A noblewoman unwed has two options,' he continued, going to the hearth and kicking at the logs to wake the fire, as if that might overcome the fire that had begun to burn in his loins. 'To marry or to take the veil. You must choose one, Isobel, for if you do not, the King will command—'

'Which *king* are we talking about?' She came to stand in front of him. 'The rightful king? Or the usurper?'

They were standing almost toe-to-toe now, like enemies at close quarters on the battlefield. The top of her head came level with his chin and, for an alarming instant, Edmund had an urge to kiss that glossy, untidy hair. Mayhap let his mouth dip lower and taste those full, ripe lips too, as for the first time in four years his body craved the carnal pleasure he'd denied it for so long.

'You must accept the inevitable, Isobel, as must I.'

'*You?*' she snarled, as viciously as those hounds of hers doubtless did. 'I hardly think you'll have much trouble accepting the situation! You've gained everything you wanted even though you have no right to any of it. And stop calling me Isobel!'

Edmund flushed, not least at the reprimand of his use of her name, as once more desire flared up inside him. She was beautiful, she was spirited, she was brave, and she was passionate. Everything a man should want in a wife, everything *he* might want—if Mariette hadn't destroyed his dreams, his capacity for trusting, for loving.

'All the life I've ever known has been here in this house,' she was saying now, her voice quivering with emotion. 'I would rather die than surrender Mistlecote, Edmund Deverell! And neither will I take a husband, nor be shut away in a nunnery. I refuse!'

The words were final but Edmund saw her eyes fill with unshed tears, granted, and tears of hate and fury and resistance, perhaps, rather than sorrow or fear. But they made his heart heave all the same.

Moving past her, he went to the window and pressed a

palm against the lintel, remorse twisting in his gut. This woman hadn't even been born when this house was stolen from his family, and now he'd come marching in to turn her whole existence upside down. But that didn't mean he should be feeling compassion or pity—or desire—or anything else.

Mistlecote was finally his and he would not let Isobel sway him, less still let her touch his heart, as suddenly she threatened very much to do.

With a sigh, Edmund dragged a hand through his hair. This wasn't going to be as straightforward as he'd thought, when he'd reined in on the hilltop an hour ago, his victory over the house of Calvert complete.

How wrong he'd been!

'If a nunnery is not to your liking,' he said, steeling himself, 'and you have no man in mind to marry, then Warwick will have to find a suitable match for you.'

Isobel heard the words—the ultimatum—as if from a great distance, somewhere so far away from here that she'd never even imagined it existed. And yet, it was real. The words were real. The stony face that turned towards her, the light from the window making its hollows and shadows seem like that of a demon risen from hell, it was all happening.

Right here, right now.

She lifted her chin, felt nausea fill her throat, but forced her voice out through shaking lips. 'A Yorkist match?'

'Ideally, or, if not, someone who favours neither one side nor the other, but who would be loyal to the next king.'

'I will not marry anyone, Yorkist or otherwise,' Isobel said, holding his cold stare. 'I do not wish it.'

She'd said those last words to her father once, when a

particularly persistent suitor had asked thrice for her hand. She'd been eighteen then and, having devoted her life to caring for her father and brother, chosen to continue to do so. She'd had to remain at home in order to give Tom the love and protection their sire—lost in grief after the death of her mother in childbirth—could not.

In taking on the role of both parents to her brother—which she was glad to do, since there was no one else—she'd discovered a freedom that was too precious to relinquish, and the power to do as she pleased, make her own choices, lead her own life.

But now it seemed she would be given little choice at all and her freedom was at an end.

'My mother is Prioress at the White Ladies in Brewood.' Deverell's voice broke into her thoughts. 'I could ask her if you might be placed there.'

Had he not heard her? Or did he not want to listen, or to care? Either way, she had to keep control, be cunning, cleverer than he, and not give way to the terror that had closed about her heart.

'I heard your mother had entered a nunnery on your father's death,' Isobel said, with deliberate intent. 'Did she choose that fate—or was she too forced to take the veil against her will?'

Her attack succeeded. Hot colour swept into his cheekbones and his mouth tightened. In fact, his whole body tightened, as if every sinew had pulled taut like a bowstring.

'It was a long time ago…but no, she was not *given* a choice.'

The reply was ground out as if through clenched teeth and his arrogant gaze was now turbulent, like an angry sea. For the first time since his arrival, Isobel saw raw emotions, violent emotions, and in them, a weakness that she might attack.

'Was she alone too? No protector, no people she could have gone to?'

She herself had no people to go to either but, unlike that unfortunate woman, she would not go as quietly, nor as meekly. She would fight her fate to her last breath before she would submit.

With a cruelty she'd never have believed herself capable of, Isobel pushed the point of her invisible sword home. 'Was your mother helpless, Edmund Deverell, without defence or recourse? Was she also a victim of men who cared nothing for her wishes or her happiness?'

Deverell's reaction was not what she'd expected. His face went completely white, as if all the blood had drained out of him. His features, so harsh only a moment before, changed into such a mask of pain that she flinched. A pain that threatened to soften her hate, shake her determination, evoke a pity that he didn't deserve. He was the invader here, after all, the traitor to his king, the enemy under her roof, the destroyer of her whole life.

'No, she had no one.' He was so still he might have been turned to stone, his tone empty and yet full of feeling. 'My father was dead, my brother and I in France, banished from the realm by King Henry.'

'Because your father was a traitor.' She tried to infuse relish into the word but somehow it fell short. 'As you are.'

'My father was no traitor!'

'He was no lover of the King, was he?' Isobel forced her tone to mockery. 'Else surely his claim to Mistlecote would have been upheld in the trial by combat, you and your brother would not have been banished, and your mother would still be free.'

The blue-grey eyes focused suddenly, as if he'd returned from somewhere far away, and his stance became alert again, strong, like a warrior advancing onto the battlefield. 'We have wandered far indeed from the topic we began on. It is *you* we were talking about, Isobel.'

She felt the advantage she'd gained falter. 'But you cannot deny the similarities between your mother's fate and mine.'

'My mother was a widow, you are a maid. There are worse fates for an unmarried woman.'

Isobel's heart began to race as he moved to stand so close she could have touched him. 'Should a woman, whatever her status, not be free to choose her own fate?'

'You *are* free to choose, Isobel.' Deverell's gaze was locked on hers, no trace now of the emotion she'd just glimpsed there. 'It is merely that your choices are limited to two.'

'Neither of which is a choice at all!' she countered. 'Either is abhorrent to me.'

'I agree, you would be wasted in a nunnery.' He gave a slow nod. 'But a beautiful and accomplished woman can marry well, even without a dowry.'

Isobel stifled a gasp as she saw something else in his eyes, something very different to anything she'd seen before. Appreciation of more than just her situation.

'Do you think me beautiful and accomplished, then, Edmund Deverell? Or so plain that a nunnery is the best I could do?'

'You know you are beautiful, Isobel, so why ask it?'

They stared at each other, the silence crackling louder than the logs in the hearth and the hairs at the back of her neck lifting in the breeze that came in through the window. Or *was* it the breeze?

'Was your mother beautiful?'

He nodded, his gaze dark on hers, a flush of colour on his face. 'Yes, she was beautiful. At nought but fifty, she still is.'

There was a multitude of feeling in his quiet reply. Sadness, pride, and things Isobel couldn't even begin to guess at. A sort of perturbation descended upon her, as if the words had landed on the calm surface of a lake and whipped up a storm. From the moment she'd stepped outside the gates to confront him, she'd known that resisting this man would be far from easy. But little had she suspected that it was not just her home but her whole self that she needed to protect.

For he incited feelings in her that she'd never experienced before. Responses that had come without warning and so she'd not been prepared for them. He was different to those suitors who'd come to ask for her over the years, men who had neither interested nor attracted her. And none of them had ever affected her in the way Edmund Deverell did, he who was not a suitor at all but her enemy.

Isobel felt the blood drain from her face and then rush back again, leaving her cheeks hot and her breath hard to draw. Could she actually be...was she really *attracted* to him?

And even as she retorted to his remark, with a scorn that was toothless now, she knew her advantage was gone, stolen away from her, as smoothly as her home had been.

'And is she *happy* in her nunnery?'

Edmund wished he could answer that honestly, but he could not. The mother he'd known was gone and in her place was a remote, untouchable saint of a woman, as distant from him as an angel in heaven.

'She has found serenity,' he said, 'and is respected and loved by her sisters.'

Isobel's gaze held his, unafraid, curious, but noticeably more veiled now than it had been before. 'I know nothing of serenity, but being respected and loved does not mean that she is happy.'

The opinion was one that Edmund shared but the shrewdness of it caught him off guard. Isobel's situation was not exactly like his mother's, however, and she could have a future of contentment and safety if she was wise enough to choose it. If she was not…then Warwick would order him to choose for her, decide her fate as if he really *was* indifferent to her happiness.

Except he wasn't indifferent at all, no matter how much he tried to convince himself that he was. No matter how immune he'd thought himself to women, he was not—at least not to *this* woman.

Why not? Was it her perfectly shaped face, her luminous eyes, the rich darkness of her hair? Edmund didn't think so—after all, he'd beheld women far more beautiful than Isobel Calvert and resisted. Was it her body, then, slender, high-breasted, alluring in a simple and modest blue gown that had seen better days?

A sudden image of Mariette flashed through his mind. She'd favoured blue too, a colour that had complimented her golden hair. Though there'd been nothing modest about *her* gowns, quite the opposite. That had attracted him at first, being young and lustful, and in love, but later her flaunted flesh had offended him because he'd found out that it wasn't displayed only for his pleasure but for the pleasure of many other men.

Perhaps it was just as well that Isobel took the veil, if she was as modest as she appeared! But in the wake of that, another vision took the place of the first—Isobel in the garb of a nun, her glorious hair hidden forever, or even shorn, her eyes lowered meekly, that vital body restrained to a shuffling walk, and her sharp tongue dulled by the repetition of constant prayer.

A pain struck at his heart. Yes, his mother was serene, at peace, seemingly content, her past life forgotten, her only living son along with it. It had hurt him to discover that, and the bite of rejection still cut deep. But even more painful was the loss of the vivacious, laughing, warm being that had been his mother.

Try as he might to be glad she was at peace, a part of him hated what she had become. Hated the religion that had taken him from her, even if it had saved her life and her sanity at the time, when *he'd* been unable to aid her at all.

And now…could he really endorse such a fate for Isobel, even if he'd not been commanded by the Earl of Warwick to do so, and at once? A woman he'd found to be spirited and passionate? A woman of beauty and courage who, despite all his inner armour, had awoken a part of him that had died with Mariette?

With a shake of his head, Edmund tamped all those questions down. Isobel Calvert wasn't his responsibility and her fate was her own concern. She didn't have to become a nun, she could marry a man of her choice, be happy, have children, live a long and prosperous life.

He turned and strode to the door, taking with him the scent of rose and lavender. The perfumes that his senses knew Isobel used on her skin and hair. Luxuries that she would not be allowed in a nunnery, of course, if that was the fate she chose.

'I expect to hear your decision on the morrow.' He threw the ultimatum over his shoulder as the hounds followed growling at his heels to see him off. 'Have it ready.'

Chapter Three

The next morning, Isobel rose later than usual after a deep and nightmare-ridden sleep, dressed quickly, and drank a cup of wine. Then, as she did every morning, she consulted her book of hours, her star charts and cast her horoscope for the day.

The sun was in Pisces and her sign, Leo, was in the fifth celestial house. Her horoscope told her she should not have anything to do with fire, nor let blood from the arms, nor build anything out of wood, but it was good to plant trees.

Isobel sighed, put her charts away, then plaited her hair and wound it up under a clean coif. Today of all days she needed the wise guidance of the stars, but none of what they'd told her seemed to have any relevance at all to her current predicament.

Sitting on her bed, she stared at the wall, absently stroking Orion's head, aware that sooner or later she'd have to leave the sanctuary of her room. Go out and face Edmund Deverell and pretend…hope…that those reactions she'd experienced yesterday were false, born out of her predicament, and nothing more than that.

That he was a powerful presence and a force to be reckoned with was undeniable, but that did not mean she was attracted to him. He was merely…different to the men she'd encountered before, that was all. He'd taken her by surprise when he'd marched through Mistlecote's gates and into her life and she'd reacted instinctively, irrationally. But now she would be better prepared to resist him—in every way.

Since there was no point in delaying, Isobel fastened a cloak about her shoulders and went out into the hall, her hounds leaping ahead of her. The tables had already been cleared away, telling her she'd missed breakfast, not that she could have eaten anything. Edmund Deverell hadn't come yet to hear her decision—which she hadn't made nor intended to—and she was determined to give him no opportunity to ask.

The outer courtyard was sunlit and full of Yorkists and, if she hadn't realised it before, now she saw how vastly outnumbered her own people were. The day-to-day business was going on as usual despite the upheaval, and no one had waited for her orders or instructions. Doubtless, they'd already been given them by Deverell or that vile Frenchman he'd brought with him!

Seeking out Ned, Isobel discovered him sitting on the low wall that enclosed the herb garden, watching two Yorkists draw water and fill buckets from the well near by. Sitting down beside him, she breathed deeply of the aroma of autumn herbs—rosemary, thyme, sage and lavender.

She loved herbs, and flowers, scents and colours, and autumn was her favourite season—but this autumn seemed tainted now, like the fruit rotting on the trees in the orchard. Since the household was depleted, there hadn't been enough people left to eat all the apples and pears, quince and berries. At least not until now.

With a silent sigh, Isobel looked into the lined face of the man at her side and realised he'd become an old man, as if overnight. 'Good morning, Ned.'

'Good morning, mistress,' he replied, but his tone was old too. 'It is a fine day.'

It *was* fine, and promising to be warm for November, but despite that there was a chill of foreboding in the air. Ned would be no help in resisting the invaders and nor should she expect him to be. She really *was* alone, one woman against more than thirty enemy soldiers—and their leader.

'I see these Yorkists have made themselves at home,' she said bitterly.

'And quick enough too!' A spark of fire lit in Ned's voice. 'Come from Calais they have, and not only do they have the manners of heathens, but most of them don't even speak the King's English!'

Isobel placed her hands on the warm stone beneath her and looked upwards to the window of the room that had previously been her father's, and then her brother's but now usurped by Edmund Deverell. Her chamber lay adjacent and she'd heard him pass by her door earlier, on his way to the hall, his steps sure and his presence like a hammer at her heart.

'And where is Edmund Deverell this morning?'

'I believe he is inspecting the farms, mistress.'

The two farms attached to Mistlecote were not large but now, with the household grown, perhaps Deverell had plans to expand, and plough more land, raise more stock. But at least his being absent for the time being gave her time to think of a plan, a way to resist, even though as yet she could see none.

'Have you any instructions this morning, mistress? That French upstart told me I may not be steward for much longer, due to my age, but while I am I will do your bidding as I always have done, as I did your father's.'

'I will speak to Deverell about that, Ned.' She placed a

hand on his arm, finding it thin below the sleeve, and anger bubbled up inside her. If Ned was dismissed from his post, what could she do about it in reality, when she too might be dismissed? 'Will you take my hounds out into the fields for some exercise?'

'Orders have been given that no one is to pass beyond the outer gates today without permission.'

Isobel cursed below her breath. Was there to be no end to this arrogance? 'Then please let them run around the orchard and gardens. I will speak to Deverell about the gates too.'

Ned rose and called the hounds to heel while she made for the kitchens to give instructions for that day's meals. But once there, she found not only her own two cooks but also another occupant—a man as big as a bear—who was busily stirring a boiling pot.

'What is the meaning of this?' She turned to her chief cook and pointed. 'Who is that?'

'He is called Jacques of Calais, mistress.' The apology in the answer was subordinate to resentment. 'The new cook that came with the Yorkists. He does not speak our language, but he cooks well.'

Isobel spoke French but didn't trouble to greet the Calais man. Rage boiling inside her, hotter even than the pots over the fire, she told her youngest cook to core the quinces thoroughly. Then, with feet of clay, she made her way back up the wooden stairs to the bailey and turned for the stables to check her mare had been seen to, as she did every morning.

None of the Yorkists looked at her, except for sly glances beneath lowered lashes and hat brims, less still acknowledged her with any sort of reverence. However, as she neared the armoury, a man sitting in the doorway, fletching arrows in the sun, issued an imperative whisper.

'Mistress Calvert!'

Stopping in her tracks, Isobel recognised the fletcher as Robin of Talgarth, one of the manor men who'd come with Deverell and who apparently had switched allegiance after the battle at Northampton. Somehow, it was the crowning insult of a morning that had already proved too trying, and the sun hadn't even reached its zenith yet.

'Are you addressing me, you knave? If so, don't bother. I have no time for traitors!'

'It is not how you think it is, mistress.' With a furtive glance around the courtyard, Robin took a piece of cloth from inside his jerkin and showed it to her. It was her brother's coat of arms—the golden griffin rampant.

'I tore it off my sleeve, as they commanded me to do,' he said, thrusting the badge back out of sight. 'But I keep it even so.'

Isobel's heart leapt. Could she possibly have an ally? Or at least, a source of information? 'I thought you had sided with York?'

'No, indeed! Your brother thought it wiser—'

She interrupted him. *'Tom is alive?'*

Robin nodded and motioned her to move out of sight within the doorway behind him. Isobel shrank into the shadows, hope and suspicion vying in equal measure.

'How do I know you are speaking the truth?'

The man reached into the pouch at his belt and drew out a ring. 'Your brother bade me give you this and to convey what he dared not write.'

She took the ring and stared down at it. It was indeed Tom's—a silver band set with a garnet, red for Lancaster. 'You might have taken this off his hand, were he slain,' she said cautiously. 'Speak truthfully or not at all.'

'I tell you truly, mistress, Lord Calvert was alive when

last I saw him, though he was sore wounded at Northampton. Adam Ewyas and I were making our way homewards after the battle…you have heard all about that, no doubt?'

'Yes.' Isobel curled her hand over the ring, pressing all her faith into its cold, hard curve, 'but we have had no word of my brother at all. If you know something, tell me quickly!'

'We were in the thick of it, every one of us fighting alongside your brother. Then Lord Grey—curse him— changed sides in the midst of the battle and overwhelmed us. Our lord's horse was killed under him and we had to scatter and run for our lives.'

'You left him there?'

Robin bowed his head. 'We fled the field, those of us left alive, and those were few enough. Adam and I made it across the river, which was swollen with heavy rain, and hid all that night in some woods. At daybreak, we went back to look for his body, certain he must have perished.'

Isobel clutched Tom's ring tighter, until the stone dug painfully into her palm. 'Did…did you find him?'

'The horse was there, dead, but he was not. There were folk everywhere, combing the battlefield looking for their kin, aye, and scavenging from the dead too, the Devil take them! Then we heard that a wounded Lancastrian nobleman was being cared for in the house of White Monks at Merevale.'

'Was it Tom? Is he there still, at Merevale?'

'It was he, and he was alive when last we saw him, though he had lost much blood, and broken a leg besides.'

Isobel moved closer, eager to hear. 'You said he sent a message for me?'

Robin nodded. 'To tell you that when he was well enough, he would make his way back here. We were to try to get home but if captured we were to pretend to offer our allegiance to York in return for our lives and continue to work for Lancaster.'

Isobèl felt her legs go weak with relief. Tom was young and strong—he would not die uselessly in a monastery so far from home! 'If my brother mended of his wounds, he might have left Merevale by now,' she whispered. 'Did he say what he meant to do?'

'If Mistlecote was fallen to York, he would ally himself to those still loyal to the King and fight on.'

Mistlecote *had* fallen! But pray God, the next battle, when it came, would rise it up again.

Robin went on. 'The Tudors in Wales, and the lords of the north, are staunch for Lancaster, and even now—'

The Welshman broke off suddenly and hissed a warning. Taking an arrow from the quiver beside him, he recommenced his fletching just as the voice of Edmund Deverell came, loud and clear, and very near.

'How goes the fletching, Robin?'

Isobel froze and pressed herself back against the wall, sure Deverell must see her, for he was standing just outside the door, so close she could feel him. Robin got to his feet and, leaning casually against the door jamb in front of her, handed over one of the arrows.

Deverell took it, his flaxen head dipping to study the arrow. 'You have great skill in this craft, I see.'

'I should do, Sir Knight. I learned it from my father, who was also a fletcher, as was his father before him.'

'Then I am doubly pleased that you saw sense and came over to the side of York.'

Isobel almost smiled at the irony. Little did he know that Robin—for surely he had proved now he was still loyal—

was pulling wool over his eyes as neatly as he'd bound goose feathers onto that arrow shaft.

Deverell took another arrow out of the quiver, evidently not satisfied with the standard of just one example. The sleeve of his tunic was rolled up to the elbow and she stared fascinated at the flex of the muscles beneath the flesh, the gleam of sunlight on the hairs that lightly dusted the surface of his bronzed skin.

'I see you favour goose over swan, Robin.'

'Most of the time, Sir Knight, though it depends on the type of arrow.'

The two men conversed on, about the different feathers used for fletching, the virtue of the longbow over the crossbow. Isobel felt her gown begin to stick to her back and a spider fell from above onto her shoulder and began to crawl its way down her bodice.

But worse was to come. Dust filled her nose and a sneeze began to build. She clapped a palm against her lips, but it was too late. The sneeze came out like a cannon shot.

'A-tish-oooooooooooooooo!'

Edmund had known Isobel was there, of course. He'd detected, above the usual odours of leather and linseed, the same sweet floral scents he'd noticed graced Isobel's hair and skin in the hall yesterday. Now she'd given herself away with that sneeze and he didn't know whether to be amused or sorry for her.

Dismissing the Welshman, he leaned against the doorway and folded his arms. 'Good morning, Isobel. Have you been in here all night?'

Immediately she appeared out of the shadows, brushing a cobweb off her sleeve. 'Of course not!' she retorted, her head high, but her cheeks pink. 'I have newly arrived.'

'To inspect the fletching of arrows?'

'And why should I not? This is still my manor.'

'Why not indeed?' Edmund didn't address the last part of her statement. It wouldn't be her manor for much longer, which was all to the good, as his senses sharpened and his blood quickened. Clearing his throat, he noted wryly that his voice was not as steady as it ought to have been. 'Your friend Robin is a good fletcher.'

'Since he's gone over to the Yorkist side, he is hardly a friend of mine!'

'Even so, the two of you seemed to have much to talk about.'

Her gaze slid away. 'I… I was asking him about the whereabouts of my brother.'

'And what did he tell you?'

'Nothing.'

'Why hide yourself inside the door to speak to him? Why didn't Robin make your presence known to me?'

'You must ask him that! And while we're asking questions, I have several I want to ask of you!'

Edmund sensed the stench of deception in the air. Men who changed allegiance to save their own lives had no qualms about changing back again when the tide turned. He would keep a close eye on Robin of Talgarth from now on.

'Ask,' he said, 'and I will do my best to answer.'

'To begin with, why have you put your cook in my kitchen?'

'Because the household is greatly increased and he is too good a cook to let go to waste.'

'And why is my presence ignored by your men? I have run Mistlecote for nigh on fifteen years, first for my father, and now for my brother.'

Edmund inclined his head. Her brother was irrelevant

and she herself would not be mistress here for much longer. 'I have seen how well this house is run,' he conceded, since it was the truth, 'and also the farms and forests belonging to it.'

'Is it true that you intend to dismiss Ned?' She hurled not questions now, but accusations at him. 'And why are my people not allowed to go outside the gates?'

'Your steward is far advanced in age and clearly failing in health and strength. As for your people, they are free to come and go as they please, as long as they tell the guards where they are going and why.'

'Does that freedom apply to me?'

'Of course,' he said graciously. 'You are not a prisoner here, Isobel.'

'I suppose you expect me to be grateful for that boon!'

Edmund held her gaze, the hate in the green eyes almost tangible, but he could hardly blame her. 'I expect nothing, only your compliance.'

'That you will never have!' She folded her arms, a belligerent and, at the same time, defensive action. 'But even so, I wish to go outside the gates today.'

'For what reason?'

'My mare needs exercising.'

Edmund nodded. 'Then I will ride with you, as my courser needs exercising too.'

Her expression went from haughty to horrified and then she gave a scornful laugh. 'Are you afraid I will run to the nearest Lancastrian stronghold and raise an army against you?'

'You will not find any Lancastrian strongholds within fifty miles of here,' he informed her. 'Most of the nobles in these parts, except for a stubborn few, have seen the wisdom of supporting a strong York against a weak Lancaster.'

Her eyes blazed but beneath the fire Edmund glimpsed desperation. 'Then they are cowards all, in that case!'

He shrugged. 'It is not as simple as that, Isobel. Some men will sway with the prevailing wind, yes, but others search their hearts deeply before changing their loyalties.'

'And what would *you* know about hearts?'

The question was bitter but he ignored it. He knew all about hearts—those that were hard, those that were soft, those that were false...and those that were foolish. He included his own in the latter.

'In any event, riding together will give us an opportunity to speak further about your decision, assuming you have made it?'

'No, I have not!' Her head turned and he could almost see her mind searching frantically for a response, an excuse, a lie even. 'Perhaps I will not ride today after all.'

Edmund bit back a smile, though behind it rose impatience. He needed her gone from here as soon as possible. The longer she remained, the harder it would be to oust her, and it was already far from easy. She clearly wasn't going to leave without a fight and he had no stomach for fighting women. But it wasn't his stomach that concerned him.

His sleep the previous night had been a troubled one, interspersed with unwanted physical desires and inappropriate visions of not sending her away at all, but of letting her stay, at least long enough to find out if that mouth tasted as delicious as it looked. If her hair would spill like silk into his hands if he loosed it from her coif and braid. If her body was as supple as it appeared beneath those old-fashioned gowns she favoured.

Nocturnal lust had never troubled his dreams once in the last four years because his marriage to Mariette had doused all desire in him. But now, since he'd ridden in here yesterday, it seemed some remnant of lust remained, dormant, unwelcome but not extinguished. And last night, in his dreams, Isobel had become the object of it.

'Then perhaps we can ride tomorrow?' he said, silently cursing that simmering, insistent desire. 'If your mare can wait another day?'

She drew an audible breath as, from the stables, one of the horses neighed—her mare, mayhap? Frowning, she chewed her lip, shifted from one foot to another, folded her arms about her midriff.

Intrigued, he waited, but she seemed so undecided, or rather trapped, that he felt the heart she'd insulted soften. It wasn't that he was hard of heart. He was not in most matters, but had learned to use his heart rather more wisely than he'd once done.

'Could it be that you are afraid to be alone with me, Isobel?' he asked, aware that goading her into riding with him wasn't a wise use of his heart but allowing it anyway. 'I am your enemy so it would be understandable that you might feel you cannot trust me, were we to be alone.'

'Afraid?' She arched an eyebrow in clear contempt. 'I am afraid of nothing! And no, I do *not* trust you—why should I?' There was a moment more of hesitation and then she nodded curtly. 'But very well, ride with me if you must, but I would prefer we do not speak at all.'

Edmund inclined his head. 'Then I will be silent, if you insist, though it will be a tedious ride indeed in that case.' But even as he said it, he knew there would be nothing tedious about riding with Isobel. 'I wonder which one of us will weaken, and speak, first?'

Her look could have withered an oak. 'It will not be me,

I assure you! I'll need to change into a riding gown,' she said, spinning away, her voice as brittle as glass. 'Meet me at the gates in half an hour.'

Chapter Four

The silence was getting on Isobel's nerves now. They had been out for hours and, at first, she'd simply enjoyed the freedom, the feel of the sun on her face, the thrilling motion of the mare below her. They'd galloped along the wide swathe of green that traversed the valley floor and picked their way through shady woods and around the edges of crop strips newly harvested.

They'd followed the River Teme so far west that from the crest of a small hill the great bell tower of St Laurence's Church in Ludlow could be seen, dimly in the distance. There, they'd lost Sirius in a thicket as he'd followed some scent or other, and had spent ages looking for him.

And all the time, as she'd bade him, Edmund Deverell said not a word!

Finally, Isobel could stand no more. Drawing Luna to a halt, she turned in the saddle and glared at him. 'Speak, for the love of God!'

He drew his courser to a halt alongside, his knee brushing hers. 'What would you have me say?' His grin was both audacious and triumphant. 'If it is any consolation, the silence was grating on me too, so shall we call our wager equal?'

'I did not agree to any wager, as I recall!'

'No, that is true,' he agreed, his indulgent tone making her feel even more childish. 'So what topic shall we talk of?'

'Anything, as long as it is not tedious and has nothing to do with…decisions of any kind!'

Isobel couldn't bring herself to say the hateful words—marriage or a nunnery—although she was aware that, even during the pleasure of the ride, those words had been there all the time, keeping pace with the beat of hooves and the rustling of autumn leaves as they fell from the trees.

Never had she felt so trapped, so helpless, her life reduced to two options that would only entrap and disempower her even more. For doubtless the Earl of Warwick, or Edmund himself, would marry her off to some man who was both a stranger and a Yorkist, or else, as she had no wealth of her own, place her in whichever convent would deign to take her without a dowry.

'Why don't you tell me something about you, Isobel? That, I suspect, is a topic far from tedious.'

Isobel nudged Luna into a walk again. Was he jesting, or being serious? Either way, she was as reluctant to talk about herself as she was to give him a decision she'd not yet made. 'There is not much to tell,' she replied dismissively, 'at least no more than you must already know.'

'I know nothing beyond the fact that you are John Calvert's only daughter, and that you have—or had—one brother.'

The inflexion of the past tense came as a painful reminder that, for all her conviction to the contrary, Tom *must* have died from his wounds in that monastery. Though surely, if that was the case, would the monks not have sent word? Perhaps they were Yorkists too!

'I refuse to believe my brother is dead,' Isobel retorted, 'so please do not refer to him as if he were!'

'As you wish.'

But even that compliance sounded so final, so hopeless, that the horizon suddenly blurred in front of her eyes as she turned her mare homewards.

'Your mother, the Lady Blanche, died some time ago, I believe?'

Why, oh, why had she broken the silence if all he meant to do was remind her of what she'd lost, and what little was left to her? 'Yes,' she replied shortly. 'When I was a child.'

The breeze grew stronger, playing with the horses' manes, driving crispy curling leaves across their path. It played with Deverell's hair too, since he was bare-headed, though Isobel herself had wound her hair tightly up inside her coif.

'How old were you?'

'Four.'

'That must have been a very difficult time for you.'

His tone was sombre and Isobel could feel his eyes on her face, though she kept her own eyes fixed on the road ahead. 'I don't remember her very well.'

'I didn't ask if you remembered her, Isobel. I asked if it was difficult for you.'

'Yes, of *course* it was difficult,' Isobel said, still not meeting his waiting gaze. 'My mother died in childbirth, leaving Tom newly born and my father heartbroken and disconsolate. How could it *not* have been difficult, for us all?'

Deverell, instead of being satisfied, probed all the more. 'Who raised you both?'

At least that was something easier to answer. 'My brother had a wet nurse, of course, and my father's widowed sister came to live with us. She stayed with us until she married again, some eight years later. After that, I looked after my father, and Tom.'

'But you would have been only twelve then, still a child.'

Isobel shot him a scornful glance. 'Girls are often already wed at that age, and even quick with a child of their own. My father was content to allow me to run Mistlecote, and remain at home, and unwed.'

'And you preferred that to marriage?'

'Yes.' She couldn't help it, since it was too good an opportunity to let pass. 'I still do!'

'Why?'

The question caught her off guard and her reply this time was defensive even to her ears. 'I *could* have married, since more than one suitor asked for my hand, but I refused them.'

'Because you found them lacking?'

Isobel suppressed a sigh of irritation. 'None of them were appealing enough to make me leave Mistlecote,' she said, simply, since it was the truth in part. 'I was happy as I was and my brother needed me.'

Until now she'd never thought of those years since she'd passed her twelfth summer and grown into womanhood, almost without her realising it. They had gone by so quickly, it seemed, though it hadn't felt like it as her life had fallen into a pattern of duty, and familiarity, and purpose. Now those years rushed upon her all at once as Deverell probed deeper still.

'You said he had a nurse?'

'Only until he was eight years old, but it was more...' She paused, unwilling to reveal so much to this man she hardly knew. 'Tom was still a child.'

'As were you...'

Isobel shrugged. 'I was old enough to take responsibility and I did so.' There was no reason she should explain anything but suddenly she found herself doing exactly that. 'It wasn't that my father…*blamed* Tom for my mother's death, but rather that his son reminded him too much of her loss, his pain. And I think, because of that, he couldn't feel anything at all for him, only a cold indifference, and so…'

'So you gave your brother the affection and care that your sire could not?'

'Yes.'

'Did you not consider taking a husband when your brother grew to manhood?'

'No,' she replied shortly. 'I did not.'

'Had *he* married,' Deverell went on, 'it would have been impossible for you to continue as mistress of Mistlecote in any case.'

Her fingers tightened on the reins. 'Tom is but twenty yet.'

'A man old enough for marriage…and there cannot be two mistresses of a house.'

Isobel darted a glance at him. 'If you are trying to dislodge me from my manor with insinuations, you are wasting your time.'

And yet, she *was* dislodged, or soon would be, for all that she dug her heels in. She would be cast out of her home and tossed into a sea of uncertainties and fears, unless she found a way to prevent it.

'I am insinuating nothing, Isobel, although I can't help but wonder. While you were being responsible, and capable, and devoting yourself to looking after your father and your brother, who looked after *you*?'

The question struck like lightning, so startling that Isobel jolted in the saddle. Something closed tightly around her throat and, for a moment, she couldn't breathe, let alone answer him. Silly tears came from nowhere to burn behind her eyes and she pushed Luna into a gallop, desperate to hide both the shock and the emotions that came in its wake.

But the wind in her face, the thrill of speed, the illusion of freedom, didn't hide anything at all. Instead everything became starkly and unbearably clear. All her days she'd known who she was and what she wanted, or what she'd thought she wanted. She'd known what her duties were, the role she must play, and she'd been content with her existence, never looking for anything different, anything more.

But now Deverell had come and shattered all that and, even worse, had forced her to confront things she'd never even recognised before.

He was close at her side, his courser easily keeping pace with Luna, his body leaning forward, strong and firm in the saddle, in total control of both himself and his steed. There was no fleeing him, nor her fate, perhaps not even her own self, no matter how fast or how far she galloped.

Suddenly the mare veered violently to the side and, too late, Isobel saw a hare shoot out of cover of the long grass. Orion and Sirius set off in hot pursuit and, unprepared, her thoughts preoccupied, she couldn't react in time. The reins slipped from between her fingers and she felt daylight between her and the saddle. A flash of blue sky dazzled for an instant and then she hit the ground with a sickening thud.

Edmund reined in sharply and turned his horse to one side as Isobel fell almost beneath its hooves. Flinging himself out of the saddle, he rushed to where she lay and dropped to his knees beside her.

'Isobel!'

Her eyes were open, although they were staring upwards, and her gloved fingers were digging into the grass beneath her. Gently placing his hands on her shoulders, he gave her a little shake. She blinked and focused.

'Luna!'

Edmund didn't even spare the mare a glance, though he was aware it seemed none the worse for the mishap and was cropping at the grass near by. The hounds, having given up their chase of the hare, were returning at a bounding run.

'Your mare is unharmed, but you…are you hurt?'

'I don't think so, no…' A grimace shot across her features. 'I'm not hurt, merely winded.'

'Even so, lie still a moment to be sure.'

Her gown had ridden up and her lower legs were exposed, stockinged to the knees. Her feet were booted, and one leg was twisted at an awkward angle. Carefully, Edmund straightened it and then felt along the thigh, knee, shin bone and down to the ankle. He found no breaks anywhere, nor swelling either, though doubtless there would be bruising on her body, beneath her clothing, which he could not see.

Suddenly her leg twitched under his hands and, sitting up, she pushed him aside and drew her skirts down to her feet. 'What are you doing?'

Edmund sat back on his heels. 'I was checking lest there were any bones broken.'

Her coif had come off and her braid undone, leaving her hair loose to tumble down over her shoulders, and her face was a ghastly shade of pale. 'Did I ask you to? I told you I'm not hurt!'

She struggled to her feet, ignoring the hand he put out to help her. 'If I *had* broken my leg, I would have known it!'

Rising to his feet too, Edmund looked at her keenly. Even if there were no broken bones, the smudge of dirt at her temple indicated that she'd hit her head. 'A fall from a horse at such speed is a daunting experience,' he said, 'no matter how skilled a rider one is.'

'It is not the first tumble I have taken, nor is it likely to be the last.'

She was brushing grass and dirt off her clothing now, her movements seemingly unhindered by any hidden pain or dizziness. There were leaves entangled in her hair here and there, and Edmund couldn't resist plucking one free.

'You have some leaves in your hair,' he explained as Isobel frowned at him. 'I was just removing one.'

'Oh…' Colour flooded her face then ebbed again. 'I can do it myself.'

She drew her hair forward over one shoulder and removed a small twig, her fingers working quickly, almost impatiently. Her hair was longer than he'd thought now that no braids confined it nor coif concealed it, and fell full to her hips.

Edmund itched to help her disentangle those glorious locks, to seek out the debris she could not reach. But since his help was clearly not welcome he stayed his hand, for a moment at least. All around the air was silent, only the gurgle of the river and the singing of birds, and the sound of the two horses grazing side by side. There was something so innocent and yet so sensual in the way she was arranging her hair that he felt himself grow warmer than the day warranted.

Granted, the sun was still strong and the breeze light, but that did not explain the heating of his skin, the burning sensation of his blood as it rushed faster through his veins, the pulling of the sinews in his loins. Finally, unable to resist any longer, he reached out and removed a leaf that was clinging to the crown of her head.

'You have missed one.'

Isobel's eyes were a little unfocused still, as if her head did indeed ache, though she was not pale now at all. Instead there was a flush on her cheek and, at her throat, Edmund saw a pulse begin to beat fast and strong as she stiffened and drew herself upright.

'Oh…well, no matter,' she said, haughtily. 'That will suffice, and now…we should go.'

Isobel spun away, almost tripped over the hem of her gown, and then righted herself, and looked around for her coif. Her head was beginning to throb and she realised, despite her denial, that she must have hit the ground hard. Well, at least her fall had knocked some sense into her. Gone were the irrational tears that had come in the wake of his penetrating question and in its place now burned indignation. Who'd looked after her? She herself, of course, as she did still!

And a headache, though discomforting, was nothing compared to the mortification she'd felt as he'd laid his hands on her. A touch she'd been only dimly aware of while she'd been dizzy but now, even though his hands were nowhere near her, she could still feel them, as if in hindsight— the gentle way he'd felt over her leg, the tenderness with which he'd plucked those leaves from her hair.

No man had ever touched her…not like that…not in such an intimate manner, and, dazed or not, the contact had shaken her far more than the fall from Luna had. Powerful responses had resulted, ones that she didn't understand, ones which had unsettled her, frightened her though not with any kind of fear she'd ever known before.

'Your coif is here.'

Isobel turned, saw him holding it out to her, hesitated. The thought of taking it from him, their hands touching, was suddenly too dangerous to contemplate. But the alternative, as he stepped forward, sent her into a fluster.

'Would you like me to tie it—?'

'No!' she replied hastily and, snatching the coif from him, bundled her hair up under it anyhow and secured it as best her trembling fingers would allow. 'I can manage.'

'I'm not sure that you can.'

Meeting his eyes again, Isobel saw them twinkling, his lips twitching in a smile as, sure enough, unruly strands of hair refused to stay where she'd put them. With a scowl she pulled her coif off again and shoved it into the pouch tied to her belt. 'Shall we go?' she said coldly.

Retrieving Luna, she paused as another obstacle faced her. How was she to mount with no mounting block or stable lad to help her? She could hitch up her gown, of course, as she'd done many times in order to mount, but only when alone. Doing so now would mean baring her legs once more to Edmund Deverell!

There was nothing for it but to ask him to help her, even though it rankled that, on this occasion anyway, she couldn't look to herself. 'If you would help me mount…'

He came immediately and, stooping, linked his fingers together, ready for her foot. With the reins in one hand, and her skirt firmly in the other, Isobel stepped into his waiting palms and felt herself lifted into the air as if she weighed nothing.

'Thank you,' she muttered ungraciously as she settled herself in the saddle. 'Shall we resume?'

He gave a nod, his hand on Luna's withers, his eyes narrowing with undue concern. 'But perhaps rather more slowly?'

Isobel nodded in return. She didn't feel like galloping anyway, since her head was pounding, and that question of his still hovered unsettlingly over her heart. She *hadn't* needed anyone to look after her as she'd been growing up, never even sought or expected anyone's help. So why did his worried gaze now trouble her so?

'Naturally. I would not let Luna get hot and sweaty again so close to home,' she said dismissively. 'We will walk the rest of the way.'

They rode in silence for perhaps half a league, Isobel keeping her gaze fixed firmly ahead where Mistlecote's walls appeared, quite near now. But, out of the corner of her eye, she studied him. He sat a horse well, she had to admit, with a natural and easy confidence rather than the arrogance she'd imagined. His hands were gentle, though commanding, on the reins, and the sway of his hips and shoulders disturbingly compelling.

'How is your head?'

Isobel glanced sideways at him and away again. 'You need not be concerned. If it hadn't been for the hare, it would not have happened.'

He shrugged but, as they rode on, she felt his eyes return to her often, linger, thoughtful and penetrating, making her breath hard to draw and her palms grow moist within her gloves.

She knew men gazed lasciviously at women and sometimes women—the brazen and shameless sort anyway—gazed right back, but she wasn't one of them. Edmund Deverell's stare evoked different feelings in her, not ones of uninterest and distaste at all. Strong feelings of wanting to return his stare, being drawn by a force almost too strong to resist.

A force that, at last, she obeyed, and turned to face him. 'What are you staring at?'

'You, Isobel.'

To her amazement, he flushed, the sharp cheekbones turning decidedly scarlet. And between them something seemed to stir the air, a strange recognition of things unseen, but felt all the same.

'Do you always speak so boldly to ladies?' she demanded.

He smiled and shook his head, the sun turning his hair to dazzling gold. 'No, as it happens, I do not.'

Isobel found herself wanting to smile back, but she stopped herself, wondering why her stomach was fluttering and her thoughts reeling, as if she'd taken too much wine. 'Then why are you doing so now?' she asked, pertly. 'Are you afraid I might fall off my horse again and you'll have to pick me up once more?'

'No…it is not that.' His smile faded and his expression grew serious. 'Though I almost wish it *were*.'

Isobel didn't know how to interpret or respond to the strange remark so she said nothing at all. But it rode with them the rest of the way home, embellished by the plodding of hooves that seemed to echo her heartbeat.

A heartbeat that faltered a little as they entered under Mistlecote's outer gate, the golden walls more honey-coloured as the autumn sun sank lower, the smoke curling upwards from the tall chimneys, welcoming her home.

But Mistlecote belonged to Edmund Deverell now. It was his banner that waved proudly over the gatehouse, his grooms that came running to take their horses, his men who straightened up and looked more alert as their leader returned. Even the aroma of the stew that came wafting from the kitchens had been prepared by his cook!

Isobel slid down from the saddle and, in a moment of rebellion, ignored the Yorkist man who stood waiting for her reins and beckoned to one of her own. Then she turned to Edmund Deverell and her moment of rebellion vanished as he lifted his fingers to her temple.

'There is a bruise forming here. Does it pain you?'

'No.'

His touch lingered, his eyes bored into hers and his breath was coming rather quicker than before. And, all at once, Isobel saw it and recognised it, doubting it even as she did so. But surely she was not mistaken! What else could cause him to look so wrong-footed, so awkward? What else would make his voice and his hand shake so, and his cheeks turn crimson?

'All the same…do you wish me to send my physician to you?'

'No…' she replied again, her pulse beginning to race. Could it be true though? Could it really be desire? Did Edmund Deverell—her hated enemy—desire her? 'But thank you all the same for the offer.'

His fingers finally fell away from her temple to curl into a ball at his side. 'Then I will see you at the supper table tonight?'

There was a distinct note of expectation, of command, in the remark. Isobel had intended to sup in her room, as she had the previous night. But suddenly, a thought occurred. If he did desire her…could she…should she encourage it? Use his desire against him to get what she wanted? To remain at Mistlecote?

A man who lusted after a woman might become a slave to his lust. He might grant all sorts of requests in the hope that she would succumb and give him her body. She'd seen it happen to Tom when he'd become smitten with the pretty daughter of a visiting Welsh lord once, several years ago. He'd been like a moon-calf for days while Mirain was under their roof, and disconsolate for weeks when she'd left again, his ardour scorned, his heart broken, or so he claimed.

If Tom—so stalwart and sensible—could become weak and easily manipulated because of passion, could not Edmund Deverell also? There was only one way to find out. Taking her courage in her hands, Isobel nodded, sending him a little smile, noting the surprise in his eyes.

'It will depend on whether my headache improves,' she said lightly, and then with more weight, 'but, yes, I hope to be at the supper table tonight.'

Then she turned and, calling to her hounds, walked away towards the hall, knowing he watched her go. Never in all her days had she imagined she would—or even could—play the coquette with a man. It was something unfamiliar, alien to her nature, something she'd never wanted and never needed to do.

Until now.

Edmund watched Isobel walk away with long, graceful strides, her hips swaying, her hair tumbling down her back like a waterfall of dark fire as the sinking sun lit the courtyard. A sort of fire consumed him too, one that had been smouldering inside him since the moment he'd laid his hands on her. A fire that flared even higher now as already he anticipated suppertime with an excitement that sent his blood gushing in torrents through his veins.

The thought of Isobel sitting at his side at table, her flesh merely a gesture away, her eyes simply a glance sideways... Her presence alone ignited desires he'd long since believed he'd eliminated, a weakness he'd long since conquered.

But it seemed not! Damn it! He'd been so distracted by desire, by Isobel, that he hadn't even pressed her for her decision!

Drawing a deep breath, Edmund took that omission as a lesson, and one he would not waste. If today was any indication, then every day Isobel remained would make her harder to ignore, and resist. He might reach a point where he didn't even want to resist her!

That disturbing thought vanished as Alain appeared in front of him. 'A tasty wench, Edmund. If I was a marrying kind of man, I might be tempted by her, but I think it is *you* she has tempted!'

Edmund shook his head, retorting more harshly than he'd intended. 'Then your sight is deceiving you, dolthead! Or else your wits are blunted and making your tongue run away with you.'

'Hold hard, man!' Alain, no respecter of rank, grinned unabashed. 'Since when were you so quick to bridle at an innocent observation?'

Since this afternoon, Edmund thought grimly, when he'd discovered that he not only desired Isobel but that he'd also begun to care about her, more deeply than he ought to. That moment when he'd asked who'd looked after her had touched a nerve in her, and instead of answering him she'd fled. Why?

'Observations that are as ridiculous as they are mistaken!' He forced a grin too, though it felt like a grotesque grimace. 'But neither am I a marrying kind of man these days, Alain, as you well know.'

His sergeant had heard of his ill-fated first marriage during a drunken evening together in a tavern. 'Naturally, but now you have gained your manor, you will need heirs to keep it, and I can think of no more enticing a woman to provide you them than she, Edmund.'

The Frenchman's eyes narrowed pensively as he too gazed after Isobel's retreating figure. 'Marriage to the

Calvert girl would unite your two families, as well as ensure her loyalty to York. Think upon it, man! I would in your place.'

Alain was right, of course, heirs would be required, one day, to follow him and hold this manor in perpetuity. But that day was far in the future and any wife he eventually chose would not evoke any feelings in him beyond fidelity and affection.

Someone unlike Isobel, who, in a few short hours, had almost disassembled the defences he'd built up around his heart over the last four years. Did that not prove that those defences were inadequate, or else had not been threatened so perilously until now? And did that not come as a warning he must build them higher still?

As he walked slowly into the hall, Edmund reached mentally for the stone and quicklime with which to commence that building, but somehow they would not come to hand. Instead, his heart sensed again the fleeing vulnerability he'd glimpsed in Isobel and his fingers felt the silken warmth of her hair as he'd unwisely plucked away those errant leaves.

He should have left the leaves where they were and his heart well out of it!

Chapter Five

That evening, Isobel put on a murrey-coloured gown that was a little lower in the neckline and a little tighter in the waist than those she normally wore. Taking up her mother's mirror, she combed her hair until it shone, then she peered closer and inspected her skin. She was pale—since it was the time of her flewsa—and there were lines of anxiety under her eyes, but her lips were full and well-shaped and needed no balm or tincture.

She ran the tip of her forefinger over her mouth, tracing its curve, wondering how Edmund's mouth would fit there, what it would feel like. Immediately, her cheeks became anything but pale and there would be no need to colour her complexion with angelica at all at this rate!

At least those strange feelings she'd had that afternoon were gone, replaced by a cool and clear intent. After all, they must simply have been the result of her fall, her dizziness and confusion, and before that the seeking questions that had seemed to expose her very soul. But now she had the weapons she needed.

Plaiting her hair into two thick braids, Isobel noted how well the colour contrasted with the whiteness of her throat. The swell of her breasts at the neckline of her gown looked too naked, however, and so she put on a necklace hung with a large ruby pendant.

Then, placing a gold circlet studded with pearls on her brow and looping a chain belt low on her waist to emphasise her slender shape, she turned for the door. But there she paused, the changes in her body sending mixed feelings through her—trepidation, a sort of delight, and a new sense of power.

Discovering Edmund Deverell's lust, which she knew all men possessed, was an opportunity she must not waste. If he could become so distracted at the feel of a woman's hair, or her body, then he could also be pliable, perhaps even biddable, and weak, while she would be strong.

She must be strong enough also to overcome, or at least suppress, the distractions of her *own* body. Strong enough to ignore and deny the physical responses she'd experienced that afternoon as he'd evoked in her an awareness of a man for the first time in her life.

Her sex and her cunning were her only advantage over this Yorkist invader and she would not let that disturbing awareness weaken her advantage. She had everything to gain and nothing to lose, for he would send her away sooner or later. All she had to do was detach herself from any unwelcome responses and wayward thoughts, focus on using her femininity, her allure—which he appeared to appreciate—to get what she wanted.

As Isobel entered the hall everyone got to their feet, which was so unexpected she almost dashed back out again. Was the reverence because this was the first time she'd appeared at the table since the Yorkists had arrived the day before—or because she'd been riding alone with Edmund Deverell that afternoon and all were agog now with speculation?

Deverell took her hand and gallantly seated her in the chair to his right. As she composed herself, spreading her skirt out around her legs, Isobel made sure the outline of her thighs was visible, noting the drop of his eyes, and the quick lift a moment later.

'May I serve you, Isobel?'

She murmured a response in a tone that she hoped was worthy of any courtesan. 'Thank you.'

He speared a leg of roast duckling from the platter and put it on her plate. Isobel noted the slight shake of his hand as he filled her goblet with wine and a secret smile tugged at her lips. Was it so easy, then, to affect a man? Did a woman need only to sit close to his side, wear a gown that both revealed and concealed at the same time, flutter her eyelashes and grant him a rare, but encouraging, smile to set him all fingers and thumbs?

'Has your headache gone? No other after-effects from your fall this afternoon?'

'Yes, thank you, Sir Edmund.' Isobel laid the thickest of emphasis on the title, one which she'd never used before. 'And no, no after-effects at all.'

She had to admit that he looked elegant this evening, far removed from the dusty serviceable soldier's attire he'd worn during their ride. Now Edmund Deverell wore a snow-white linen shirt beneath his doublet, with a dark green surcoat over, giving a striking contrast through the slashes in his sleeves and at his cuffs. The hose on his legs was of fine black wool and his thigh-length leather boots were highly polished.

'Good.' He took up his meat. 'I am pleased to hear it.'

He wore no rings on his fingers, she saw, no adornment whatsoever to dim his undeniable masculinity. She knew nothing of masculinity, of course, apart from what she'd noticed over the years growing up alongside her brother and his friends, but she was a quick learner. And now she had to learn, quicker than ever before, all there was to know about masculinity.

'And, my tumble aside…' Isobel took up her leg of roast duckling, pausing to speak before biting into it '…I enjoyed our ride together very much…more than I'd expected to.'

The effect of her words was not the one she'd expected or hoped for. A frown settled on his brow and there was no shake of his hand now as he lifted his meat to his mouth. Was she being too obvious, too friendly? Was he puzzled by this change in her attitude towards him? Was her gown too clingy, too immodest?

Isobel wiped her fingers on her napkin and, as he still made no response to her previous remark, added to it.

'I don't know why I managed to fall off as I did,' she said, infusing a hint of pride into the remark. 'I am a better rider than that and Luna does not often take me by surprise.'

'Mayhap you were distracted?' His gaze didn't meet hers. 'Your mind on other things?'

'Possibly,' Isobel replied, aware that her mind had indeed been on other things. But now…was her advantage slipping away even before she'd properly gained it? Had something happened since this afternoon? 'Perhaps we can ride out again tomorrow?' she ventured. 'My mare was too fresh today, which is why she shied. Usually I ride her for miles every day.'

'Perhaps.'

His tone was cool and, taking a sip from her cup, Isobel glanced around the hall. Nothing seemed untoward, everyone was eating and drinking, no unease was evident, no undue tension in the air, or at least no more than she supposed was usual for a house under occupation. The servitors were going about their duties and, at the head of the table to her right, a minstrel was tuning a lute.

'Would you like some music, Isobel?'

The clipped, too polite question only confirmed that something had indeed happened, though she knew not what. Perhaps he thought she was babbling, or too eager for his company when she'd shunned it so blatantly before.

Isobel nodded. Novice that she was, she must have been far too obvious, clumsy even. 'Music might make the hall a bit more jolly,' she said, 'So yes, by all means, let us have music.'

Edmund beckoned to his troubadours, who immediately rose from their seats and positioned themselves in the middle of the room. He waited until the first song—a French love song—was ended, and then turned to Isobel, refilling her wine cup, and his too.

'Do you find the hall unjolly, then?'

She met his eyes, her own slightly wary, an uncertain smile on her lips. 'Not unjolly...perhaps unfamiliar would be a more apt description.'

'Does it not look as it always has?'

'Of course.' Her head turned away and she took a sip of her wine. 'It is the company that has changed.'

Edmund studied her profile. It wasn't only the company that had changed—Isobel had changed too. He'd sensed it the moment she'd walked into the hall like a queen, dressed in a gown that was as beguiling as it was beautiful. Of a rich, wine-coloured velvet, with long, hanging sleeves that revealed the snug sleeves of the kirtle below, the garment hugged her body like an embrace. The intricate lacing at the back had his fingers itching to undo it and, while the neckline wasn't indecently low, it emphasised the swell of her breasts until he could almost feel them in his palms.

Lust—desire—admiration— had hit him, one after the other, right in the middle of his chest. And, in the wake of all those unwanted responses, the ghost of Mariette had risen up before his eyes. His appetite had vanished and an irritation had settled instead in his stomach at the knowledge that he could be so easily affected.

Isobel was still smiling as she listened to the music, and the scent of rosewater on her skin, even the lingering aroma of grass on her hair, invaded his nostrils and sent his senses spinning. Her mouth was even more lovely when she smiled, and it drew him as if by an invisible thread to look at it, again and again, to imagine its taste, its texture. And when he wasn't drawn to her mouth, he sought her eyes, as they sought his, like a promise calling him into a deep and dangerous forest, where once more he'd find himself ensnared.

'Is anything amiss, Sir Edmund?'

Even that—especially that. The courteous, formal yet over-familiar use of his title was new—and somehow wrong, false. And as he shook his head, a falsehood too, since there was something very much amiss, Edmund knew then what it was.

Tonight, Isobel reminded him of Mariette. Her gaze, her tone, the way she held herself, the deliberate coquetry, which admittedly fell far short of his former wife's mastery of the art. The demeanour that could change with the weather, or be suited to her moods. The whims so meekly but so cleverly put that they had tied a rope around his neck and led him like a lamb to the slaughter.

Even now, as Isobel dropped her knife onto the floor, feigning dismay, she evinced the same attempt to wheedle her way around him as Mariette had used. Perhaps even the reticent manner in which she'd revealed her childhood that afternoon had all been cleverly played out for him!

Gallantly, Edmund retrieved the knife, of course, from where it lay between their chairs, but as he straightened again his eyes fastened on the outline of her body, the curve of her hip, the small waist and high, round breasts. As he placed the knife down next to her plate, her hair—bound with silken braids—glinted like bronze in the candlelight and dazzled him until he yearned to lift a lock to his nose and breathe in its fragrance.

Isobel was beautiful, she was beguiling, and he would be lying to himself if he tried to deny the desire she evoked in him, desire she doubtless recognised and was prepared to take full advantage of. But he wasn't that foolish and love-blind youth any more. He was older and wiser, master of himself and of his heart. Only once in a lifetime could a man endure the pain and the shame that followed when love unmanned him and then destroyed him. And once was more than enough for him.

Tearing his gaze from hers, Edmund turned it to the troubadours, who stood clutching their lute and tabor as if undecided whether to retire or to resume. At his nod they took up an amorous song popular among soldiers in field camps in France. The lyrics were in French, of course, and he glanced sideways at Isobel. Did she know French? he wondered. Her face was impassive, but when the men who had come with him from Calais joined in the refrain, the blush that crept slowly up her cheek gave him the answer.

As the song ended, to loud applause, he asked Guillaume and Raoul for something gentler, and more fitting for the ears of a lady. The troubadours obliged and a dreamy atmosphere gradually replaced the robust air of a moment ago.

However, as the notes floated up to the rafters and the lyrics mourned a love lost, Edmund wished his request back.

The song was one that Mariette had sung often, at least in the early days of their courtship, before he'd realised she sang other songs too, some bawdy enough to make even the most hardened soldier blush.

Isobel spoke suddenly at his side. 'The song is very sad, is it not? Do your minstrels not know any English songs?'

In truth, the song was not to his liking either, since it sang of a man who lost his sweetheart to his enemy and, unable to live with the loss, chose death on the battlefield. They were lyrics he'd understood well, once, for his passion for Mariette had been so intense that he might well have sought a quick end in battle than go on living without her.

'They do indeed know many English songs and will, of course, play some for you.'

Edmund requested a happier tune in the language that was, after all, his own, then sat back and looked around the hall. The oak panelling glowed darkly and the tiled floor shone ruby red. The tapestries that hung at intervals were elaborate and expensive, and the mullioned windows reflected the firelight back into the room. Along the walls, candles flickered in tall holders, and from the hammerbeam ceiling hung a *couronne de lumière*—a metal corona holding a dozen more candles.

His hall. His home. The one he'd dreamed he'd bring Mariette to one day—before he'd learned she preferred the slums he'd rescued her from.

Isobel's voice came again, breaking into his morbid recollections. 'Perhaps, having spent so long in exile, you prefer French melodies now?'

'That sounds as much an accusation as a question,' Edmund said, meeting her eyes. 'Is it one?'

'Perhaps it is,' she mused. 'Or mayhap I am envious, as I myself have never left England.'

'I cannot recommend exile as a way of seeing the world, but it contains many lovely lands.'

'How many have you seen?'

'France, of course. Spain, Burgundy, and Italy…the northern states anyway.'

'I think I would like to see more of the world, as long as I could always return home any time I chose.'

Their eyes held as the music flowed on, seeming to get louder, rising to the hammerbeam roof and drowning out everything else in the hall—the sound of voices, of cups and plates and knives, the legs of a bench scraping on the floor as someone moved place.

His bench, his hall, his home and, at his side, the woman he must oust from *her* home, for there was no place for her here. It should be simple. It had been simple yesterday, before he'd ridden through autumn meadows with her. Before he'd asked her about herself and she'd told him, albeit unwillingly, and showed him a vulnerability which now seemed at odds with her brazenness tonight.

The music stopped suddenly, interrupted by the flinging open of the hall door. One of the guards on duty strode in and approached the high table, holding out a parchment, rolled tightly and bound with red ribbon.

'This has just arrived, Sir Edmund. The messenger waits for a reply.'

Edmund broke the seal, which he'd recognised at once. The message was momentous if not unexpected. At his side, Isobel leaned forward, her scent distracting him from the words he read.

'What does it say?'

'It is from the Earl of Warwick,' he said. 'From London.'

'The King…?'

'Still in captivity.' There was worse to come, at least for her, so she might as well hear it straight away. 'The message concerns Richard, Duke of York.'

Edmund met the wide green eyes, fearful eyes now, all coquetry gone. But it was just as well. The news in the missive was all the more reason to see Isobel settled in a nunnery, out of harm's way should war come to Mistlecote, or else married to some lucky man, on whom she could practise her charms to her heart's content.

'On his return from exile, six weeks ago, the Duke made a formal claim to the throne before Parliament. It was not accepted outright, but an Act of Accord, proclaimed on the last day of October, has named him King Henry's legal and rightful heir.'

'The Prince has been disinherited?' The words were more of a gasp as Isobel's hand went to her throat. 'But… but that is not right nor just. It is impossible…unthinkable!'

'Unthinkable or not, Isobel, it is so.'

Edmund sensed the excitement building in the hall, even though he'd not yet made an announcement, as men looked towards him in expectation, others with heads together in speculation of what the letter contained. Before he told them, however, there was more he had to impart, not to the waiting company, but to Isobel.

He held her waiting eyes, saw the parting of her lips, felt her breath quicken and come warmly to his face as she leaned closer, as if to ask what he had to tell her. His heart began to race, so fast he felt light-headed, and his mouth dried, even as the words filled it.

'There is something else in this missive that you should hear…'

Edmund heard his voice come oddly in his ears, as if the

words came from outside of himself, not from within, the sentences they formed going in and out of focus, becoming indistinct, nonsensical, impossible.

'Warwick advises me that the Lord of Ledwyche has heard of your…circumstances and has expressed interest in taking your hand in marriage.' The fingers that held the parchment tightened to stop them shaking, the same instinctive way they tightened on the reins when he rode into battle. 'He holds a large estate near Ludlow and is a widower, his wife dead some years now. He wishes—'

Chapter Six

Isobel didn't wait to hear the rest. The whole room seemed to shake and heave as she pushed herself to her feet, her fingers gripping the edges of the table and her legs hollowing beneath her.

'M-marry George Ledwyche? The man is ancient!' Her voice trembled so much she could hardly speak. 'Is Warwick mad?'

But Deverell merely shrugged. 'Naturally, Warwick will allow you to enter a nunnery, if you decide on that course instead of marriage.'

Nausea rose up into Isobel's mouth. Suddenly all her finery and coquetry seemed both ridiculous and humiliating, and ultimately pointless. Edmund Deverell was on his feet now and calling for quiet. The hall fell silent, everyone eager to hear what the message had been. They didn't have to wait long.

'Richard, Duke of York, has been formally and legally declared, by his peers in Parliament, as the rightful heir to King Henry, who will retain the crown for the remainder of his life.'

Cheers began even before he'd finished imparting the news, and there was a banging of cups and stamping of feet and slapping of backs—at least among the Yorkists.

Her own people sat mute, their expressions a mix of shock, disbelief and fear, all emotions she too shared.

Deverell held his hand up and silence fell once more. 'On the death of the present king, the Duke of York will succeed, as will all his heirs after him. Also…' He cleared his throat, as if a lump had risen and settled there. 'Also, the proceedings of the Parliament at Coventry a year ago, after Ludford Bridge, have been set aside, and all Yorkists are now free of attainder and of the slur of treachery.'

Cheers broke out again, even louder than before, but Isobel hardly heard them as her own fear deafened her. Surely this sealed her fate? Her delay in making a decision was irrelevant now, since Warwick had made it for her. She would either become George Ledwyche's wife and be chained to an old man for the rest of his days—or *hers,* should she die first of sheer misery!—or spend her life in a similar prison behind the walls of a convent.

A cold hand closed around her heart and breath failed her as someone among the Yorkists started up a chant, 'Richard of York to be King! Richard of York to be King!' Soon all his comrades had joined in, one of the musicians that had played the lute so beautifully only moments ago now striding up and down the hall banging a tabor.

Isobel's head began to pound. 'I… I feel unwell,' she muttered, to no one in particular, and nobody paid any heed anyway. Groping her way around the table, she made for the door to the solar, her hounds following. The troubadour fell in behind her, banging his drum in time to her footsteps, and worse, his companion ran to join in the fun. Pipe in hand, he danced before her, playing a silly tune she recognised as a child's skipping song.

Blindly she pushed him out of the way, so violently that he fell flat on his rump, causing even more hilarity around the hall. Resisting the urge to flee, though she dearly wanted to, Isobel lengthened her strides towards the door. Orion and Sirius began to bark but even their noise was drowned out by a cruel taunt that was taken up with glee by the Yorkists.

'Run, bitch of Lancaster! Run right hale! For the Duke of York is hot on your tail!'

The door was just there, in front of her, but her hands fumbled with the latch. She pushed and it opened so abruptly that she all but stumbled through it, just as Edmund Deverell's voice boomed out like thunder.

'Quiet!'

Silence fell immediately, as if everyone realised they'd gone too far, and then she heard him call her name.

'Isobel! Wait!'

Isobel ignored it and hurried on. She'd nearly reached her chamber when she felt his arms close about her. Furiously she fought him but he held her tight against him, saying words that she couldn't hear over the sound of her blood pounding in her ears, the barking of the hounds, and of her own voice too.

'Devils! Knaves! Curse them all! How dare they speak so to me? How dare they make fun of me? I hate them… I hate the Duke of York and I hate Warwick…and I hate you!'

He turned her in his arms so that her face was against his chest, his heartbeat even louder than the drum that had chased her from the hall, his hand cradling the back of her head, as if she were a child having a tearful tantrum.

'They will be reprimanded for their insolence, Isobel, I promise you.'

Furiously, Isobel lifted her eyes to his, intent on telling him to release her, her palms pressing themselves against him, pushing him away. For all the quiet calm of his voice, the gentle hold he had on her, his gaze was like a tempestuous sea. And even through the raging of her own storm, she saw the same thing she'd seen there that afternoon. Desire.

'Isobel...'

His voice was not calm now as his body hardened against hers and his arms tightened. He was strong, warm, alive, ardent and Isobel couldn't have pushed him away now even if she'd tried her utmost.

Her body came alive too, as if the contact with his had lit a spark deep inside her, engulfing her in flames. Her heart filled her chest, until she thought it would burst with feeling, as slowly his head dipped towards hers. A moment of stillness, when even the noise in the hall—that had started up again on his departure—faded to nothing.

And then his mouth took hers, not soft, nor soothing, nor comforting, but with passion, a kiss of pure hunger. Isobel's legs went weak, though not in the way they had when she'd left the table. And instead of pushing him away, she curled her hands into his clothing and, with the same hunger, kissed him back.

It was like nothing she'd ever experienced before because she'd never been kissed like this before by any man. She heard herself moan and didn't know why she did so but at once his kiss deepened, grew even more demanding. The taste of him sent her head spinning and she cleaved closer, a yearning she didn't understand taking possession of her.

'Isobel...'

He said her name again, on a groan, and then his lips left hers and found her throat. Her head went back and she closed her eyes, clinging on to him as a host of sensations swept her away. An ache yawned low in her belly, between her legs, an ache so intense that it pulled at every sense, every inch of her skin, every pore of her body.

And then Isobel felt his hand close over her breast. The whole world seemed to explode and reform into something new, something thrilling. Her heart soared and her senses sang and her blood began to rush through her veins in a torrent of fire. It was so powerful, so consuming, so terrifying that she froze in utter shock for an instant before reality hurtled back.

'No! No!' With a mighty heave she pushed him away. 'Let go of me!'

Edmund released her at once and he took a step back, his hands dropping to his sides. His eyes shone brilliantly, dark as night, and his breath came fast and furious. Then Isobel saw him reassemble himself, piece by piece, as she knew she herself did, except not quite so quickly or so easily.

'I apologise…forgive me. I did not intend…that to happen when I followed you.'

'What *did* you intend, then?' Her kissing him back wasn't supposed to happen either! And neither was this reaction, this excitement, that made her voice quiver and her limbs shake. 'To insult me as your men did? To have some fun by treating me like…like…a whore?'

His face paled, as if all the blood had drained from his body. 'That is not at all what I intended,' he said. 'Nor ever would intend. But what did *you* intend, Isobel, when you put that dress on? When you played the coy and the coquette at table? Didn't you *intend* for me to kiss you tonight?'

Isobel's hand flew to her throat. She hadn't thought beyond beguiling him into giving her what she wanted— leave to remain at Mistlecote. The implications of getting that want met, what he would demand in return, the price she would have to pay, or that in the paying *she* might demand things too—things she should not want at all… No, she hadn't thought that far ahead, but clearly she should have done.

'I wore the dress because I *like* it,' Isobel said, since it was partly true. 'And even I, in my innocence, know a man should wait for a lady's invitation before he kisses her and not think he can grapple her into submission!'

There was a beat of silence before Edmund replied, his tone clipped. 'I was not grappling with you, I was trying to—'

But the words were left unfinished and, with a violent shake of his head and a few muttered words that she couldn't hear, he turned abruptly on his heel. He didn't return to the hall, however, but went out of the little door at the end of the corridor that led upwards to the battlements.

Turning for her room, Isobel flung herself over the threshold, slamming the door shut behind her. Then her knees finally gave way and she slumped to the floor. 'That wasn't supposed to happen at all!' she repeated out loud but failed to convince herself all the same. 'Not like that!' And as Orion and Sirius came to lie down beside her, their dark eyes troubled and confused, she burst into tears.

Up on the battlements, Edmund pounded his fist on the stone rampart, once, twice and then again, on the third time feeling a flint break the skin. The quick pain didn't help, and neither did the words of reproach he hurled at himself under his breath.

'Fool! Dolt! What in God's name did you think you were doing?'

There was no answer to that, not from he himself, let alone from a higher deity, but he didn't really need one because he knew full well what he'd been doing without having to ask. When Isobel had fled the hall, the ridicule of his men chasing her through the door, something had snapped in him, and anger and disgust at the behaviour of his soldiers had been the least of it.

He hadn't even stopped to think before leaping to his feet, snarling at the company as he strode from the hall in her wake. It hadn't occurred to him to consider his actions, to temper his reactions. All that had mattered was to go after her, comfort her, reassure her.

But instead he'd taken her in his arms and kissed her. And worse, his body had come to ardent life at the first touch of their lips. Desire had flowed through his veins as her breasts brushed his chest and their hearts had begun to beat urgently and in unison.

Even now his heart continued to thunder, his blood still gushing hot and his loins aflame. But his mind, at least, was clear. It hadn't been solely lust, or simple outrage on her behalf, that had spurred him in Isobel's wake. It hadn't been, as he'd declared in vile defence, because she'd flirted with him at table, worn that dress, used her body, her eyes, her voice so enticingly.

He'd *cared* about her feelings, he'd cared that she'd been insulted, humiliated, hurt. And he'd felt all of it as keenly as she must have done because…she *mattered* to him. She mattered very much, more than she should, more than he wanted her to.

With a groan Edmund dropped his head into his hands. He had to send her away, and soon. Tomorrow—tonight if he could. Either to marry George Ledwyche or to the nearest nunnery, as long as she was gone from here.

He groaned again. When had it happened? Desire—well, he was fully aware of when *that* had happened without having to ask, but this caring? He hardly knew Isobel, after all. He'd only met her a day ago, when she'd been merely a name, a problem to be solved, an inconvenience to be dealt with, as kindly as possible, and then forgotten.

But now…now she'd become so much more and it seemed to have occurred in the space of a few isolated and unwise moments when he should have known better. That afternoon, when he'd listened to her talk, heard or perhaps imagined the things she hadn't revealed, seen her vulnerability, her pride, her courage. When he'd threaded his fingers into her dishevelled hair and then lifted her into the saddle.

Concern had changed to desire and that desire had simmered beneath his skin all day long until tonight when his lips had touched hers. Touched and then begun to drink like a man dying of thirst.

Was that what it was? Was it simply because he'd not bedded or even kissed a woman for over four years that had made him lose all control? Allowed his body to feel, to want, to drive him to thoughts, to actions, to needs that he should have, and once *would* have, curbed?

The man on watch trudged past him, with a grunt of greeting and a curious look, doubtless wondering what he was doing up here, in the dark, holding his head in his palms as if he'd taken too much wine at supper. But Edmund couldn't even blame it on that, could he? He'd barely been able to drink, eat or even breathe after Isobel had walked through the door, those cursed hounds at her heels, wearing that murrey-coloured gown of a hue richer than *any* wine.

Her long sleeves trailing, the ruby between her breasts, the golden circlet around her forehead, a fashion that was outdated now, but on her…on her it had been as if a breath of fresh air had suddenly rushed into his lungs, clearing his mind, refreshing his soul, exciting his senses.

It didn't matter now whether she'd been playing the coquette or not, or her reasons for doing so. Because, at that first glance, he'd felt more vital, more alive even than he'd felt on the day he'd first set eyes on Mariette…

The name of his wife served at least to cool his blood a little. He'd lost his head over Mariette and soon had lost everything else because of her. His name, his pride, his respect and the respect of his men too. And here he was in danger of doing the same thing all over again.

Dragging in a breath, Edmund pushed himself upright, his mind and his body his own again, or nearly so. Bidding a curt goodnight to the watch, he turned for the stairs and for his bed, his resolve set once more upon its course.

Isobel must go on the morrow.

Isobel didn't know how long she'd been sitting on the floor of her chamber, her back against the door, but her legs and arms were stiff. Her eyes at least were dry because she hadn't allowed herself to weep for long. What was the point, since she wasn't even sure what she wept over? The news of Richard of York, the insult she'd suffered in the hall, her flight from her own table, then that kiss with Edmund Deverell that had stunned her completely.

Never before had she responded to the attentions of a man but instead had ignored it or treated it with the disdain it deserved. So why hadn't she done that with him? Why had she welcomed it, returned it, enjoyed it?

Sirius was asleep and snoring, but Orion still watched her with concerned eyes. He was the father of Sirius, who was Tom's hound, really, but always more hers. The younger always followed the older, just like her brother had followed her lead as they were growing up. Oh, how she missed Tom and how she needed him now, he who'd always needed her, until he became a man and went to war!

But Tom was gone, as her father was gone, and with him the reason—the excuse—she'd been hiding behind all her life to avoid things she didn't understand, didn't know, and therefore feared. And now, with Edmund's coming, and her own responses to his presence, those things had found her out. They were here, daring her to face them, and embrace them. The things of the world which, all her life, she'd ignored, dismissed, denied.

On impulse, she reached out and flung her arms about Orion's neck. 'Oh, sweetheart. I wish you could talk.'

He licked her face, offering comfort, but of course, he could give her no wise counsel. Only she herself must decide upon what looked now, after Warwick's cruel message, to be her unavoidable future—marriage to a stranger old enough to be her grandsire or a life behind the walls of a convent.

Getting to her feet, Isobel took off her gown and replaced it—carefully, since it had been her mother's—in the coffer. Then she went to sit at the little table where earlier she'd combed her hair and inspected her face, and removed her circlet and the ruby pendant, placing them back in the jewellery casket, beside Tom's ring.

Tears welled again as the garnet twinkled in the candlelight but she pushed them firmly away, since it wouldn't help to give way to hopelessness, now of all times. Taking up the mirror, she inspected her appearance again. Her hair was tousled, her eyes were red and her cheeks still flushed, both from the flight from the hall and from what had followed.

She looked like a strumpet and doubtless that was how Edmund Deverell saw her too. Perhaps that was why he'd kissed her in the first place, taking advantage of her vulnerability, her confusion. Perhaps she'd played her part all too well and had incited a reaction from him that was too male, too powerful, too frightening to ever risk playing again.

Because her plan that night had gone disastrously awry. She was no good at such games, whereas he was clearly a man of the world. She'd been so naïve that she'd fallen at the first stumbling block and, instead of outwitting Deverell, had found herself helpless in his arms.

From the hall next door, the revelry grew louder as the night progressed, and the Yorkists doubtless toasted their would-be king. The songs became bawdier, the language of the soldiers coarse and lewd, drifting through the wall and making her blush all over again. Was Deverell there too now, singing and swearing with the rest of them?

Knight or not, he was as lustful as them all, and perhaps worse than them despite his fine manners and speech. For what man took advantage of a woman in distress as he had? Pretending to offer comfort in order to take what he wanted? What man…?

Isobel's mind lingered on the word. That was what he was, after all, a man, much like any other. Driven by desires, admiring of the female sex, taking what he wanted, when he wanted it. And he'd wanted *her*. She'd felt it in his body, in his lips, heard it in his voice, seen it in the darkening of his eyes.

And, worse, she'd known herself to be driven in the same way. Each and every time he'd looked at her, touched her, and then, tonight, kissed her, she'd *wanted* him to. She'd wanted to feel that awareness again, to know that excitement, to experience the carnal responses he'd awakened in her that must have always been there, undiscovered, dormant, safe…

She'd known her cheeks had also flushed, her eyes had darkened too, just as his had done. And, in doing so, her body had betrayed the fact—to her if not to him—that she desired Edmund as much as he desired her.

But she didn't want to be desired, by him or by anyone else. She didn't want to lose possession of herself as she so nearly had done this night. She wanted to be free, in control of her destiny, safe, as she always had been. Yet how could she be any of those things if she was married to a man who would regard her, and use her, as his property, as old George Ledwyche would surely do?

Worse even at his age, he might bed her and get her with child!

The convent, then? Could she really bear that, since it would be a sort of prison too, that once inside, she could never leave, not until she died? But at least there she would be safe from the overpowering and frightening feelings she'd felt in Edmund Deverell's arms. There she would not know, not ever again, the responses his kiss had evoked in her, the longing to know more, to know *him*, intimately, desperately and completely!

Many hours later, when the moon had risen high, and the revelry from the hall had long since ceased, Isobel took out her star charts, her book of hours, her astrolabe and cast then recast her horoscope. By the time the moon had slipped into the purple hue of dawn, she'd finally made her choice.

The following morning, her resolve shaky but as strong as it ever would be, Isobel sank to her knees in front of the altar in the little chapel that led off the solar block. She prayed here every morning but today it was different. Today she was going to tell Deverell that she wished to go into a convent. Not the one where his mother resided, though, for that would only remind her of him, but somewhere far away, where she need never see or think of him ever again.

On her knees, she prayed for the religious conviction that up to now she'd lacked, observing the mass only superficially, with her mind and her lips, but never with her heart. But the words she tried to say sounded empty, meaningless, even nonsense, so she rose and went into the aisle to the right of the altar, where lay the tombs of her grandparents, and her mother and father.

Away from the window, it was dark but she could still make out her mother's effigy. The small, delicate face that she barely remembered now, but which they said was just like hers, the hands pressed together in eternal prayer. Her figure was painted in blues and whites and golds, though the colours were muted in the gloom. Her father's effigy was as yet unpainted, the grey granite of his fine figure even more indistinguishable beside that of his wife.

Isobel bowed her head. Would his effigy ever be completed now the Yorkists held Mistlecote? Or would both her parents' tombs be dismantled to make way for the new lords of the manor, their precious bones within tossed into a common grave outside the walls? If her brother still lived, perhaps he could reclaim the manor someday, when Lancaster finally triumphed over York, but that day would be too late for her.

The air was thick and stale in the chapel and, suddenly unable to breathe, she lowered herself to the floor and sat with her back to the cold stone. Without, the manor came to life, dawn filtering in through the glazed window above the altar, spilling its light over the tiled floor. Birdsong greeted the rising of the sun, as yet unseen beyond the walls, but it was soon drowned out by the voices of men, the clinking of utensils and tools, the stamping and neighing of horses in the stables as they awaited their breakfast.

Sounds Isobel had heard every morning of her life, but this morning it all sounded different. She *was* different today and, once she left here and went into a convent, she would never be the woman she'd been ever again. She'd never even *be* a woman, not one of flesh and blood and wants and needs and loves and hates—a woman she'd never wanted to be.

Until last night when ignorance had become knowledge and even her fear had been eclipsed by a craving to be just like any other woman. To know a man…to desire a man… to lie with him…

Then other sounds came to her ears—those of the door opening and a footfall ringing quick and sure. Isobel leapt to her feet just as the light from the window illuminated a figure framed in the doorway. Not speaking, not moving, just staring at her as if he'd never seen her before.

A long moment passed and then Edmund Deverell closed the door quietly behind him and walked towards her.

Her heart thundering in her chest, Isobel rose and moved forward to meet him, the decision she'd made last night beginning to seem unreal now that she was about to speak it out loud. Then it had been logical, practical, a solution that was safe, if bleak…but now it loomed before her like an endless, horrifying living death.

But she mustn't panic, nor give way to the terror that gripped like a vice around her heart. She had to do what was necessary, for it was the only way. She had to adhere to her choice, tell Deverell her decision straight away, before he said the thing that doubtless *he'd* come here to say to *her—choose or he'd choose for her*!

Isobel dragged in a breath, locked her fingers tightly

together, and flung up her head. He halted in front of her, his face stern in the shadows, his mouth grim as his lips parted, as if he did indeed mean to say it without preamble, without inviting either an argument or a refusal.

She got in first, but not with the words she'd intended to say at all. Instead, others, quite different, and totally shocking, shattered the quiet tranquility of the chapel.

'Will you marry me?'

Chapter Seven

Edmund heard the words echo around the walls, saw them dance like the dust motes in the beam of light from the window, then they slammed into his head as if Isobel had wielded a mace not a question. A question that surely he'd mistaken, or imagined…or dreamed.

'Will I marry you?' he repeated, stupidly, his mind reeling from the blow, as if it really had been physical, not verbal. 'Is that what you just asked me?'

'Th-that is indeed what I asked you…yes.'

With the altar behind her, and the window above, Isobel might well have been a spirit, not a woman of flesh and blood as she spoke again, her tone almost imperative now, instead of the tentative one of a moment ago.

'Well? Will you?'

Edmund felt the air rush back into his lungs, unaware until then that he'd stopped breathing. 'You are asking me to take you as my wife?'

She gave a sharp nod of her head. 'Yes.' There was a pause and he saw her wipe her palms on her skirts. 'So… what is your answer?'

As she waited, his gaze followed that little nervous gesture of her hands, saw them ball into fists, until her knuckles showed white against the dark green wool of her gown. Then something burst inside him, like a canker full of poison.

Laying his palms flat on the cold, hard stone of the altar, Edmund tried to absorb the myriad emotions that swept through him. Confusion, disbelief, suspicion, excitement, hope and fear. 'Why?' he asked, at last, when some of those feelings, at least, had settled. 'Why do you want me to marry you?'

'Because I do not want to become a nun… It would… I could not be confined in such a way.' She spoke without looking at him. 'And neither do I wish to marry the Lord of Ledwyche, which would be a prison too, but of a different sort.'

'But you wish to marry me?'

There was a moment of hesitation, as if his question was unexpected, and then she shook her head. 'No, but the only way I can remain here…in my home…is to become your wife.'

Her response, even though said haltingly, sounded so reasonable, so practical that Edmund almost wondered why he'd never considered it himself. Why he'd not given it serious thought even when Alain had observed it would be a sensible move. In those moments when he'd touched her, kissed her, *wanted* her…he'd not let himself go that far. Perhaps if there had been no Mariette he *would* have considered it, even imagined them marrying for love, not for any practical reasons.

But there *had* been Mariette…

'I have been married once,' he said, 'and I have no desire to marry a second time.'

Isobel had been looking away from him, down the aisle to the door at the end, but now her head turned towards him. 'You are married already?'

'I said I *was* married,' Edmund corrected, 'but am no longer.'

'Is she…?'

'Yes.' Despite the distance, the healing, of four years, he flinched as he said it. 'She is dead.'

'Oh. I'm sorry.' There was a little silence before she spoke again. 'Did you love her?'

'Yes.'

Edmund didn't elaborate. How could he say he'd both loved *and* hated Mariette, with equal and extreme passion, but now he felt nothing? How could he explain that the heart that had beat so ardently then was now hollow, filled with only pity and regret?

'If we were to marry…it wouldn't be for love, naturally. It would be a practical arrangement, of advantage to us both.' Isobel was speaking again, deliberately, carefully, as if her thoughts were forming only an instant before the words. 'I would keep Mistlecote and you would have a wife who would give you heirs…sons… I presume you want them?'

Edmund lifted his gaze to meet hers. 'Yes, some day I will require heirs.'

'Then why should I not be the one to give you them? I think…' A flush mounted her cheek and she moistened her lips with her tongue, nervously. 'I believe that you feel some sort of…desire towards me…do you not? Why else would you have kissed me…like you did last night?'

'Why indeed!' The bitter retort was out before Edmund could stop it. He didn't want to desire Isobel. He didn't want to desire anyone. For in the wake of desire, who could tell what might come next? But he would not lie to her, nor to himself. 'No, Isobel, I cannot deny that I desire you. What man could?'

Her gaze flared and then her lashes lowered. 'I don't think I could…ever feel…*that* for you, but I would be prepared to lie with you, until you begot a son.'

'A coupling to seal a bargain, is that it?'

The words were cruel, though he didn't intend them so, and her flush deepened. 'You were right, last night, when you accused me of playing the coquette. I was trying to…to…'

'Seduce me?'

She shook her head. 'No…well, I hadn't thought of it quite so clearly as that. But I sensed you were not…indifferent to me, as a woman, I mean, and if I could use that in some way to keep Mistlecote, well…you see?'

'I see very clearly, Isobel. You meant to use my desire to induce me to let you remain here.'

'Yes…' She nodded. 'And then when that message came from Warwick, and I heard that Lord Ledwyche had asked for me, it all went wrong.'

'And you think marrying me will make it all right again?'

Isobel's eyes clouded. 'I don't know…but it would give us both the things we want. I would not expect, nor look for, the love you had for your first wife. I do not wish for *any* sort of love from a husband.'

Yes, it was immensely practical when she put it like that—cold, unfeeling, safe. Yet still Edmund hesitated. She wouldn't speak so confidently if she knew the folly of what she was saying—the danger.

Love, like desire, was not something you could decide you wished for or not. Love, and desire too, came at you, out of nowhere, regardless of whether you expected it or not, or wanted it or not. Love chose *you*, not the other way around, and once it had you in its grip, nothing could save you, or set you free—until the person you loved killed it.

'Do you want Mistlecote so much that you would settle for a loveless marriage, then?' Edmund studied her profile, her head turned away now, a little frown upon her brow. 'Would you lie with a man, give him your body, submit to his demands night after night, and expect nothing in return?'

Isobel shrugged, but he saw it wasn't the careless gesture she clearly intended it to be, and he could also see how effective his deliberate words had been. If she really meant to do as she was proposing, she needed to be fully aware of the cost—as he would be.

'If I married Ledwyche,' she went on, 'it would doubtless be a loveless marriage too, with a man old enough to be my grandsire, and I would have to endure all that and lose Mistlecote all the same. And, since I have never lain with a man... I have no expectations.'

Edmund turned his eyes to the window, the shattering of colours through the stained glass only serving to confuse him further. Why was he filled with rage all of a sudden? Was he still angry at Mariette after all these years, angry that she could still affect him so? Or was he angry at Isobel for putting this temptation in his path now when he'd thought himself beyond it?

'Ledwyche might die soon and leave you a wealthy widow, and the mistress of another home, with money to live on for the rest of your life.'

'He has sons from his first marriage—do you think they would allow that? No, they would shut me up in a convent before old George's body was even cold in its tomb!'

She turned so that they stood side by side, laying her palms on the altar too, her gaze earnestly seeking his. 'I want Mistlecote, Edmund, and no other home will do for me. Besides which, would not a union between us settle the dispute between our families over this manor once and for all?'

Edmund pushed himself upright and strode down the nave to the door, not to exit, but just because he needed to clear his mind of her scent, his senses of her allure. Away from the realisation, too, that her proposition was as tempting as it was sensible, and also one that the Earl of Warwick would favour.

Mistlecote was a Yorkist house now—*his* house—and the estate fully returned to his family. Isobel's brother's inheritance was therefore invalid. If Thomas Calvert had fought for York, it might have been otherwise. But it was not otherwise and nothing would alter that—unless Lancaster proved the eventual victor when this war was over.

But if they were to wed, Isobel *could* stay here, his hold on the manor would be *doubly* secure, and the quarrel between their two houses *would* finally be settled regardless of whether her brother was alive or dead. And, since this place meant as much to her as it did to him—perhaps even more—could he not be kind and consent?

And, in plain truth, the thought of Isobel married to an old man, or imprisoned in a nunnery, was as abominable to him as it was to her. He *would* need heirs one day if he was to keep what he'd gained and pass the inheritance down. Only a fool would refuse such an offer from a beautiful woman, one that it would be no hardship to lie with… quite the opposite.

But that was where the problem lay, was it not? He'd always envisaged a faceless, nameless wife to give him sons. A woman he wouldn't love and who wouldn't love him, and once the necessary had been achieved they would live separately from each other, albeit under the same roof. A woman he would respect, of course, even find some affection for, were she sweet-natured and good, but a woman who would never possess his heart.

But it wouldn't be like that with Isobel. He'd want to live his life with her in every sense, to sleep at her side every night and wake up with her every morning. He'd want her face to be the first he saw on his return when he was absent from home, her arms to welcome him, whole or wounded, from the battlefield.

He'd want to love her and he'd want her to love him in return. To have his heart and give him hers in exchange. Make their marriage not something she had to endure but something filled with pleasure and companionship and affection—all the things he'd never had in his marriage to Mariette.

And that was precisely why he could not marry Isobel. He'd learned the bitter lesson that love could not be trusted and if you were foolish enough to believe it could, then you would pay the price eventually. For in the wrong hands, the wrong heart, love could destroy a man and there was nothing he could do to defend himself.

Striding back towards Isobel, Edmund steeled himself to say as much—though not in those revealing words. She was still standing before the altar, her head high, watching him intently. Her hands hung by her sides, her fingers tightly clenched, as if everything depended on his answer.

Everything *did* depend on his answer, of course, for her at least. How much courage had it taken her to ask him what she had? How much dignity had she sacrificed, how much hope was burning in her breast, right at that moment? And how afraid was she that the answer she would hear would not be the one she wanted, the one she needed?

Hope, dignity, fear, beauty, courage—all the things he'd recognised in her, from the day he'd arrived, and on so many occasions since. The qualities that had enabled her to resist him at her gates that first day, to ride that wild mare of hers like the wind and still rise to her feet after a fall, to allow her to humble herself and ask for his palms to help her mount.

The qualities that made her a woman any man would be proud to have as a wife—any man but he.

'I could not make you happy, Isobel, you must understand that,' Edmund said, forcing the words out from lips that didn't want to form them. 'And I cannot ever come to love you.'

'I am not happy now,' she said, 'and neither could I learn to love you. So…since neither of us wants or is capable of love, would ours not be a suitable union?'

'In one sense, yes,' Edmund agreed, feeling his resistance ebbing as temptation flowed stronger. 'But there are other aspects of marriage to consider when a man thinks of taking a wife.'

'Men have…carnal needs that a woman does not.' Her lashes flickered but her gaze never left his. 'I understand that. I am not a child.'

No, she was not a child. She was a woman, one he already desired, and who might come to desire him in return, given time.

'So…' She was studying him intently now, as if trying to read his mind, perhaps even succeeding in doing so. '*Will you marry me, Edmund Deverell?*'

Still Edmund wavered. She, even more than he, needed to be absolutely certain. 'Is it really what you want, Isobel? Tell me truly.'

'Truly?' She gave a brittle little laugh. 'No, of course it

is not what I *want* at all! It is what I *need*. Besides, it is the only means to avoid an even worse fate! This way at least allows *me* to choose my *own* fate.'

For the first time since he'd entered the chapel, Edmund felt a smile pull at his lips, though there was nothing humorous about the situation. It was dangerous, fraught with obstacles, and it could turn out to be the worse fate for both of them. It could also be full of excitement, and pleasure, and mutual respect, liking even, and he suspected that there would never be a moment of dullness, or tedium, no matter how long their marriage lasted.

'In that case...'

He paused as a quick thrill of anticipation ran through him and his stomach hollowed with fear. But, even as he wrestled for a moment with those conflicting reactions, his mind sharpened on something. With Mariette, it had been instantaneous. He'd loved her the instant he'd seen her and there was no pausing, no questioning, no doubts at all—until it was too late.

Now he was all doubts but did that mean he should say no—or ignore those doubts and say yes? Were those doubts there because he was older and wiser now and would never again be that love-blinded, hapless cuckold? No, he would not, for this time, he could—he *would*—enter into marriage with his eyes wide open and his heart firmly shut.

'In that case,' he said again, his mind made up, 'I will marry you, Isobel Calvert.'

Her face paled and, for an instant, a look of panic, followed by terror, rippled over her features in quick succession. Then, inclining her head, she lowered her lashes and murmured something that he didn't catch.

'What?'

The green eyes lifted again. 'I said...thank you.'

She didn't look as if she wanted to thank him for anything at all and, once again, Edmund felt a flurry of doubt. But he dismissed it and, now that he was decided, and was never one to second guess his decisions, he held out his hand. After a little hesitation, she took it, her fingers trembling, her palm clammy.

Slowly he drew her towards him and, just so that she and he himself were sure, touched his mouth lightly to hers, in a kiss completely different to the possessive one of the night before. Her lips were cold and, suppressing the urge to prolong the kiss and banish that chill, Edmund lifted his head again.

Then he checked himself, swiftly, keenly, thoroughly. No tightening of his body, no rush of blood, no increased heartbeat, just a sort of warmth that was pleasant, reassuring.

'Shall we wed a week from now,' he said, 'at Martinmas?'

The nod of her head was barely there. 'Yes. Let it be at Martinmas.'

A thousand times during those eight days before Martinmas Isobel asked herself what had she been thinking? Why she'd proposed marriage instead of a nunnery? Why she hadn't changed her mind during the intervening time, even after the banns had been read?

She could have done. She still could, she realised, even today as she prepared for the journey to Tewkesbury, where their wedding would take place. Her maid, Hawise, whom she'd recalled a few days ago—since a married woman would not expect to see to her own needs—placed her cloak on her shoulders.

Barely twenty, Hawise was a pretty girl, who'd been her maid since her husband, a Mistlecote man, had died out hunting after being gored by a wild boar. There was no warmth between them though, a distance which had little to do with the differences in their standing, Isobel suspected, but more to do with her maid's shyness, which was acute. However, today the excitement of going to Tewkesbury had loosened Hawise's tongue.

'They say the abbey is lovely, mistress, though I've not seen it myself.'

Isobel had been in the abbey before. Once when she was a child then again after her father's death, when she'd gone to pay the monks to say masses for his soul. And tomorrow she would enter it again—as a bride.

She descended the stone steps from the hall and walked through the arch into the outer bailey to find Edmund waiting for her. His face flushed as he came towards her, a smile of greeting on his mouth, his eyes finding hers. He was handsome in his riding gear, a short cloak billowing from his shoulders and his head bare. Isobel's heart did a funny sort of flutter despite the apprehension that gripped her.

'Are you ready, Isobel?'

No! The word leapt to her tongue but came out—as her words in the chapel had done—quite differently. 'Yes, I'm ready.'

He took her hand and, even through their gloves, the contact sent a thrill along her nerves. As he'd done that day they'd ridden out and she'd fallen off, he stooped and cupped his hands for her to mount. Like then, he looked up at her, his hand on Luna's withers, but the expression in his eyes was not of concern now but rather something that was impossible to read.

Had he too felt misgivings this last week?

'We will reach Tewkesbury long before dusk,' he informed her. 'I have sent a man ahead to engage rooms for us in the Crowne, a good inn, very close to the abbey.'

As she gathered up the reins, Isobel didn't care where they slept this night. The following night, her wedding night, was the only thing that occupied her mind. 'Yes,' she replied, nonsensically, as he'd not asked her anything.

He arranged her skirts more snugly around her legs, a liberty he would not have dared take that day he'd helped her into the saddle after she'd fallen off. Now, as her husband-to-be, doubtless he thought he could touch her as he liked.

'It is well you have dressed warmly for the journey,' he said, smiling up at her, the bright day reflecting in his eyes. 'The weather has turned colder.'

It *was* cold, but as they rode out under the gateway, Hawise and four of Edmund's men accompanying them, Isobel felt as if she'd been turned to ice. For the first time since she could remember, she was not in control of her destiny, a destiny she'd thought was laid out, never to change, because she'd chosen it so. Even her astrolabe and star charts had mirrored her choices, making her sure always of the future, keeping her safe in the present.

How naïve she'd been in her comfortable bubble of bliss. For now the future was anything but certain. Even the next few days were filled with terror, for she'd have to face her greatest fear. Not just the physical part of the bedding—that she could and would bear—but the other…the surrendering of her freedom, and her will, to another being.

The ending of her life as she'd known it and the entering into another life that she knew nothing about at all. Suddenly it was as if everything that had gone before had been false, fooling her into confident complacency. And fate was demanding payment for that respite by demanding she face them all at once.

On her wedding night…

Chapter Eight

The abbey at Tewkesbury had been chosen for the ceremony, the reason being—so Edmund told her—that the Earl of Warwick would give her away, since she had no father or brother, and the chapel at Mistlecote lacked the grandeur and the capacity for the occasion and presence of such a great earl.

There was another reason too. Near Tewkesbury was the seat of the staunchly loyal Lancastrian family of Throckmorton. Holding the marriage of a new and powerful Yorkist in the area, and the figure of the Earl of Warwick in the town, would send a message to them, and to all the other nobles in the area still adhering to Lancaster.

Isobel noticed little of the magnificent edifice that swallowed her up as they'd entered. The vows already said at the church door, she'd walked along the aisle at Edmund's side, oblivious to the vaulted ceiling overhead, with the central bosses of the life of Christ and the beautiful Angel Choir. Oblivious to the brightly painted stone pillars and the glorious hues of the stained-glass windows that filled the abbey with light.

Oblivious too to the tombs of the dead knights, abbots and lords as they passed through the north ambulatory to the Lady Chapel beyond, with its beauty and glory and colours and candles. Oblivious even to the presence of Abbot John Galys, who stood in all his finery before her, bestowing his blessing upon them and upon their union.

Behind them, the Earl of Warwick looked as satisfied as any proud father might be. Isobel had disliked him on sight, though she couldn't deny the charisma that had won him not just the respect of the nobility but the affection of the common folk too. It was said the whole of London was his, and the people flocked into the streets to see him, to touch the hem of his cloak or the spurs at his boots as he rode by.

Isobel got the impression he didn't like her much either as they sat at table during the wedding feast in the Crowne Inn. The hours passed slowly and yet far too quickly. She ate sparingly, made polite conversation when anyone spoke to her, and longed for the feast to end—while at the same time dreading the moment when it would.

Edmund had been reserved too and likewise had spoken little, and even then it was more to Warwick or to the Earl's father, Lord Salisbury, than to her. The Abbot who'd married them was the other occupant of the high table that filled one end of the hall, and it was touching how, perhaps sensing her misery, he tried to put her at her ease.

Even so, Isobel only paid scant attention to his conversation, her gaze more often than not wandering over the room, seeking a way out that was too late to take now. There were three other tables, the one at the end, facing the high table, housing half a dozen beggars, bearded and roughly dressed, and even rougher of manners.

For her wedding feast was also the feast of Martinmas, in commemoration of St Martin, the patron saint of beggars, drunkards and the poor. For that reason, Warwick had invited a handful of the unfortunates of Tewkesbury to dine with them. They ate greedily and she could smell the gutters of the town on their clothes and bodies even from where she sat.

One of them, a younger man than the rest, his face half hidden by a filthy beard, stared frequently and insolently towards the high table. He was dressed in monk's robes but from the staff propped against the table at his elbow, he was clearly a mendicant friar who lived by wandering, preaching and begging for alms.

Of the other two tables down the centre of the room, one seated Yorkists and the other Lancastrians, and Isobel didn't have to hazard a guess as to the reason for that arrangement. The Yorkist table was grand, and boisterous, the lords Audley, Grey and Croft splendidly dressed, as were their wives. The Lancastrian table, lower down the hall and rather more sedate, comprised the Throckmorton brothers and their wives, and Thomas Cornwalle of Burford. All of them looked as if they were at a funeral not a wedding.

The Throckmortons had been friends of her father's, but when Isobel looked towards their table she met only cold stares in return. Doubtless they had all unanimously condemned her for going over to York and betraying her house, her brother, and her parents' memory.

Then, all at once, the feast was over and she was walking on Edmund's arm through to the bedchamber that awaited them. In the same way she'd approached the altar, Isobel moved as if in a trance, her head high and her eyes fixed in front of her, seeing ahead an ordeal to be endured and survived.

Hawise was waiting to prepare her for that humiliation and it was then, as she stepped over the threshold and saw the bed made ready, the covers rolled down, the sheet pristine white in order to best show the result of her loss of virginity, that Isobel's nerve broke.

'I don't think…' she said, whirling and seeking Edmund's eyes for the first time that day. They locked on hers and she harnessed her dignity as best she could. 'What I mean is, I would prefer it if we were left alone, to see to ourselves. Everyone else, Hawise too, may go.'

Behind Edmund, in the doorway, the guests were gathered, having followed them, as was the custom, to see them to bed. But, to her relief, her new husband gave a nod and turned to Warwick.

'My bride and I wish to forgo the usual practices and, with your leave, my lord, we will see ourselves into bed.'

The Earl laughed and slapped him on the shoulder. 'You are a knave to deny your fellows their sport, but you and your bride shall have your wish.' He cast a lascivious glance over her then winked at Edmund. 'Enjoy your nuptials night, *mon brave,* and plant your seed deep!'

As the door creaked shut, Isobel fought down a wild sense of panic. The floorboards beneath her feet shook as merriment recommenced in the hall and, to her horror, her legs began to tremble too. Edmund saw her fear—how could he not?—and his voice was quiet as he moved to a side table where a jug of wine and some sweetmeats sat.

'Would you like some wine, Isobel?'

She shook her head. 'No. I would rather we didn't tarry over what…what must take place.'

He glanced over his shoulder, irony in his eyes. 'You mean, best get it over and done with?'

'If you like.' They both knew that she was his wife now and he could do whatever he wished without troubling to care what she thought about it. 'Why postpone it, after all?'

He poured a cup of wine for himself, drinking deeply before turning around again. 'We have not spoken much to each other this last week.'

'There was nothing to discuss. We had made our agreement and I needed to say no more about it.' Isobel lifted her chin, determined not to let him see how she quaked. 'Had *you* needed to say something?'

'Not really, no.' There was a pause. 'But I had begun to think that you had regretted your proposition, since you became so distant.'

'I am here, am I not?'

'Indeed you are.' He narrowed his eyes speculatively, as if he wondered if she really *was* there. 'You look very beautiful, Isobel.'

'Your appearance is also very fine,' she said grudgingly, but truthfully. He wore a rich blue surcoat over his woollen doublet, patterned with a swirling gold design and sleeves that hung open from the elbow to show the sleeve of the fine linen shirt below. Black hose covered his legs and feet, the shoes showing just a hint of a point at the toe.

Isobel had never seen him so handsome, nor so unguarded in attire, and she had to admit that, as a husband, he was undoubtedly a better prospect than old Ledwyche would have been.

'I didn't say you look fine, Isobel. I said you look beautiful.'

The compliment brought a blush to her cheeks. 'Thank you...but you don't have to say such things.'

Putting his cup down, he came to stand before her, so close that Isobel detected the hint of soap on his skin. Despite the pleasant aroma, she flinched, sure now that he'd decided enough time had been wasted on idle talk, even though he himself had wasted it.

'I think you are not used to compliments, are you?'

How could he read her flaws so easily? 'I have never sought compliments,' she said stiffly. 'I do not trust them.'

'I concur. Actions usually speak louder, and often truer, than words.'

Then, before she'd realised what he intended, he took her face between his hands and lightly touched his lips to hers. It was such a tender, almost innocent kiss, yet so full of intent, that Isobel jerked herself free.

'I… You took me unawares!' she accused. 'I wasn't ready.'

'But I have kissed you before this…*twice* now.'

'I know…' She didn't miss the inflexion that reminded her of that passionate kiss in the passageway of the solar. 'But tonight is different, is it not?'

Edmund's gaze dropped to her mouth, lingered, and Isobel had to dig her toes into the floor to stop herself fleeing from it. But she couldn't flee. She'd made her choice and now she had to see it through.

'Of what are you so afraid, Isobel?'

Edmund saw Isobel's face turn even paler than it had been a moment before. Had she thought he hadn't noticed her feelings? All day long he'd sensed the mix of unwillingness, resignation and determination, underlying all of which he'd sensed fear.

'I am not afraid.'

But he didn't believe her brave, almost reckless retort. As a soldier he knew fear well—his own as well as the enemy's—so well that he could almost touch it when he encountered it. Naturally, as a virgin, her wedding night would doubtless be daunting, but there was something else, something more in the rigid stance of her body, its secrets still hidden by a wedding gown of pale jaune.

'If it is of any comfort,' Edmund said, 'I am afraid too.'

Her eyes widened in surprise but, leaving her to take that

admission as she liked, Edmund moved away, dousing the candles until only the two that flanked the bed remained alight. He didn't hurry. He didn't speak. He didn't even look at her. But he knew her gaze followed him all the while.

Then he took her hand and led her to the bed. 'Is it of this you are afraid?' he asked. 'If so, it is understandable, and natural.'

Isobel didn't answer him. It was as if she'd gone far away, as she'd been all day, all through the last week, in fact. As if she were there in body, but not in spirit, not in her soul. Not as her real self but rather like an imitation.

'It can be daunting…the first time…' Edmund went on. 'But it can also be pleasurable.'

The hissing of the candles was loud and, along the corridor in the hall, the feast continued raucously. But here in the room there was a strange sort of quiet.

'Pleasurable or not,' she replied at length, still from that distance that separated them, 'it matters little as long as it is quickly over.'

Edmund didn't know whether to smile or sigh or sob. His first wedding night with Mariette had been so easy because he'd been young, unscarred by love, full of passion, of hope, of expectations. He'd been no virgin then, having sown his first oats at the age of sixteen, but it had come as a complete shock to discover that Mariette was no virgin either!

He'd asked her about it, and believed what she'd told him, since he'd been naïve if not innocent. That her mother had forced her into the same sordid occupation, that she was grateful to him for saving her from a life of whoring, that she'd love him forever. But as the months passed he'd discovered that had been only the first of many lies. And, as time went on, and his love died, he stopped believing even the smallest of them.

'Are you…waiting for me…to disrobe?'

Isobel's halting question brough Edmund back from the past. The vision of the room in that Bordeaux inn of eight years ago vanished and Isobel, not Mariette, stood before him, more beautiful even than his first wife had been. Would she too fool him, humiliate him, hurt and betray him?

It was too late to ask those things, of course, and whatever or whoever his second wife proved to be, now was not the time to dwell upon it.

'I am waiting for nothing, Isobel. And I will disrobe you, since your gown, though sumptuous, is too intricate for you to do it alone.'

Moving behind her, he lifted the heavy fall of her hair forward over her shoulder and began to undo the lacing of her gown. His fingers were clumsy at first as the ties were indeed intricate, but, working slowly and meticulously, he revealed bit by bit the soft linen shift below.

The laces undone to the small of her back, Edmund inched the gown away from her body and let it drop to the floor. He paused, then touched his fingers to the nape of her neck, heard the intake of breath she gave, felt the quiver of her flesh.

'Turn to me, Isobel.'

She complied, turning fully around in the pool of jaune velvet at her feet, all beauty bathed in candlelight. Edmund caught his breath, cleared his throat, and swallowed. 'Are you warm enough?' he asked, unnecessarily, since a merry fire blazed in the hearth.

'Yes.'

'Then I will continue.'

Lowering himself to his knees, Edmund removed one soft leather slipper and then the other. Untying the garters that held up her woollen stockings, he removed them too and, still on his knees, he trailed his fingertips up over her calf. She gave a little gasp and he felt her hand touch his shoulder and then hastily lift again as he rose to his feet.

'Your turn now.'

Her gaze flared. 'My turn?'

'To undress me…if you wish to?'

She hesitated, eyeing his clothing as if it might bite should she touch it. Edmund waited, anticipating the touch of her hands, his skin quivering just at the thought of it. Finally, she nodded, but warily, as if he'd given her a task that might prove not just distasteful, but difficult too!

'Very well. I will.'

With hands that visibly trembled, she undid the belt at his waist, clutching it in her palm for a moment, as if unsure what she should do with it. So Edmund took it from her and dropped it to the floor.

'We will tidy it all up tomorrow,' he said.

Stemming the impulse to do the rest himself, he remained still as Isobel divested him of his surcoat—a wedding gift from Warwick—with the same concentration with which she'd dealt with his belt. Dropping the surcoat to the floor too, she reached next for the points at his doublet, where they fastened to his hose. There her hands paused, hovered.

'I'm not sure how to…'

The admission melted his bones. 'They need to be untied, point by point.'

Confusion became concentration once more as she undid the points one by one, and unbuckled the strap across each flank. Then his doublet too joined the pile of clothing mounting on the floor.

To save her blushes further, Edmund pushed his hose down his legs, removing his shoes at the same time. When he was standing only in his braies and linen shirt, his manhood hard and erect, he switched roles again.

'May I remove your shift?'

She stared at him in astonishment. Had she expected him to take her like a bull to the cow, swift and rough and for one purpose only? Even after four years of abstinence, even though his blood was coursing through his veins, Edmund wanted this night to be much more than that—and he wanted her to want the same.

'I will…do it myself.'

Taking hold of the hem of the garment, she lifted her arms over her head, bringing the shift off in one bold motion, and at last she was standing naked before him. The apprehension in her eyes was still there, and her face had gone from pale to pink. Edmund's heart did a little leap as, with even more boldness, she jerked her chin downwards to where his manhood strained impatiently.

'Your turn now, I believe.'

Her words were a challenge, spoken with bravado almost, and they didn't dispel her obvious nerves. It would have been easier, after all, to bed her bull-like and have done, because this tentative forerunning was pleasing, exciting, intoxicating and as new to him as it was to her.

Like all soldiers, he'd bedded whores and camp followers by the dozen once he'd come of age. As a husband he'd been unswervingly faithful to Mariette, despite the fact she'd been anything but faithful to him. Now, as a man, for the first time in his life, as he dispensed with the remainder of his clothing he felt himself being stripped naked in more ways than one.

Her eyes grew wider still and her cheeks now were scarlet as she beheld his nakedness. In his chest, his heart swelled with an emotion that stopped his breath for a moment.

'I promise I'll not hurt you, Isobel.'

Gently, Edmund took her hand and, their wedding rings winking in the candlelight, placed her palm, hot and trembling, flat on his chest.

'Do you feel the beating of my heart?'

She nodded and, after a moment's pause, he moved their hands lower, so her palm rested on his stomach. 'And can you feel how the air fills my lungs?'

Her reply was almost a breath. 'Yes.'

Edmund felt his heart thundering in his chest now, as inch by inch he guided their joined hands down over his abdomen. This time it was *his* turn to drag in a gasp when, with his hand instructing hers, she wrapped her fingers around him.

'And can you tell how much I want you, Isobel?'

Chapter Nine

Even in her innocence, Isobel could indeed tell how much he wanted her! Aware that something momentous and terrifying occurred on a woman's wedding night, she'd asked Hawise—four years younger and already wed and widowed—what would happen, down to the smallest detail. But her maid's advice had been insufficient, her experience of marriage brief, and her carnal knowledge even scantier than her own, which was based on the coupling of animals on Mistlecote's farms.

So she stood, unprepared and without armour, let alone clothing, her heart thumping until her whole body shook. Not just with apprehension—and a tingle of fear too— but with a sort of excited curiosity. As his hand fell to his side, leaving hers free to do as it wished, Isobel found her fingers longing to move, to explore, to discover. So, tentatively, she stroked her palm upwards, along the length of his manhood, then down again, drawing forth a low sound from his throat.

'Again.'

Isobel complied and with fascination watched the sensations ripple over his face. His chest rose and fell in rapid motion and, within her palm, she felt him grow as hard as iron.

'Do you want me too, Isobel?'

She swallowed, excitement spiking, curiosity growing, tempered still by fear of the unknown. *Did* she want him? How could she know? She was prepared to lie with him, tonight, and every other night should he insist on it, but *wanting* to do that…? Wanting the intimacy that she'd always shunned because it was alien to her nature, unfamiliar, and therefore frightening…?

Edmund's breath caressed her face and the candlelight in the room reflected back at her from pupils grown large and dark. Had he moved a step nearer—or had she? Perhaps both of them had moved, for now there was hardly any space at all between their two bodies.

'I cannot tell yet,' Isobel replied, his ardour, his essence, the desire that emanated from him engulfing her. 'But I am ready to fulfil my side of the bargain.'

Something flickered across his face, but was gone so quickly that she couldn't read it. 'Is that all?'

'Is there more?'

'There might be. Pleasure, I hope, for one.' His hand brushed lightly over her breast, causing her to snatch a breath. 'Shall we find out?'

So many questions but no answers—or rather, there was *one* answer at least. If she was to keep Mistlecote, she had to lie with him, this night, and other nights, until she gave him an heir. She had to face and conquer fear, exchange ignorance for knowledge, embrace this new experience which she, after all, had chosen.

Isobel nodded, though far from firmly. 'Y-yes.'

His gaze grew darker still, his breathing even quicker, as he drew her down upon the bed and came to lie beside her. Beneath her, the covering was thick and soft and warm, and instinctively she curled her fingers into it as her whole world began to shift far too quickly.

'W-wait.'

'I will wait as long as you want me to.' A steady hand cupped her cheek. 'Brides are allowed to be nervous on their wedding night. Bridegrooms too.'

'Are *you* nervous?'

He nodded. 'Did you think I would not be?'

'But you have been married before.'

'One wedding night is not like any other,' he said, 'nor is one bride like any other.'

She thought of that other bride, the one he'd married, the one he'd loved, the one he'd lost. Had she been beautiful, that woman? So beautiful that he would love her always? Was he already comparing her to his first wife and finding her lacking? Would it matter to her if he did?

Isobel knew she was not beautiful, nor feminine, nor alluring as other women were. She was not soft, and compliant, and meek, but headstrong and wilful. She preferred hunting and hawking and riding than playing hostess and dancing and all the other diverting pastimes she knew noblewomen pursued.

Edmund didn't know her any better than she knew him. They'd only met a little over a week ago. What had she been thinking when she proffered marriage to this man who was a stranger as well as an enemy? And, for all the persuasion she'd put forward that day in the chapel, how could this union ever really succeed?

Panic began to build inside her as her thoughts ran from one disastrous scenario to the next. And then all thoughts, and panic too, subsided as he stroked her hair back from her temple, moving closer so that she felt the warmth and texture of his flesh. His fingers trailed down her cheek, her throat, over one breast, her arm, his touch so light that at one moment it tickled and the next incited.

Despite the glinting eyes and rapid breath, Edmund seemed in no hurry. At each new place he touched, his mouth kissed hers, with a gentle pressure but no demand. One moment became two then three until, to her surprise, her body grew supple, languid, relaxed.

'Do you want me to continue, Isobel…or to stop?'

Heaven help her, but she *did* want him to continue! She *should* want it to stop, she *should* want to be anywhere other than where she was. But suddenly he didn't seem like a stranger, nor an enemy, and even their bargain had been forgotten as a yearning, a craving almost, took possession of her.

'Yes…' Isobel nodded, her senses winding tighter and tighter until she thought they might snap. 'Continue…'

'When we join, there might be a moment of pain, but it will pass very quickly.'

'I know…'

Hawise had told her *that* much, but it didn't seem to matter now as his lips brushed her temple, her cheek, her mouth, and his hand moved to her stomach, rested there, poised.

'Are you sure? Because soon it will be too *late* to stop.'

Isobel stared up at him. His hair glowed like gold in the candlelight and his eyes were compelling, mesmerising. A shock ran through her as she seemed to see Edmund in a way she'd never seen him before. As if by baring their bodies, they'd bared their innermost souls to each other too.

'Yes… I'm sure…'

His hand moved lower, over her hips and abdomen, and then closed over her womanhood. Isobel gasped and gripped the bedding beneath her as everything else retreated—the room, the noise from the hall, the world outside the window, the glow of the candles that bathed their entwined forms.

All of it disappeared into darkness as she closed her eyes and arched her hips upward into his palm, needing the fulfilling of something inside her that she hadn't known until now was empty.

'Don't stop, Edmund...'

And as he moved over her, penetrated her, bringing a little pang of discomfort that was gone so quickly she hardly noticed it, Isobel didn't surrender herself to something she'd always feared. Instead she welcomed it, embraced it fully, embraced *him* with all her being, until there was no fear left. Only pleasure, only completeness.

Afterwards Edmund rolled onto his back, stared up at the ceiling, and mentally checked himself. His body still resonated with the ecstasy of release, his limbs were heavy, his blood cooling and his loins bathed in a delicious, keening ache.

All that he'd expected to find in the aftermath of carnal pleasure. But now there was something else too and it took him a moment to locate it. A sort of quiet within, a calm...a sense of peace. His heart was intact, he knew that much, so what had brought this restful stillness he'd never experienced before after joining with a woman, not even with Mariette?

The name brought another realisation. When Isobel had told him, bluntly and with resolve, to get it done quickly, that she was ready to keep her side of the bargain...that had hurt, because it was a comment more than worthy of any his first wife had uttered!

Yet...as he'd entered her body, feeling her maidenhead

break, the little gasp of pain she gave piercing him too, Edmund had sensed at once it was different to how it had been with Mariette. And, as he'd shifted his hips to accommodate the tilt of hers, sinking until he was fully home and the snug heat of her closed around him, he'd been *certain* it was different.

He'd held himself still, letting her adjust, to forget the little snap of pain and begin to experience only the pleasure. As their eyes held, he'd felt something that went beyond the carnal—a sort of arrival at a place he didn't know he'd been travelling to, or why.

Now, at his side, Isobel sighed and slipped into sleep. The candles had burned out, so he couldn't see her clearly, but he didn't need to, having discovered every inch of her. Even when he'd closed his eyes, he would still see her, as if when he'd entered her body he'd also penetrated her soul, and she his.

Edmund gave a sigh too but, unlike Isobel, didn't slip into sleep. Instead he lay awake until the first glimmer of dawn showed outside the window. Then, getting out of bed, quietly so as not to wake her, he washed and dressed swiftly, and drank some of the wine left from the night before to curb the growling of his empty stomach.

When the bell from the abbey tolled Prime, he went back over to the bed. Isobel still slept, her body unmoving, her breasts rising and falling gently as she breathed. Her tousled hair was spread out on the pillow, and upon her pale cheek her long lashes looked even longer.

Something jolted inside him as he looked down at this woman whom he'd known for so short a time yet now seemed he'd known forever. How could that be? Unable to find an answer to that, instead he shook her gently awake. 'Isobel.'

Her eyes flew open, unfocused for a moment, and then she sat up, hastily dragging the coverlet up over her body. 'Is…is it morning already?'

'Just after Prime. Warwick and I are meeting some of the local lords at the Abbey Guesthouse this morning.' Edmund sat down beside her, reluctant now that the hour had come to leave. 'I will be occupied until midday at least, so you have several hours to yourself.'

'Oh… I see.'

Isobel stared at him as if she didn't see at all, however, and, pushing away guilt too now as well as reluctance, he went on. 'I am sorry to have to leave, Isobel, especially this morning…but it is unavoidable.'

'There is no need to apologise. I would appreciate some time to myself anyway.' She looked over at her clothes, which he'd laid neatly on a nearby chair, and a blush stained her cheek. 'What is your meeting about?'

'Local loyalties and how far they can be trusted.' His leaving seemed even more unappealing now as the light grew stronger, flooding in through the window, illuminating her beauty. 'Go into the town, if you wish, to the market, but do not go alone—take Hawise with you.'

Edmund bent his head and kissed her, as he'd been longing to do since the moment she'd awoken. A kiss of parting, from a husband to his new wife, it was chaste enough, but his body fired even so. Unlike the previous night, however, in the throes of their coupling when she'd kissed him back with ardour, with hunger, now her lips were resistant, unyielding, cold almost.

Rising to his feet, he pushed away a fleeting disappointment. The morning after was always going to be awkward and he'd been prepared for that. But he hadn't prepared himself for the way she avoided his eyes, held herself rigid, clutched the bedding right up to her chin.

Was it because he was leaving her, this morning of all mornings, or because she already regretted the night before? Rued marrying him altogether? It had all happened so quickly, looking back, and out of necessity, and neither of them had discussed the future after that agreement made in the chapel.

They would have to speak about it soon, of course. They would need to map out their married life as he would plan his battle strategies. No detours into unwise feelings, no wrong words that might lead them awry, no mistakes to entrap them in the quagmire of love. Strategies that ensured that, no matter what his body and mind experienced, his heart would remain intact.

Testing that strategy now, Edmund touched his fingers lightly to her cheek, gratified to find his hand steady, his head clear, even if his blood flowed slightly warmer, slightly quicker, than it should have done.

'Are you well this morning, Isobel?' he asked, desperately searching for the right words. 'Are you…comfortable?' Happy was a question too far. 'Is there anything you wish for?'

Her eyes met his, as cold as her mouth had been, and she shook her head. 'No, there is nothing I wish for, Edmund.'

'Then I will see you at noon.'

With that, he strode to the door and out over the threshold, closing it behind him without a backward glance, words he *could* have said burning like lime on his tongue. He *could* have taken her in his arms, not carnally, but with kindness and affection. He *could* have told her of the pleasure he'd experienced last night, pleasure he hoped she experienced too.

He *should* have told her that, for all their differences, for all that their marriage had been a mutual and beneficial arrangement, he would do his utmost to be a good husband to her.

But if he *had* done, what would she have said in return?

Isobel sat in bed, hugging her knees to her chest, while Hawise bustled about the room, folding away her wedding gown and laying out fresh clothing for their journey back to Mistlecote later that day. Outside the window, the town was busy, with the rasping noise of cartwheels, the ring of hooves, the sing-song of voices in the street. In the stables below, she could hear a groom whistling as he tended to the horses, and from the river behind the inn came the sound of ships being loaded and unloaded.

The daylight streamed in through the paned window, casting coloured beams of light over the bed, warming her body. A body that, after last night, Isobel hardly recognised now. It wasn't just the ache, though that was there, a sort of subtle residue, not unpleasant, of the fact she was no longer a virgin. There was no bruising of her skin, as she'd heard sometimes happened during the bedding if a husband was indifferent or, worse, brutal.

Edmund had been neither. On the contrary, he'd been so gentle with her, so tender in the taking of her maidenhead, that the swift pain had been immediately forgotten. Everything had been forgotten—their bargain, Mistlecote, the war—as her flesh had come alive and her mind had blurred into a sort of dreamlike state.

A state so unfamiliar that, at first, it had seemed to be happening to someone else, while she herself looked on, observed from a distance as Edmund kissed, and caressed, penetrated and possessed her body.

Until that moment when he'd stilled, deep inside her, and their eyes had held and everything had sharpened to a brilliant point of clarity. And, in an instant, Isobel had gone from knowing nothing of men, and never wanting to, to knowing this particular man with a certainty that went beyond knowing.

What was that? How had it been possible to know someone like that, when you didn't really know them at all? And what had happened this morning, when she'd awoken to find him fully clothed and on the point of leaving, like a stranger after a brief night of copulation?

'Will you wear the russet gown, madam, for the journey home?'

Home. Isobel felt the word like a knife in her heart. Yes, she'd got what she wanted from this union. She would be mistress of Mistlecote now and no one could ever take it away from her. But she would also be Edmund's wife, until the day she died—or he did. And at that moment uncertainty rushed in.

Because, in reality, she knew him no better today than she had when he first arrived at her gates. But now she didn't know who *she* was any longer either! All the fears, all the dread, all the ignorance she'd clung to in her unmarried state had been met and overcome, but this changing of herself in more than just a physical sense was something she'd not expected.

'The russet will do as well as any other,' Isobel said, watching Hawise place her wedding slippers into the travelling bag too, remembering how Edmund had taken them off her feet, the soft trail of his fingers up over her leg, the sensations that simple, yet so intimate touch had evoked.

Sensations and responses she'd surrendered herself to with an ease, an eagerness even, that now, in the light of day, seemed unreal, shocking. Was it the intimacy, the vulnerability, the openness that had broken down the invisible barriers that had been between them before? Barriers that had melted away and been discarded along with their clothing? Or was it simply that carnal knowledge of another person stripped bare the inside as well as the outside?

If she and Hawise had been closer, or even of the same age, Isobel might have asked her maid if it was always like that the first time—the knowing, then the unknowing, the intimacy of the bedding then the strange and frightening remoteness of the morning after. But she didn't ask. Perhaps it was better not to know, not to anticipate, nor prepare, since this coming night, back home in Mistlecote, she would doubtless find out.

It was gone noon when, after wandering around the town, not buying anything or even looking at the wares for sale in the market, Isobel made her way back to the inn. Despite the early sun, it had now started to rain and, her hood up and her head bowed against the weather, she couldn't see where she was going properly and so collided violently with someone coming towards her.

'Oh!'

It was a monk, his cowl pulled low over a bearded face, his habit dirty and threadbare, with travel-worn shoes on his feet. He was carrying a pilgrim's staff, which fell to the ground as the impact knocked him off balance. Aghast, Isobel stooped to retrieve it just as the monk did the same, and his hand closed not over the staff, but over hers.

'Isobel!'

She looked up into the eyes of the mendicant friar who'd sat at her wedding feast the night before and glared at her with such hostility. Except it wasn't he—it was Tom! Stupidly, she stared at him, her mind lurching backwards and forwards, her heart beating so fast that she felt dizzy.

'T-Tom?' Isobel gasped, her breath catching in her throat. 'Is it really…you?'

Retrieving the staff, he helped her to rise and then pushed his hood back. The face she knew so well, and had never thought to see again, appeared. Last night he'd been sitting too far away, and the lighting had been insufficient, and the beard too good a disguise, but now there was no mistaking him.

Shock turned to joy and Isobel stretched out her arms to embrace him. 'Tom! Oh, Tom!'

But he held up a warning hand. 'We must be careful. Yorkists are everywhere in this town.'

'But…where have you been all this while?' A thousand questions rushed to the tip of her tongue. 'Why didn't you send word you would be here in Tewkesbury?'

'There was no time even if I'd been able to.'

His brow creased as someone pushed past them, rude and unheeding, and Isobel saw lines on Tom's face that hadn't been there before. He was thin, almost emaciated, and with horror she realised he was leaning heavily on his staff now.

'Your leg…' she gasped, remembering. 'You broke it…'

'My horse fell on me in the battle.'

'Robin told me…and also that you had made it safely to a monastery somewhere.'

The rain had started to fall harder and, with a quick look around him, Tom drew her under the eaves of a merchant's shop. 'The monastery at Merevale. I left there a month ago.'

'But why did you not come home?'

'How could I?' Beneath the beard, his mouth curled with contempt. 'I heard that Mistlecote had become a Yorkist house but I never dreamed, Isobel, that you would become a Yorkist wife!'

Isobel gave vent to a cry of outrage. 'But not a willing one! Surely you don't think that?'

Tom swore under his breath. 'Then the bastard forced you?'

'No. I made a bargain with him, to keep Mistlecote. It was marriage or a nunnery, so what else could I do?'

A host of emotions filled his gaze. 'But to marry a Yorkist traitor! And the worst of them, a Deverell! Our enemy! Was Mistlecote worth *that*, Isobel?'

Isobel felt tears brim up, threatening to spill over and merge with the rain that spattered her face. 'It is our home! Your inheritance! I had no choice, Tom. Would you rather I went meekly into a nunnery? I was alone, powerless, so I did the only thing it was possible for me to do, and—'

But there was no chance to say any more. Her name came again, not from Tom's lips this time, but from somewhere behind him. Somewhere close. And, looking over her brother's shoulder, Isobel saw Edmund striding towards them.

'It's my husband,' she whispered urgently, grabbing Tom's sleeve. 'He's coming this way!'

'Quickly, give me some coin.' Tom held his hand out. 'I am biding with the Throckmortons for now, but am bound soon for Wales. I will send you word from there when I can.'

With a shaking hand, Isobel fished some silver out of her purse and handed the coins over. 'Here… I hope this will help you.' Her voice broke. Why did Edmund have to come now? Why did he have to come at all! 'Go…and I pray you find some shelter from the rain, good brother.'

Tom nodded farewell, his expression mirroring the anguish of hers. 'God keep you…sister.'

And then he was going, shuffling down the street on his staff, and Edmund was standing where, a heartbeat ago, her brother had stood. The rain fell heavier on Isobel's face, though out of necessity she stemmed her tears, but the accusation was out before she could stop it.

'You have returned early from your talk with the great Earl of Warwick!'

His brows rose. 'I have returned at the hour I said I would.'

Sure enough, the abbey bell began to toll. Isobel silently counted every one of the twelve notes, as Edmund's gaze left hers and followed Tom's retreating figure.

She longed to turn and look too, yearning to wring just one more precious moment out of this miraculous encounter with her brother. But she dared not. It would seem suspicious to show such interest in a stranger, and Edmund's musing words proved her right.

'Was that not the young mendicant friar that sat at the low table at our feast last night?'

'Was it? I don't think so,' she said carelessly, terrified that Edmund might actually go after Tom and find out if he was the same. 'The town is filled with beggars, it being Martinmas.'

'Perhaps it wasn't he after all, then,' he said with a shrug, 'though the limp and the build of the man are similar.'

Isobel shrugged too, the joy of seeing Tom again made bittersweet by the cruel briefness of their reunion. But her brother was alive! He was well, if lame and so thin it was a wonder he stood upright. But why was he in Tewkesbury? Why was he dressed as a monk? Why had he been at their wedding feast last night and here again this morning?

'Perhaps it *was* he, after all,' she said. 'What does it matter if it was?'

'No matter at all.' Edmund stared down at her pensively for a moment and then held out his arm. 'You are getting soaked standing here, and so am I. Let us dine and hope the rain stops for our journey home.'

Home! Unlike earlier, the word brought no knife twisting in its wake now. Mistlecote was still her home. Meeting Tom today *must* be an omen, a sign that the tide would turn soon for Lancaster, and for her.

And, an hour later, as they rode homeward, the rain from the west that drove even heavier into her face seemed an omen too. Rain that would wash away the confusing feelings, the closeness, the pleasure of the night before. Rain that would douse the sensations, the needs, the responses, the sense of oneness that had seemed even more intimate than the joining of their bodies.

All those things that had happened to her last night must never be allowed to happen again. Her husband was her enemy and always would be, and their marriage didn't change that. She wasn't changed either, only physically, and she didn't know Edmund at all, really, for all that she'd bared herself to him, and he to her, in the carnal sense.

And, as she'd discovered, the carnal was as transient as it was powerful. It wouldn't last and it would wither with time. For now, and for the future, there was hope again. Tom would come home and he and Lancaster would drive York out. Everything would be as it was before.

And in the meantime, even if those responses of last night *did* come again when darkness fell and Edmund possessed her body, she would resist them with all her might. Drive them out too and send them so far away they might never have existed.

Chapter Ten

'Margaret of Anjou is reputed to have left Wales and gone to negotiate an alliance with the Scots.' That night, after supper had ended, Edmund sat late at table with Alain, informing him of the things discussed at the meeting with Warwick in Tewkesbury. 'It is said she is angling for a marriage between her son and a sister of the Scottish king.'

Alain grinned. 'Think you King James will be so foolish as to enter into such an alliance?'

Edmund considered before replying. 'My guess is no. Not now York has won such support throughout the land. With Duke Richard being formally declared as Henry of Lancaster's heir, I don't think he'd risk such a move.'

His sergeant took a mouthful of wine. 'What other news?'

'The Tudors are said to be mustering their forces in Wales, with the intent to join up with a Lancastrian counter-attack in the spring.'

'Who says so?'

'John Dwnn, a Yorkist lord and a neighbour of Jasper Tudor in Pembrokeshire. He has his ear to the ground and is pledged to send us word whenever he has it.'

'And the Earl of Wiltshire?'

'Still in Holland, recruiting troops from France and Burgundy to bolster his own Irish forces.'

'Was Edward of March at Tewkesbury too?'

'No, but Warwick says he will be coming to these parts before Christmastide.'

Alain chewed over that thoughtfully. 'Then this is where we will fight next, on the border with Wales?'

It was a hope, not a question, but if Alain was looking forward to the coming conflict, Edmund was not. He sat back in his chair and nursed his winecup. The hall was empty at this late hour and, despite the fire, a chill hung about the rafters, like a residue of the rain that day.

Torrential, it had battled them all the way home from Tewkesbury, leaving them soaked to the skin. Isobel had retreated to a hot bath on arrival and requested her supper be sent up to her room. They'd not spoken since.

A weariness fell upon him as the darkness without encroached. The months ahead would give York plenty of time to muster as well, before the fighting resumed in the spring. The resumption of war at least would bring action, and a relief from idleness, but there was a long winter to get through before that.

Months of secret activity when men could move freely in the dark, recruit soldiers and commandeer horses and weapons. Weeks when the snow might lie so deep it would be impossible to venture outside the walls at all. Days when there would be nothing to do but sit and think and wait.

Nights when a man and a woman could lie, warm and comfortable amid the furs, naked in each other's arms, bathed in intimacy and pleasure. Would he and Isobel lie in such a way during those endless winter nights or...?

'So...how does marriage find you the second time around?'

Alain's question brought Edmund out of his reverie. 'I have only been married a day!' he retorted, a little too quickly. 'It is far too early to tell.'

His sergeant eyed him keenly. 'You look much preoccupied for a man newly wed, that is for sure.' He grinned. 'Was the bed sport displeasing?'

'If the rumours from Wales are true,' Edmund replied, taking a mouthful of wine, unwilling to discuss Isobel with the only man he called friend, 'we will do well to be preoccupied. Warwick has tasked us with recruiting men in the locality and keeping an eye on any Lancastrian subterfuge here.'

He could read Alain well now after their years together, and, although he sensed the Frenchman wanted to ask more about his marriage, he didn't. 'The Throckmorton brothers?'

Edmund pushed his cup away, the taste of wine suddenly sour. 'Also Lord Cornwalle of Burford, the Scudamores of Kentchurch, and some Lancastrian sympathisers in the town of Hereford.'

'In which case, Adam Ewyas will prove his worth.' Alain made a lewd, and very French, gesture with the fingers of his left hand. 'I've not met a more wily knave in my life, not even among the Bretons! Can we trust him though?'

The day after he'd come across Isobel speaking so secretly with Robin of Talgarth in the doorway of the armoury, Edmund had sounded out Adam Ewyas. The Welshman had been only too eager to betray his countryman, and even more eager to take on the role of spying for York while pretending loyalty to Lancaster. Nothing had come his way yet of any actual plot but Adam had revealed that Robin was in contact with Jasper Tudor, and other Lancastrians in Wales.

'Time will tell, but I think so, as far as we need to, anyway.' Edmund pondered a moment. 'The other Welshman, Robin of Talgarth…no,' he said. 'We cannot trust him at all.' And nor could they trust Isobel, though he left the latter unsaid.

That night Isobel descended the stone steps from the turret and, returning to her chamber, placed her astrolabe carefully down on the table. Hawise, sitting at the hearth repairing a tear in some stockings, glanced curiously at the object but made no remark.

The rain that had fallen that day had cleared soon after supper, leaving a brilliant array of stars. And, learning that Edmund was in deep conference with his sergeant in the hall, she'd made good use of those stars on the parapet above.

At the fireside, Isobel held her frozen hands out to the flames. 'You may retire to your bed now, Hawise.'

The girl looked up in surprise then put away the sewing. 'Do you not wish me to help you undress?'

'No, it is late and you must be tired from our journey today, as am I.'

'Will I inform Sir Edmund that you are awaiting him?'

'I am *not* awaiting him.' As her maid's brows lifted, Isobel gave a hasty explanation. 'After our inclement journey today, I imagine he is already abed.'

'I haven't heard him pass by in the corridor yet.' Hawise paused at the door. 'Well, goodnight, madam.'

Madam! Would she ever get used to that title? 'Goodnight, Hawise.'

When her maid had gone, Isobel took out the wooden chest she kept hidden in a little niche in the wall, covered by a tapestry. Then, spreading out her charts and book of hours on the table, she began her work.

Tom's horoscope was better than she could have hoped. Aries was on the cusp of the fifth and sixth celestial houses, ruled by the moon and Saturn respectively. Given her brother's birth day and time, she concluded that it was good for him to begin anything that would end shortly.

That sounded promising if the war proved to be short—but what if it turned out to be long? She continued his horoscope and found he could send messages and letters and go on a pilgrimage. That must mean his journey to Wales and his promise to send word would both be successful.

Isobel cast next her own horoscope. Her sign was currently in the twelfth house, also ruled by the moon, and this was a good time to speak to lords and monarchs! Well, she had no opportunity to speak to either—unless the traitorous Warwick counted, and, since she had no intention of speaking to him ever again, that made no sense.

She cast on for a moment, then stopped, shook her head, stared in disbelief. The stars were rarely wrong but surely this time they were. No, something definitely was in error—she must have miscalculated somewhere. So she cast it again but the result was the same.

It was good to get married!

A knock came at the door and quickly Isobel gathered up her charts, in her haste knocking the astrolabe to the floor. She retrieved it just as the door opened and Edmund appeared on the threshold.

'What do you want?' Clutching the astrolabe behind her back, Isobel glared at him. Why hadn't she bolted the door before she'd begun her work, as she normally did? 'It is late indeed to come to my door and disturb me!'

Without answer, or asking her permission to enter, he

stepped into the room and closed the door behind him. The hounds, stretched before the fire, jumped up, but they didn't growl as they went towards him, and Sirius even wagged his tail.

Edmund fondled the silken ears and smiled at her. 'It seems I am forgiven by one of these fierce hounds, at least.'

'Sirius was always too trusting.' Isobel placed the astrolabe down on the table, trying to hide it with her body, her face flaming as she remembered how his hands had fondled *her* the night before! 'Hawise told me you were engaged in talking to Alain?'

'I was relaying to him the matters that Warwick and I discussed at Tewkesbury.'

'And now you have come to discuss them with me too?'

He shook his head 'The hour is late and I am weary with talking politics. I didn't intend to disturb you at all, Isobel, but, seeing candlelight beneath the door, I came to bid you goodnight.'

'Oh… I see.' Isobel felt suddenly disconcerted at a feeling of not relief, but deflation. 'Then…goodnight, Edmund.'

But he didn't leave. Despite her efforts to conceal them, he'd obviously seen the astrolabe and other objects on the table and now he crossed over towards her.

'You study the stars?'

It was pointless denying the fact. Just as it was pointless to deny the sudden racing of her heart, the quickening of her senses. 'I think that is evident!'

'How did you learn the art?'

'I taught myself from an ancient book one of my ancestors brought back from Constantinople, where he went on the last crusade.'

'A dangerous pastime, especially for a woman, as doubtless you know.' He frowned. 'Why do you practise it?'

'Because I find it fascinating.' Isobel lifted her chin. 'Besides which, there is nothing superstitious, less still to do with witchcraft, about it. The stars help us avoid mishaps and disasters, or at least prepare for them.'

He traced his fingers over the astrolabe as he'd traced her body last night, exploring its design too, with care and consideration. 'It is a thing of great beauty, this. Where did you get it?'

'My father's blacksmith, dead now, made it from instructions contained in the book.' Isobel felt herself warm to her subject. She hadn't had opportunity to talk like this about her passion since Tom left. And talking of the stars at least distracted her from other things!

On her charts, she indicated the points of the midheaven and ascendent, the planes along which the planets travelled. 'Here are the twelve houses,' she said. 'And here are the equator and the ecliptic.'

'How does that help you cast your horoscope?'

'I use the astrolabe to find the ascendant at the time and date of my birth, then find the divisions of the celestial houses and where the planets are within them, and then consult my book of hours.'

'You make it sound both impressive and seductive.' He met her eyes just as she looked up at him. 'But I don't think I would place my trust in how these instruments and tables interpret celestial objects we know nothing about, less still place my faith in horoscopes.'

'Then how do you prepare for the things that happen in your life?'

He shrugged. 'By planning what I want to happen and reacting appropriately to things that I cannot plan for.'

'But wouldn't you rather be certain of everything?'

'I have found it is impossible to be *certain* of anything, Isobel.'

He'd looked tired when he'd first entered her chamber but now his face was as alive as she'd felt her own to be when she'd been telling him about the stars. There was the scent of soap on his skin, for he'd bathed on their return earlier today, as she had. Involuntarily her mind's eye saw him as he'd been the previous night—his naked body tall and powerful, his golden skin, the taut muscles and hard loins, the silver scar across his flank, which she'd been too shy to ask about.

Shaking her head, Isobel tried to dismiss the image, as she tried to dismiss his scepticism, and failed at both. 'I could not bear to live a life I had no control over.'

'And do you have control, Isobel, really? Did the stars tell you of this war? The death of your father? My coming?'

'No...' she admitted, far too aware of his presence as she defended her beliefs. 'Sometimes it is difficult to interpret exactly what the stars mean.'

He gave an odd smile. 'How convenient!'

'Just because the stars do not reveal everything, it doesn't mean they should be ignored.' Isobel gave vent to a sudden impulse. 'Let me prove it by casting your horoscope!'

'My horoscope?' His brow arched. 'I would rather not know a future that may or may not happen.'

'Do you prefer to meet your fate unarmed, then?' she challenged. 'Or perhaps you are afraid of what I might see in your stars?'

'Such as what?'

'Things you have not shown me as yet.'

As she said it, again her mind flew backwards, not just to images now, but to sensations—the press of his flesh against hers, his weight upon her, his scent, the feel of him deep inside her at the moment of bonding.

'Very well, then.' He gave an indulgent tilt of his head. 'Cast it and let us see.'

Spreading out her charts, Isobel tried to ignore the other things he'd revealed to her last night. The unexpected tenderness, the consideration that had surprised her, the pleasure, the awakening to something that she feared now, at this moment when they stood so close, would never sleep again.

Her own womanhood.

'What is the date and hour of your birth?'

'The thirtieth day of November, the fourth hour after midnight.'

'Sagittarius, then, the Archer,' Isobel calculated, looking for his sign on the ecliptic. It wasn't there. 'Your star is hidden this time of year, being a spring and summer star.'

She pored next over the divisions of the celestial houses. 'But currently your sign is in the ninth house, ruled by the sun. At this time, it is good to begin battling and fighting...'

'I don't need the stars to tell me that!'

No, Isobel imagined he did not! The realisation sent a little shiver down her spine. 'Don't take any medicine. It is a good time to buy horses, and also to travel eastwards on business.'

'As to that...' He perched himself on the edge of the table, leaning his weight on his hands, looking suddenly much younger. 'I have no plans to take medicine, nor to buy any horses, and my travels are certain to be westwards, not eastwards.' A note of amusement edged his voice. 'But by all means, read on.'

But Isobel couldn't read on because her breath had lodged in her throat, stopping all words, as a result of what she saw next. *In this sign one will find much good. One can make friendship among enemies.*

She peered harder, but worse was to come!

It is good to get married.

'Th-the meaning of the stars is…is not so clear now,' she said. This mirroring of his horoscope and hers could not be right, surely? 'Because it is the winter season, your sign is not fully visible.'

Edmund sent her a dubious grin. 'Then it seems we must wait for spring and summer.'

'I will calculate again, if you like,' Isobel said, trying to ignore the brush of his sleeve against hers, the way the candlelight turned his hair to gold. 'More is sometimes revealed on a second, or even third, reading.'

'What do you expect to see that you have not already seen?'

Him! Only him! Even though it was only out of the corner of her eye, and that eye fixed on the astrolabe in front of her, Isobel saw him as clearly as she'd seen him the night before. The fact he was fully clothed now didn't make any difference to the sense of intimacy, of connecting, of wanting that swamped her now, as it had then.

'Well,' she said, her heart beating erratically in her breast, 'there *is* something else here, something I didn't see at once…'

And there *was* something else. It was incredible but she wasn't inventing it. It was there, in his stars, the best prediction she could have wished for.

'The stars advise not to have intercourse too often or there will not be any children.'

'What?' His gaze narrowed. 'Where does it say that?'

'Here.' With a trembling finger, Isobel indicated the place on the chart. 'That is what it says! And from that

I think we should not lie together again…at least not too often…since it might be difficult to conceive of a babe.'

Edmund stared at Isobel, his mind reeling. Up until then it had seemed like a game, a meeting ground of pleasant frivolity after her chilly reception of him. An unexpected moment of reconnection to bridge the distance that had grown between them as they'd ridden from Tewkesbury.

'Besides, Hawise says that in many marriages people lead largely separate lives by day…and by night.'

The comment was dismissive, as if he were just a hapless villein at a country fair who'd crossed her palm with coin in return for his fortune and now she was done with him.

'Hawise says far too much in my view!' Edmund ran a hand through his hair and forced his thoughts to come together. 'She is correct, but few go their separate ways so soon after leaving the altar!'

'I am not insisting that we go our separate ways.' Isobel was placing her paraphernalia in a niche in the wall. He saw her pause, draw a breath, before she turned to face him again. 'I am saying that we should heed the stars and observe a period of…abstinence.'

Edmund searched her eyes, but they slid away, towards the hearth, the window, the door, back to the hearth. Anywhere but towards him. And, as she pulled a tapestry down over the niche, it was as if she hid herself too, not only her astrolabe and charts.

Crossing the room, he took her chin and compelled her to look at him There was something else here, he knew, something he didn't understand. 'Very well, Isobel. If that is what you wish, then it will be so.'

'I don't… I mean…the stars know best.'

'Do they?'

'Yes, they do.' She turned her head so that his hand fell away. 'And, after last night, I could be with child already, in which case it would be harmful to...have intercourse.'

Intercourse. Edmund repeated the word to himself. A cold word that didn't relate to the act itself, at least not the way it had been between them the previous night, when it had been anything other than cold.

It *had* been cold with Mariette, always, although he'd been too calf-eyed to see that, at least at the beginning of their marriage. He'd seen everything, eventually, of course—her indifference to his lovemaking and then her absence from his bed while she graced the beds of other men.

And here he was, at the beginning of another marriage, one that already seemed to be racing towards an ending. Was Isobel—now she'd got what she wanted, as his first wife had—doing exactly the same?

'And how long do you wish this abstinence to continue?'

She met his eyes and shrugged. 'I don't know!'

'A night? A week? A month?' Edmund pursued. 'Six months...forever?'

'Do we need to decide that now?'

'You're the one who likes to be certain of everything, Isobel. To know exactly what will happen, and when, to be prepared.'

'Well...yes, that is so.'

'Then how long?' Edmund asked again, a sense of rejection making his tone harsher than he intended. 'Tell me and I will comply with your wish.'

'Well...perhaps a month...?' As he stared down at her he could almost see the calculations in her mind, as quick and as deft as her star calculations had been. 'And by then, of course, I will know if I am with child or not…and, if I am…well, our bargain will be complete.'

Edmund felt his heart twist. 'And afterwards?'

'What do you mean?'

'Will you go on obeying the stars, whatever they tell you?'

Her eyes flashed with annoyance. 'I suppose you think I should obey *you* instead!'

'No, I have come to know you well enough not to expect that, and neither would I want it that way. I would rather you do what you wish to do.' Edmund stepped in closer and felt her gird herself as if he'd drawn his sword against her. 'So what *do* you wish, Isobel?'

He waited and, as the silence stretched out, he detected a turmoil in Isobel, as if, instead of stating a wish, she grappled with some immense and impossible decision. And when an answer finally came, it left him in turmoil too—a turmoil all of his own making.

'I… I wish for you to leave my room.'

Edmund flinched inwardly, as if a door had slammed in his face, and four years rushed together and connected the past with the present. Anger piled into his chest, crushing his heart and stopping his breath, but, spinning on his heel, he did as she wished.

He sat sleepless in front of the fire in his chamber long into the night afterwards. The manor was silent, everyone abed, as was fitting. He wondered if Isobel was sleepless too in the chamber next door? Or did she sleep deeply, untroubled by the things that kept him awake?

He'd not fooled himself that their marriage was, nor would ever be, any more than a bargain mutually struck and of advantage to both of them. However, last night, as they'd joined, found pleasure and fulfilment together, he'd almost believed they could be more than that bargain required them to be.

Clearly, Isobel harboured no such hope. Perhaps their closeness had been all in his mind, and for her part it was nothing more than the sexual awakening that all virgins experienced when they lost their maidenhead to a man. And now that she was awake perhaps she found him lacking, both as a man *and* a husband, and considered their married nights only as an ordeal to be borne.

Edmund shivered and, getting to his feet, strode across to the window. He looked out and cursed the stars that seemed to shine brighter tonight than he'd ever seen them, as if to taunt him with their power.

He'd stood at his window in that house in Bordeaux on many such nights, not looking at the stars, but wondering where Mariette was, fretting and awaiting her return, resolving not to forgive her this time. But he always had... until forgiveness became impossible.

Their wedding night had not been one of closeness, though there'd been carnal pleasure in between the lies. Lies he'd believed because he'd wanted to believe in *her*, but later she hadn't even bothered to lie. Instead, she'd boasted how she'd chosen to be a whore, not only for the money, but because she enjoyed being with a different man, as often as she could.

But when she began fornicating with his own soldiers, making him a laughing stock among his men, there could be no more forgiveness, no more belief, no more love. Even when she'd died, of a despicable disease caused by her whoring, he'd felt nothing, only pity and regret.

With a curse, Edmund turned away from the stars and flung himself down on his bed. Had he once again opened himself up, if not to heartbreak, but to shame and humiliation? Was Isobel exactly like Mariette—cold, callous, deceitful?

A woman who could detach herself so completely, without feeling, only hours after her first lovemaking? And, if so, what was he supposed to do now? He smiled grimly at an irony that would have been funny if it wasn't so insulting.

Not even the stars could have predicted this!

Chapter Eleven

A full fortnight passed before Isobel was alone again with Edmund. They'd met at table, of course, in the intervening period, conversed politely, discussed manor business when necessary, but that had been the extent of their communication. Since he'd left her chamber the night she'd cast his horoscope, he'd not knocked on her door, nor lingered in her company, nor met her eyes directly, except when his own were guarded.

And today, as she walked in the walled garden, Isobel wondered why that granting of her wish, the abstinence, the *absence* of him, left her more restless as the days went on and winter crept closer. Not just restless but resentful almost at the stars for giving her exactly what she wanted— or what she'd told herself she *should* want.

But now she'd got it, she lay awake for hours every night, her thoughts seeping through the stone wall that divided her chamber from Edmund's. Her body refused to either rest or settle beneath the thick winter bedding and her thoughts went back time and again to their wedding chamber at Tewkesbury.

And, worst of all, her hands did things at night that they'd never done before! Exploring the parts of her that his hands had done, touching herself as he had and bringing forth the same pleasure he had brought her. Although it wasn't the same, not as fulfilling, not as…beautiful, and it left her incomplete every time.

Barren too, just as this garden was now as Isobel strolled between withered rose bushes, her feet disturbing the leaves on the ground. For the tenderness in her breasts and her simmering irritation indicated that her courses were near and therefore she had not conceived on her wedding night.

Edmund had gone hunting for meat for the table and no sooner had he ridden out than Robin had sent her word that he and Adam Ewyas wished to speak to her about a disease of the apple trees in the orchard.

Isobel knew, of course, that their request had nothing to do with apple trees, and her nerves grew tighter and tighter as she made a circuit of the gardens, once, twice and then a third time. The hem of her gown was damp and her fingers numb inside her gloves by the time the two Welshmen appeared.

She met them by the cluster of fruit trees in the northeast corner of the garden, where the small orchard stood. 'What is the news?' she asked quickly.

It was Robin who answered, Adam being, she'd found, reticent always. The two were as different as night was from day—Robin was lean and wiry, quick of step and wit, and Adam, though of about the same age, was already corpulent, being always first at table and last onto the training field. She didn't like him very much without knowing why exactly.

'Your brother is in Pembroke Castle,' Robin informed her, 'with Lord Tudor. They only await the arrival of the Earl of Wiltshire from Holland before marching to join up with the Queen's forces when they come south again.'

Isobel's heart surged to hear of Tom, though the other

news was already rife around the walls of Mistlecote and had been since Edmund had met with Warwick at Tewkesbury. She had heard, as they all had, that the Tudors were mustering in Wales and that the Lancastrians in the north must, sooner or later, march on London if they wanted to secure the crown.

'How is my brother?' she asked.

'Well, as far as I know. Tudor thinks highly of him, they say.' He chuckled and, to her surprise, so did the taciturn Adam. 'To think Lord Calvert was right under Warwick's nose at Tewkesbury, at your wedding!'

Isobel didn't join in the joke. If she'd recognized Tom sat at the beggar's table…a shudder passed through her. 'Under *my* nose too. If only I'd known!'

'Your brother thought it best you did not.'

A hot resentment surged up inside her that Robin should know more of Tom than she did, but she stemmed the impulse to voice it. Then, the next moment, the creak of the door in the wall that enclosed the orchard and garden had all three of them turning in alarm. Robin and Adam, more used to subterfuge than she was, recovered themselves quickly, straightening and giving their commander a bow as he approached. Isobel, however, could only stare dumbly at Edmund as, acknowledging his men's deference, his attention turned to her.

He was dressed in his favourite riding doublet and short cloak, and there was mud on his boots. His head was bare and his face bore a healthy colour, the result, she imagined, of a long chase after deer or boar.

'Good afternoon, Isobel.'

His greeting, though not warm, was cordial as he pulled off his gauntlets and tucked them inside his belt. Isobel's mind lurched back to their wedding night, to how she'd removed his belt—not this particular one but a finer one, fitting for wedding attire. Despite the cold, heat suffused her body as into her mind swept the rest of that scene, in vivid detail.

The undoing of the points of his doublet with shaking fingers, the press of his hand on hers as he guided her over his naked flesh, the silken hardness that showed her how much he'd wanted her…the shock, and the excitement, when she'd discovered in return how much she'd wanted him.

Still wanted him! Worse—she wanted him now even more than she had then! Was that because she'd denied herself the carnal pleasure he'd given her then or would she want him all the same? Would she go on wanting him, craving the pleasure like some potent elixir that, once tasted, she could not live without?

'G-good afternoon, Edmund.' Isobel cursed the breathless stammer of her voice and coughed to clear her throat. 'I hope your hunt was successful?'

Edmund took in the scene swiftly and accurately. Even if he hadn't, the expressions on the faces of the three people staring at him would have told him everything. Robin of Talgarth cleverly dissembling, Adam Ewyas cunning and vile, and Isobel…beautiful in her guilt!

His heart sank then swelled with a sort of rage. Not really at her—after all, she'd never pretended that she would be anything but a loyal Lancastrian. He'd never expected her to come over to York just because she'd married a Yorkist.

The sense of betrayal didn't stem from their political differences, nor even from her plotting, but from something much more personal. He'd invited it, of course, albeit unwittingly, that night he'd gone to her chamber and she'd cast his horoscope and, with breathtaking neatness, barred him from her bed!

'We have meat enough to see us through the rest of this month,' he replied, 'and a week or so into December.'

'That is good.' Isobel's eyes slid away and then back again, and he could almost hear her thoughts racing after the answer to a question he hadn't yet asked. 'I was seeking the opinions of Robin and Adam as to whether some of these fruit trees are diseased. They have borne little fruit this year.'

Edmund looked down at the heaps of rotting apples and pears on the ground, ungathered, since they'd been surplus. 'I thought plenty of fruit had been harvested already and turned to good use?'

Part of him wanted to believe her as he'd wanted to believe Mariette. His eyes *wanted* to see diseased trees, to ignore the abundance of stored apples in the barn, the jars of jellies and chutneys in the larder, and his heart yearned to pretend the obvious wasn't obvious at all.

'But perhaps the change in the weather has brought a blight with it,' he added, turning his gaze to the Welshmen. 'What think you?'

Robin shifted uneasily, clearly knowing far less about fruit trees than he did about bows and arrows. Adam, conversely, responded with quick confidence. 'I would prune back the worst of them, Sir Edmund, now before next year's growing season, then see what results.'

'A good suggestion,' Edmund agreed. 'Has Mistlecote a gardener?'

It was Isobel who replied, her tone more brittle than the branches of those trees. 'The men who looked after the garden and orchard went to Northampton and did not return from the battle.'

'Then perhaps Adam here can fulfil that role until we appoint new gardeners.'

'Willingly, Sir Edmund.' Adam grinned. 'I would welcome some activity over the coming winter.'

Edmund doubted the truth of that, since Adam was lazy, and welcomed nothing better than idleness, but he nodded all the same. That Isobel was plotting was certain, though he intended to do nothing about her part in the plot. Robin he would watch closely and act when the time was ripe, and Adam...of the two, Adam, though in Yorkist pay, was the more deadly.

He dismissed the Welshmen with a nod and, as Isobel went to leave with them, he laid a hand on her arm. 'Will you show me the rest of the garden?'

'There is not much to see at this time of year.' The reluctance was unmissable but the defensive tone beneath it spoke even louder. 'It is better viewed in spring and summer.'

'I cannot change the season, Isobel, but a winter garden can be as pleasant as a summer one, to my mind.' Edmund infused a point into his tone. She might have forbidden him her bed but was a walk in her company too much to ask? 'Besides, we have spent little time together of late.'

He saw her flush, as his point did indeed drive home. There was a moment of hesitation, when her resistance became almost tangible, before she nodded.

'Very well, then.'

They walked along the paths that wound through the empty flower beds, the grass damp underfoot, the air full of the freshness of winter—and of the tension that walked with them. Isobel was dressed warmly, for it was a chilly day, her slender body hidden beneath a forest-green gown and a russet surcoat trimmed with apricot edging.

As was her wont—and despite the fact that she was a married woman now—she scorned both veil and hennin, and only a linen coif adorned her head. Her hair hung in a thick plait down her back and swung to and fro as she walked. She didn't look at him once but there was a frown on her brow and her lips were compressed with what he could only assume was frosty forbearance.

Did she really dislike his company so much, out of bed as well as in it?

Despite the tension, it was peaceful in the garden, the high walls shutting out the activity beyond. It was the twenty-sixth day of November and only one or two hardier flowers still bowed heavy heads. Above, the sky was grey and the air fresh, the rain of the previous day leaving the smell of the earth sharp, invigorating.

For perhaps a full quarter-hour they walked in silence, round and round the garden, with only an atmosphere of growing discomfort between them. Edmund wondered how to break it and then she herself brought the silence to an end, stopping suddenly in her tracks and turning at last to face him.

'It will be your birth day on Sunday.'

Edmund was startled she should remember. 'The thirtieth day of November, yes.' Perhaps it was resentment that Isobel had denied him her body as much as suspicion that she plotted against him that suddenly stung and spurred him to sarcasm. 'Are you thinking of casting my horoscope anew?'

'No, but I wondered…how old you will be.'

He got the feeling that was not what she was wondering at all, but he told her anyway. 'Twenty-nine.'

Her gaze fell to a drooping rose, lingered a moment, then

lifted again. 'Also I wanted to ask if you…would like something special for the supper table…to mark the occasion?'

Edmund stared at her in astonishment. 'That is… thoughtful but I will not be here on Sunday in any case.'

'You are going away?'

He nodded. 'To the town of Ludlow.'

'Ludlow? For what purpose?'

'John Talbot, Earl of Shrewsbury, is dead, and his heir is still a boy, so the administration of the area is to pass to Edward of March. I am going to facilitate the relieving of the castle from its constable, who is Lancastrian, and placing a Yorkist in his stead.'

'Will there be opposition?'

'There may be some dissent.' Edmund gave a shrug. 'But Ludlow has always been a Yorkist town, so I do not anticipate any resistance.'

'And….when will you return?'

'After securing the town for Edward, I will be travelling on to assess the extent of Lancastrian loyalty along the border with Wales.'

'Then you may be gone some time?'

Was that a note of hope in her voice? 'Yes.'

'I see.'

A light rain had begun to fall and Edmund reached forward and drew the hood of her cloak up over her head. A mistake. As soon as he leaned in, he inhaled the scent of rose water on her hair and his breath caught in his throat.

'Though if the weather turns harsh,' he added, 'I may have to return sooner.'

'Ned thinks we will have a hard winter this year.' Her gaze moved from his to somewhere beyond him, beyond the walls too perhaps. 'The holly and rowan trees are thick with berries and the mistle thrush are already abundant.'

Edmund suspected the old man might be right, though he placed as little faith in folklore as he did in the stars. 'Did you know that is where the manor—the original Saxon one, I mean—got its name from? A sheltering place for mistle thrush, and doubtless many other birds too.'

She turned to him, surprise in her eyes. 'Was it? I never knew that.'

'It was winter when the first Deverell—D'Aueville, as it was then—made this his home, four centuries ago. I imagine Mistlecote is very pretty in winter.'

'It is.'

Her head turned away, her face hidden now by her hood. Edmund didn't need to see her features, though, to picture them. The curve of her cheek, the delicate jawline, the wide mouth and soft lips. The lobe of her ear that he'd discovered on their wedding night was a particular spot of pleasure for her. Every part of her seemed so familiar to him now, even though she herself had put a distance between them.

A distance that was not solely due to the stars. That they did not lie together because his horoscope said so was ridiculous, naturally, but he'd not argued the point. That Isobel didn't want him was abundantly obvious, but he'd known that when he'd married her.

What he hadn't expected then, however, was that he'd want her as much as he did. Knowing she was conspiring to bring about his downfall, and that of York, made no difference. He desired her even more now than he had on their wedding night, and it wasn't just physical cravings that plagued him and made him curse the heavens each and every night.

Edmund drew his hood up too, as the rain grew heavier and began to soak his hair and trickle down his face. It didn't douse desire but it did sharpen his mind. A conspiracy was one thing but she was playing a dangerous game and didn't know it. Or perhaps she knew it but placed her faith in those cursed stars, confident that Lancaster would triumph in the end.

But should anything happen to him, should he die in battle, and should York be victorious, Isobel would be vulnerable. Spies, of either side, were as hated as they were dangerous and once unmasked could face grim penalties.

So, almost casually, he gave her a warning, an ambiguous one for the sake of his own cause, but one he prayed she would heed.

'Do you really believe that Adam Ewyas knows anything about apple trees, Isobel, diseased or otherwise?'

Isobel felt her mouth drop open, snapped it shut again, and glared at him. Was he teasing her or taunting her? Whichever it was, and as lightly as they were said, there was an edge to the words that put her on her guard.

'What do you mean?'

'Just that.' His expression was unfathomable. 'He is a man that one should be very careful of.'

She shrugged but an uneasiness stirred within her. 'Are you implying he lied?'

'Whether he did or not, someone who changes their loyalties for money is not to be trusted completely.'

'That is a strange thing for you to say since you paid him to defect to York!'

'And that is exactly why I do not trust him, and I advise you not to either.'

'Why don't you dismiss him, then?'

'For now, while he is useful to me, and to York, it serves me to keep him in my pocket.' He glanced up at the sky, which had darkened as heavy clouds billowed, though the rain was as yet intermittent rather than persistent. 'I think a storm is on the way.'

Isobel blinked at the abrupt change of topic, though the sky was indeed much darker than it had been a moment ago. A rumble of thunder in the distance bore out his prediction, as accurately as any horoscope she could cast, and suddenly the air turned thick and ominous.

'Then we should get indoors, should we not?' she said, turning to go, retreating as much from Edmund as from the approaching storm. But her foot caught in a dead bramble branch, almost tipping her headlong. The hem of her gown, one of her favourites, got snagged on a thorn and, cursing, she bent to free it.

But Edmund was already there, down on one knee, unhooking the trapped material with infinite care. Examining it closely, he glanced up again. 'The thorn has made no tear but perhaps, while Adam is tending to the trees, he should be instructed to clear the brambles too.'

Isobel nodded her thanks, but curtly, another weighted allusion to Adam Ewyas annoying her as well as alarming her. Did Edmund suspect Robin too, in some way? He was on his feet again now, kicking the bramble branch away from the path.

'It would be a pity to see such a fine gown spoiled.'

'It was my mother's gown,' she said, unsure why she'd given him that information. 'Some would call it old-fashioned now, but it is well made, and warm. I like it.'

'I would not call it old-fashioned.' His eyes were dark, his lashes spiked with raindrops, as she knew her own to be. 'It suits you very well.'

And, as his voice softened, Isobel saw him suddenly as she had on their wedding night a fortnight ago. He'd gone down onto his knees then too, not to rescue her gown from a thorn, but to divest her of her shoes and stockings. Then he'd smoothed his fingers up over her calf, taken her hand in his, led her to the bed...

If she hadn't cast his horoscope, doubtless, he'd have bedded her many times since, as was a husband's due. Would she have discovered more about him then? The stars had said there was a lot of good in his sign, that if he were an enemy, he might become a friend. But how could that be, when he was her foe, and always would be?

He took her hand again now, the gesture unexpected, intimate, and as his fingers curled around hers the same responses of that night came again. Stronger, more intense now, because she knew what they meant, what caused them, where they could lead...

'Shall we go indoors?' he suggested, his feet however making no move to do so. 'Before we both get drenched?'

Isobel nodded. 'It would seem wise.'

But her feet didn't move either as the rain—cooling, fresh, invigorating—fell upon her face, and upon his. Their clothes grew damp, the scent of wet earth rising, a sort of hush settling. And in that hush came a clearing away of the confusion in her head, leaving her with one thought only, one desire, one regret.

If only she'd never cast that horoscope for Edmund, never told him its advice...for if she hadn't he might read her thoughts, her needs. He might do as she was imagining him doing at that moment—tear her mother's gown from her, right here where they stood, and give her the excitement and pleasure he'd given her on their wedding night.

But he didn't and, as the thunder rumbled again, closer now, they both moved at the same time, as if spurred on by some mutual thought. Hand in hand, they hurried from the garden and across the bailey—empty, since everyone else had gone indoors already. They climbed the slippery steps to the hall and gained the shelter of the wooden porch at the top.

And there they stood and stared in silence at each other once more. Rain dripped, and splashed, and several puddles had formed in the bailey below before Edmund spoke.

'I will be leaving early on the morrow, so I will bid you farewell now.'

Isobel's heart jolted. 'Will I not see you at the supper table?'

'Of course, but then, in the company of the entire hall, I might not be so bold, or so disregarding of your wishes, as to do this...'

'Do...what?'

In reply, he drew her towards him and his mouth took hers. The kiss, ardent and unexpected, was gone before it had even begun, but when his head lifted Edmund's stare was long and penetrating.

'The stars might have barred me from your body, Isobel, but they said nothing about your lips.'

And with that enigmatic remark he was gone too, turning and striding away into the hall without a backward glance.

Isobel stared after him, her wet clothes clinging to her body and her limbs trembling, but not with the damp or the cold. Her lips tingled too, but not with cold either, or the raindrops that dripped from her hood down onto her face.

They trembled with anguish and with need and with resentment that his kiss had ended so soon, sparking her whole body into life, then leaving her expectant and unfulfilled. But, as he'd said, she herself had barred him, or rather had let the stars do it for her.

As thunder rumbled again, and a crack of lightning lit

the sky, she looked upwards, searching for the stars that she knew were there but were invisible. And for the first time ever cursed their power. But…could they be both right and wrong? Could Edmund be both her enemy and her lover? Could she hate him and at the same time love him?

Dare she believe that he was a good man, a friend as well as a husband, even that she was *meant* to be married to him? That she could even lie with him whenever she wished it, no matter what the stars told her?

Or should she go on hiding behind certainty as she always had and shun feelings for the sake of staying safe? Risk nothing and in being safe slip back into the slumbering life she'd lived before Edmund had come and awakened her?

Even as she asked them, Isobel realised all those questions were irrelevant—and too terrible to answer, or to even try. Because anything could happen when the war resumed, and battles were fought, and men died. She herself might have to do things that were terrible too, and in the doing forget all feeling, all longing, all desire, and think only of the cold and brutal reality.

Her brother needed her support, King Henry and Lancaster her loyalty, while Edmund needed nothing from her. Only her body to warm his bed and a vessel to bear his heir.

Chapter Twelve

Isobel rode in through Mistlecote's outer gate, her fingers so cold she could hardly hold Luna's reins. It hadn't rained while she'd been out riding but the cold had seeped into her clothes and the morning mist had lingered and clung in dewdrops to her hair and eyelashes. Winter had arrived all at once, it seemed, on this eleventh day of December, and the afternoon was already rushing quickly towards nighttime.

But worst of all was the stabbing pain in her stomach that had brought her home early from her daily exercise outside the manor walls. Her head ached too and her mood was so irritable that, handing Luna's reins to a stable lad, she snapped at him because he jerked the bridle, causing her mare to snort and dig her heels in.

The moment she entered her chamber, relieved to see a roaring fire—which Orion and Sirius immediately flopped down in front of—Hawise scolded her.

'Madam! You should not venture out into the cold at the time of your courses…'tis not healthy, nor fitting either.'

'My courses have not come yet!' muttered Isobel in return. She didn't voice her worry that her bleeding was late, by over a week, in fact, which was not usual for her. But

Hawise, less taciturn these days, would doubtless jump to the conclusion that she had taken with child.

'Mayhap not,' her maid said now, 'but it won't be long, judging by your temper.'

'I do not have a temper!'

But as she stood, impatiently, while Hawise removed her damp clothing, Isobel knew that was a lie. She'd always had a temper, even as a child, though as she'd grown older she'd learned to rein it in most of the time. Now, as winter set in and confined them more and more to the manor, and the conflict between York and Lancaster brewed quietly yet menacingly outside the walls, irritation constantly prickled under her skin.

But it wasn't simply temper or irritation that had Isobel out of sorts this gloomy winter's day. It was the worry that she might, despite her conviction to the contrary, actually be carrying Edmund's babe in her womb! After all, her flewsa was never late…

Hawise threw a thick blanket over her shoulders then pushed her towards the fire. 'Sit and get warm while I fetch some spiced wine and arrange a bath.'

Isobel did as she was bid without further argument. She was too tired to argue anyway. Her bones ached and she felt as if she could fall into bed and sleep for a year, even though it was only mid-afternoon.

Closing her eyes, she leaned back in her chair, glad her maid had gone below to the kitchen, leaving her alone for a few moments at least. Mistlecote was always quiet now that the days were shorter and the bad weather meant folk remained indoors with little to do except wait for spring, keeping themselves occupied with mundane tasks to pass the day until night fell.

All except Edmund. He came and went from the manor

like the frost that greeted each dawn and disappeared at noon. Twice since his return from Ludlow eight days ago he'd set forth again on business, travelling to Hereford then Gloucester, and now Worcester, recruiting support for York and hunting out Lancastrian loyalists.

Each time he'd returned she'd not asked anything, not wanting to know what happened to those who stubbornly remained loyal to the poor King—still on his precarious throne but a mere puppet of the Duke of York and the Earl of Warwick. She'd longed to ask, to the point of desperation, if he'd discovered Tom among those stubborn, and admirable, stalwarts of Lancaster but had held her tongue.

And neither she nor Edmund had alluded to that kiss on the top of the steps the day of the storm.

On the few occasions her husband had spent at Mistlecote these last weeks, he'd left her alone at night, and instead lingered long at table with Alain, and his wine. Lying awake in bed, she'd listened to his footsteps leaving the hall and entering the solar, occasionally pausing outside her door, only to pass on. Then the closing of *his* door and a silence that seemed to echo with the distance that had grown between them.

And yet…that kiss, and the words he'd said afterwards, seemed to stretch between them, like a cord connecting them, threatening to wind in on itself and draw them towards each other.

Isobel stared into the fire. When she'd made her request of abstinence, in lucky collusion with the stars, she hadn't expected this…confusion, this regret, this longing. But the truth was she missed Edmund when he was away, and she missed him even more when he was here, under the same roof.

Hawise returned just then and, as the door opened, the

dogs jumped up from their slumber, their tails wagging. On the threshold, her maid hovered, then turned back, her curtsey telling Isobel what she'd sensed already.

'Welcome home, Sir Edmund!'

Isobel jumped to her feet too, a swift gladness flooding her heart. But only her maid entered, closing the door behind her, a jug in one hand and some bathing cloths in the other.

'My…? Sir Edmund…?'

'Newly arrived, mistress, and gone to bathe before suppertime.'

As Isobel sank into her tub, the water seemed to swallow her up and drown her in a mire of feelings, of bodily cravings, of muddled deception—all of which she'd brought upon herself, and which she saw no clear way out of. One resolution presented itself, however, when a long while later she stepped out of her cooling bath and into the drying cloth, and Hawise gave an exclamation.

'Mistress, there be blood on the cloth! 'Tis your courses come.'

So there was no babe in her womb, after all, and no heir yet for her husband. At the realisation, Isobel's stomach began to flutter at what that might mean.

Edmund would doubtless want to lie with her again soon, if only to get her with child. And if they joined once more, many times more, perhaps, until that happened, and she conceived of a babe, could she keep at bay the feelings she'd felt on their wedding night? Feelings that would surely confuse everything even more now?

Could she pretend not to feel them, hide her responses, lie to him, even as her body rejoiced at the carnal communion with his? Perhaps but, even as her mind grappled with the prospect, Isobel knew she couldn't lie to herself.

She didn't want to abstain any longer. She *wanted* to join with Edmund again. Enemy or no, she wanted him desperately, more than she'd ever wanted anything in her life.

The next morning, Edmund walked into the hall and saw Isobel sitting in a sunny window embrasure. He'd known he'd find her here, because Hawise—taking some soiled clothing to the laundry—had told him so. But as he caught sight of her, the morning sun falling down upon her, illuminating her loveliness, his breath stalled in his lungs. Her image had travelled with him constantly these last weeks as he'd ridden from town to town. But every time he'd returned, her beauty and his desire had seemed to grow and grow.

He went over to her, but, although the two hounds greeted him warmly, there was only a cold indifference from Isobel, and curt, almost resentful words.

'I'd heard of your return yesterday.'

She looked pale, Edmund noted, or perhaps it was the dark blue robe that shrouded her, revealing only her face and throat, and her hands, that made her seem so wan. Her hair hung in a thick plait over her shoulder, the simple coif covering her head making her seem even more untouchable.

It had been a month, almost to the day, since they had last lain together, and then parted, leaving an abyss a mile wide between them. On the few times he'd returned since that day in the garden, when he'd been even more convinced of her deception as well as her indifference, he'd kept to his chamber.

But each and every time she'd bade him good night at the supper table his body had clenched tight, and he'd cursed the abstinence he'd agreed to.

He sat down opposite her and tamped down on the desire that even now stirred his loins. 'Hawise tells me you are unwell?'

'No, not unwell...' Her gaze met his then slid away again. 'Just...out of sorts.' A blush warmed the ashen hue of her cheek. 'Did you accomplish all you intended while you were at Worcester?'

Edmund stroked the coat of the younger hound, who'd come to sit at his side. 'As much as I could, though the Throckmortons of Coughton are still solid for Lancaster, of course.'

'Did you expect otherwise?'

He shook his head. 'No, but I had hoped they would see sense.'

It was quiet in the hall. Breakfast was long over, the tables stacked away, the floors swept and the candles doused. They were not needed in any case, as the sun, bright and wintery, beamed in through every window.

Gathering his thoughts, Edmund stared down into the eyes of the older hound, wise brown eyes, still not quite trusting of him. Just as Isobel's eyes were when, the words ready and formed on his tongue, he looked up again.

'I have news of your brother,' he said, without preamble.

'Of Tom?' Her expression altered, the guarded mask slipping. 'You have seen him...where? Is he...?'

'Alive. It seems he survived Northampton and has made his way to the Tudor stronghold in Wales.'

'Oh.'

Edmund had expected more of a reaction, not the muted lack of interest that replaced the concern of a moment ago. 'I had thought you would be gladder to hear of him.'

'I *am* glad, but somehow I knew all along that he was alive. I...sensed it.'

'Perhaps the stars told you?'

He'd meant it flippantly, an attempt to lighten a mood that had grown heavier with every word uttered, but her gaze flashed with anger.

'I suppose you mean to hunt him down too? Like a criminal instead of the loyal man he is!'

Edmund took a breath. The truth was he was *relieved* the man had evaded him. It would have placed him in a difficult position had Thomas Calvert—his kin by marriage now—been taken this side of the border. 'I have no instructions to go into Wales, Isobel, after your brother or anyone else. But even so, he and I may well meet in battle one day.'

'I know that.' The anger of a moment ago became anxiety. 'When will it come, the next battle?'

'Not until the spring,' Edmund replied, relieved about that too. 'So we have a winter of respite at least.'

A winter of peace, albeit one that reeked with conspiracy and plot. How long had it been since he'd known a spell this long without a battle? Not once during his mercenary days, not until he'd married Mariette, when he'd found himself embroiled in a different sort of war.

He was tired of fighting, had been tired for a long time, and—while he'd been away, even if not on campaign—he'd found himself aching inside, with a loneliness that at times had been unbearable. And now he was back, it still ached, even though he wasn't alone now.

'Has anything happened here, in my absence? Anything that Alain has not already informed me of?'

'If you are asking if I am with child, no, I am not.' She folded her hands in her lap, as if to compose herself. 'My courses have come…which is why I feel a little queasy.'

Edmund touched her cheek, found it cool, though whether that was due to her courses or something else, he didn't know. 'It wasn't what I was asking, Isobel.'

Did she think he viewed her as a brood mare and nothing else? If so, she couldn't be more wrong! Their bargain, made so practically that day in the chapel, had become irrelevant almost, changed in the space of one heartbeat and the next by the intense feelings of their wedding night. A bonding that had gone much deeper than the carnal, far further than the mere bargain it had been at the start.

A bonding that he almost thought reignited as, all at once, her skin warmed beneath his fingers. And then, her lashes flickering and her gaze dropping, she turned her head to the window.

'Well, now you know, anyway.'

Her voice was defensive and attacking at the same time. If only he could read the thoughts behind it, discover if she too had felt the same as he had that night. Been alive to more than just the physical awakening of a virgin to carnal pleasure.

Discover too if she'd missed him as he'd missed her these last weeks. If she also yearned for that bonding that had been interrupted, made incomplete, then extinguished. Or perhaps that was only his lust, his needs, his torment, for she seemed oblivious to it all as she sat there like an ice queen.

But…if he bent his head now, and touched his lips to hers, would that ice begin to melt as he'd felt it do that day on the steps in the storm?

Edmund pushed the temptation firmly away and changed the subject. 'Edward of March is riding to these parts soon and he plans to sleep a night here at Mistlecote.'

Her eyes met his again, wide with shock. 'York's son is coming here?'

'For one night anyway, more if the weather is inclement and he cannot ride onwards to his destination.'

She shook her head vehemently. 'He is not welcome under my roof!'

'*Our* roof,' Edmund corrected. 'And we must *make* him welcome, Isobel, since one day he might well be our king.'

'He will never be *my* king!' With that, she leapt to her feet, her hands balling into fists. 'Let him come, then, since it is clear I cannot prevent him, but I hope you do not expect *me* to act as hostess?'

'As my wife, it is your role, is it not?'

'No! I refuse!' Isobel turned away, paced a few steps, then spun around to face him again. 'He is an enemy!'

'Edward is lord of these lands and I hold this manor in fee of him, as do you now, be he your enemy or not. As such, we owe him hospitality and cannot do other than extend it.' Edmund rose and, stepping towards her, looked down into her angry face. 'If you refuse, Isobel, you will shame me and shame Mistlecote too.'

'This is not about *shame*!' Isobel planted her hands on her hips, the sudden nearness of him as he closed the gap she'd put between them unsettling her. 'I do not support the house of York and never will.'

'But I do and I am also your enemy.'

'That is not the same thing!'

'Is it not?'

The quiet question was the truth. It was exactly the same thing—and yet it was completely different too. Edmund *was* her enemy, even more so than that son of York, since he was here, in her home, in her life, in her mind, in her...

She stopped the word before it formed in her thoughts. He would never find his way into her heart, she would not allow it, because that would only make what she had pledged to do even harder, impossible perhaps.

It was only her *body* he affected, only her *senses* that he stirred, evoking unwanted desire within her every time she saw him, heard his voice, felt his presence.

'Or are you incapable of feeling shame, Edmund?' she accused, snatching at a weapon that might keep at bay the treacherous feelings that even now threatened to weaken her resolve. 'Shame at supporting traitors against the true king? Shame at taking the spoils of an unjust war that do not belong to you? Or perhaps you do not even know the meaning of the word!'

He blanched. 'I know all about shame, Isobel, believe me. My first wife brought me nothing *but* shame and, for that reason if none other, I ask you not to do likewise over this matter.'

There was anguish in his words, anguish on his face. Edmund had mentioned his wife before, of course, but almost in a passing remark that she hadn't really listened to. But now, curiosity eclipsed even the impending visit of Edward of March.

'In what way did she shame you?' Isobel asked. 'Did she too refuse the unreasonable duties you demanded of her?'

He laughed, not a sound of humour but of harsh contempt. 'It was nothing so mundane as that. I made *no* demands of her, reasonable or unreasonable, unless you consider *fidelity* too much to ask of a wife?'

Fidelity? Did he mean...? 'Your wife was not...faithful? She took a lover?'

'A lover?' He turned away, to look out of the window, his broad shoulders squaring as he folded his arms across his chest. As if shutting himself in, shutting her out. 'No, they weren't even that!'

It took Isobel a moment to comprehend the plural. 'They? You mean she had more than one?'

'Are you really as innocent as that, Isobel?'

She recoiled at the bitterness in his tone. Hardly innocent now she was wedded and bedded! But that wasn't what he meant, was it? Curbing the impulse to reach out and touch him, she probed deeper, not just out of curiosity now but because she sensed in him, for the first time ever, an acute and awful suffering.

'Then enlighten me,' she invited. 'Talk about it—about her—if it would ease you to do so.'

There followed a silence so long that Isobel began to believe Edmund had no intention of enlightening her further, that he already regretted revealing so much of the wife he'd loved very much perhaps—revealing, as he'd done so, himself too.

Then his shoulders heaved and dropped again, and he spoke at last, not to her, but to the windowpane. 'I met Mariette in Bordeaux. She was seventeen, the illegitimate daughter of a harlot, poor to the point of destitution. I married her, not just because I fell in love with her, but to save her from…that life.'

Isobel held her breath, wanting him to go on but almost fearful now to hear what he might say because the expression on his face was so haunted, as if the ghosts that rushed back at him were too terrible to behold.

'I was young too, and idealistic despite being a mercenary, a man who fought and killed for money. And when I met Mariette, I felt I'd been…redeemed, blessed. She was so beautiful, so innocent, in her heart if not her body…or so I thought.' His head shook. 'But I wasn't redeemed, nor blessed, but deceived instead. She was anything but innocent. She was a whore, like her mother!'

'She must have wounded you deeply.'

'By the time I realised what she was, it was too late. I'd

married her and I could not put her aside. So I tried to be patient, understanding, even convinced myself at first that her lewd behaviour was meant to make me jealous, though she had no need, since I was completely beguiled by her.'

Isobel saw him swallow, once, then again, as if the words now had become too horrible to utter. So she tried to say them for him.

'But when her indiscretions became adultery, your patience ran out?'

'Adultery is one word, I suppose.' His eyes met hers, bright with pain. 'When I said she was a harlot, Isobel, I was speaking literally. She lay with men for money, brought her earnings home and boasted how easily she'd come by them. But when she started whoring with the men under my command, making me a figure of scorn and pity, even my patience reached its limits.'

Isobel tried to hide the shock on her face and tried to picture that woman instead, but failed at both. 'What did you do?'

'In the end, I left her. To stay would have been impossible, unbearable. So I gave her our home, sufficient money to live on, everything she needed, and I quit Bordeaux altogether. Six months later I heard she'd died, of a disease contracted in the brothel. An unborn child in her womb—not my child—died too. She was barely nineteen.'

'I'm...sorry.' Isobel's heart heaved with compassion. 'I never dreamed...'

'How could you?'

He'd been right in what he'd said earlier. She *was* innocent, in many ways. The world he'd described, the relationships between men and women, the sordid side of love, betrayal and deceit—those were things she'd never encountered. Never even imagined that a person could be capable of deliberately inflicting such hurt on another.

'When you spoke about your wife before…when you said you had had no wish to marry again… I thought it was because you'd loved her, and that her loss was painful, too painful to forget.'

'I *did* love her, Isobel. I loved her with all my heart, all my soul. Even when I realised what she was, I still loved her—and hated her too.' The bleakness of his words mirrored the expression in his eyes. 'And that was the saddest and most shameful thing of all.'

With that, he spun on his heel and strode from the hall. Isobel sank down onto the window seat, her mind reeling. After hearing all that, how could she shame Edmund, as his first wife had done, albeit for the minor whim of refusing to welcome a member of the hated house of York under her roof? And yet, how could she betray herself and Lancaster by extending that welcome?

She stared out of the window. The sun had begun to sink below the purple horizon and frost was already glistening in a twilit sky. It boded to be a clear, cold night outside the walls, but here inside them nothing was clear any more, and not even the throwing of extra fuel on the fire could thaw the chill that settled deep in her bones.

Isobel sat there for a long time, ignoring the house servants that appeared to light more candles and lay the tables for supper, an earlier meal since the nights had drawn in. Before today, she would not have sat like this, confused and conflicted, and completely unsure of herself. Before today, she would have had no hesitation in causing Edmund shame, and pain too, by shunning his accursed guest…but now?

Knowing her enemy, guarding herself against him, plotting his downfall was one thing. But glimpsing his past, his sorrow, his heart… Knowing that he was capable of a love that had hurt him so very much—that was quite another thing entirely.

It wasn't so simple any longer, far from it. Now she *cared* about Edmund's feelings in a way she hadn't before, and it wasn't just that he'd told her about his former wife. For she'd missed him in more than the carnal sense these last weeks. Her heart as well as her body had missed him sorely, constantly, every day and every night they'd been apart.

Chapter Thirteen

Edmund poured his illustrious guest yet another cup of wine, even though Edward had downed three already in the short time they'd been seated at table. The meal had barely begun before the young Earl of March had commented on the absence of Isobel.

'Your wife is not at home?'

'She is feeling indisposed, my lord, and sends her regrets.'

The flaxen head tilted, the golden collar of rose and fetterlock on his broad shoulders catching the torchlight. 'A pity. I hear from Warwick that she is a rare beauty, one I would have liked to see for myself.'

Edmund gritted his teeth and made no comment. The whelp's appetite for women was even greater than his appetite for good wine and rich food, even though he was only eighteen. He'd been wayward in Calais, during his months of exile, with always a roving eye, and doubtless had left behind more than one broken heart, perhaps more than one bastard child too.

But, for all his lust and splendour, Edward was a likeable lad, and an able and courageous commander in battle, as he'd shown at Northampton, when he'd captained a whole division and helped York to an easy, if bloody, victory.

'You intend to spend Christmas at Ludlow, my lord?'

Edward shook his head and bit into a leg of roast goose. 'At Shrewsbury, but thereafter I'll base myself at Wigmore, so as to keep a better eye on movement from over the border.'

'Think you, then, that the Tudors will strike sooner than we anticipate?'

'They will have to await the arrival of Wiltshire and whatever mercenary force he can gather from Holland and France.' The Earl chewed thoughtfully. 'I do not think he will come this side of Christmas, but soon afterwards.'

'And what of the Lancastrians in the north of England?'

'My father has already gone to deal with them, and with the Earls Somerset and Northumberland too. Margaret of Anjou is apparently still in Scot...'

Edward broke off, his gaze going over Edmund's shoulder, his eyes widening. Then he gave a low whistle through his teeth. 'It seems your good lady has recovered from her indisposition, Edmund.'

Edmund turned his head and saw Isobel entering through the door from the solar, Hawise behind her. She was wearing the murrey-coloured gown she'd worn the night she'd fled the supper table as his men had ridiculed her. The same night he'd kissed her for the first time.

And as she approached, a modest headdress with a veil of fine gauze gracing her head, his lips burned to kiss her again, if not her mouth, then at least her hand. Edward of March beat him to it, however. Rising, the Earl took Isobel's hand and lifted it gallantly to his mouth, his gaze latching on to hers like a limpet.

'I am glad indeed you are recovered enough to grace us with your presence, Lady Deverell. My Earl of Warwick told me of your beauty but he understated it, the knave!'

Isobel responded with a cool smile. 'Good evening, my lord. I trust you have been made comfortable in my absence?'

A smile tugged at Edmund's mouth, the avoidance of the word 'welcome' perceptible to him if to no one else.

'Immensely comfortable, Lady Deverell. You keep a good house here.'

'We do our best.' Arranging her skirts, Isobel sat and waved her maid off to her own seat. 'Though, naturally, it is not usual for us to entertain a guest such as *yourself* here.'

Edmund, retaking his seat on March's right, met her eyes, and saw a definite gleam of mischief there. Did she mean to shame him after all, not by her absence but with her sharp tongue?

'I hope this will not be my only visit to your manor, my lady,' Edward was saying now, leaning closer to Isobel than was proper. 'My castle of Wigmore is, after all, less than a day's ride from here.'

'Since you are overlord of this region, I doubt that you will await an invitation to visit us but will come whenever you please.'

Edmund tensed. Was it only he who heard the animosity? Only he who saw the frosty light in her eyes. It seemed so, since March clearly was oblivious to all but Isobel's beauty, which tonight was nothing less than luminous.

'Perhaps, when my father is king,' the Earl said, his hand hovering near hers on the table top, 'we might even see you at Westminster on occasion.'

Isobel met the amorous suggestion like a queen would the unsuitable attentions of a too-bold courtier. 'My ambition does not rise as high as all that, my lord, and, as a good Lancastrian, I doubt it ever will.'

March sat back then, a flush mounting his face but a

complacent smile still on his mouth. However, his demeanour was not as relaxed as before and Edmund sensed the mood alter slightly. His own mood shifted too, and he found himself tempted to clip the young cub about his well-shaped ears for flirting with his host's wife!

'A great pity, Lady Deverell, as are your loyalties.' March's golden head tilted. 'But I will not press you—for now—though I hope you will change your mind, come the time.'

The note of disappointment verged on displeasure, but nothing more serious. Yet it was not often, if ever, a woman had dared pour such cold water upon Edward's irrepressible ardour.

'Perhaps the time will never come, my lord.'

The Earl's eyes narrowed but his smile remained, widened even, as the repartee, far from affronting him, seemed to enliven him instead. 'York's time is nigh, my lady, I assure you of that.'

'We shall see, my lord of March.'

With Isobel's blunt use of his title, deferential and yet pointed, the repartee tottered dangerously for a moment. But, as Edmund had discovered in Calais, the boy was good-natured and generous, with an easy charm that he knew how and when to use. And now, as Edward turned to him, what could have been a difficult situation was suddenly eased.

'Your lady is loyal, and as bold as she is beautiful. I envy you, Edmund.'

Edmund inclined his head, refilled the Earl's cup, then Isobel's, and lastly his own. By this time, the music had begun and, when Edward asked his permission to dance with Isobel, he had no choice but to give it.

He watched like a hawk, however, as the two moved

around the room. And it wasn't just he who watched. Every other male present watched too, with avid eyes. Apart from Hawise, Isobel was the only woman at Mistlecote, and men without female company were like wolves who'd not had a kill for many days. And he knew himself to be the hungriest wolf of all.

A hunger that must have been etched clearly on his face because Alain, sitting at his side, leaned in and voiced as much. 'You look like a man eaten up with jealousy, Edmund—or else a fool smitten by love!'

Edmund stared speechlessly at his sergeant, and suddenly the truth dawned on him, not violently, but so softly, so lightly, that it must have been there all the time. Like a secret hidden deep in his heart, waiting patiently for the moment of recognition. He did love Isobel! He'd loved her right from the moment he'd set eyes on her.

And it was no use denying it, to Alain, or to himself any longer. 'It seems I am,' he said ruefully. 'On both counts.'

Isobel felt dizzy, not just because of the way the Earl was leading her briskly in the dance, but because of the sheer personality of the man. A force she'd sensed while they'd been sat at table, for all his languid poise and easy laugh, but one that now swept her off her feet—literally.

Edward was taller even than Edmund and startlingly handsome. The graceful body was elegantly encased in the finest clothes she'd ever seen, and supreme confidence oozed from every pore of his skin. Oh, he was smooth, this son of York—almost too smooth.

If indeed his father became king, and this boy after him, she grudgingly had to admit that one day England might well be ruled far better, and more happily, than it was at present. To her dismay, she found herself liking Edward of March, but even so, as he kept her dancing through one song to the next, Isobel's eyes and thoughts went constantly to Edmund.

Her husband was leaning forward on his elbows, his face serious, his eyes brooding yet too far away to fathom their expression. For all of March's beauty, Edmund was the more compelling, with a presence that dominated—without even trying to—all the glittering nobility that surrounded the other man. Whereas the Earl's looks were all on the surface, there were hidden depths, finer qualities, to her husband that she had only just begun to discover.

He had been surprised when she'd appeared in the hall, fulfilling her role as hostess; she'd seen that much. Now she couldn't tell what he was thinking, nor even hope to guess. But he definitely didn't look pleased that she'd favoured his Yorkist comrade with a dance.

The music ended at last and the minstrels refilled their cups, taking a rest for a while. The Earl escorted her attentively to her seat, filling a cup with wine and pushing a plate of sweet dainties in front of her.

'To restore you,' he said, with a devilish wink of his eye, 'in case I have worn you out too much with my demands.'

Isobel couldn't help it. She smiled at him. 'Not at all, my lord, but I have to confess my feet are glad of a respite!'

March turned away then, to respond to a question from Lord Stafford, one of the nobles who'd come with him, and had now left his table to join theirs. As soon as the two were engrossed, she looked at Edmund at the same time as he looked at her.

'I have never seen you dance before, Isobel.'

There was a coldness to his words, and he appeared… angry. Yet it wasn't anger that simmered in his eyes. It was more like…accusation.

'We have not had an occasion to dance, up to now,' she replied. 'Did you mind that I danced with Edward?'

'Yes.'

The frank admission made her blink. 'But is that not what is expected of a good hostess?' she said teasingly. 'Part of a wife's duties towards her husband's guests— whoever they be?'

'It is…' His jaw clenched. 'But that doesn't mean I have to like seeing you in another man's embrace.'

Isobel held his eyes, saw them darken, their expression mirroring his words. 'Not even a man who might one day be king,' she said, quietly, so that no one else could hear.

'Not even he.'

They had leaned closer with each exchange and now their heads almost touched. If the Earl of March had not interrupted them then, with a word of apology, Isobel knew their mouths might have touched too. She also knew that she'd have welcomed that touch far more than she'd have welcomed *any* guest to her home—York *or* Lancaster!

'I must leave early in the morning, Edmund, so—if it please you and your lady—may we retire now and discuss some matters of importance?'

It wasn't a request, in spite of the courteous tone, and, not waiting for a response, the Earl rose to his feet. The whole room rose with him, in honour of his status, Edmund too. He wasn't looking at March, however, but at *her*, with a blistering stare that pierced her down to her toes.

'Of course, my lord,' he said. 'We will go through to my chamber in the solar. I have made that ready for your sleep, in any case, and a chamber for my lords Stafford and Audley await below, when they are ready to retire.'

The four bid her goodnight and, on their departure, the evening ended. The minstrels packed away their instruments, the servants came to clear the tables, the men retired to their beds in the buildings outside, until only Isobel and Hawise were left.

As she walked to her chamber, her maid at her heels, Isobel's mind raced. If March was to sleep in Edmund's chamber, and the two other lords in the lower solar, where did Edmund himself intend to sleep?

It was many hours later that Isobel found out the answer to that. Alone, unable to sleep, restless with a sort of wild anticipation, she sat before the fire and watched the moon rise outside the window, pass its zenith, then start to sink again.

It had gone out of sight when the knock came at the door, startling her, and yet somehow, without knowing why, she'd been expecting it. Expecting him.

She got to her feet, the blanket she'd been shrouded in for warmth falling away, leaving her only in the kirtle she'd worn beneath her gown that evening.

'Come in.'

The door opened and there was Edmund framed in the doorway, his tall figure lit by the candles ensconced on the wall beyond.

'May I speak with you?'

Isobel felt the hairs lift at the back of her neck as excitement replaced anticipation. 'Of course.'

He entered, closing the door behind him, and crossed to where she stood. The hounds greeted him as they always did now, with wagging tails and, from Sirius anyway, a lick on his outstretched hand, then settled down to sleep again.

Edmund spoke first. 'I wanted to thank you.'

'Thank me?'

'For coming to the supper table, for greeting Edward as you did. I realise how much that must have cost your pride.'

Isobel shrugged. 'Strangely it didn't cost me as much as I'd feared it would. He is…likeable, despite his Yorkist colours.'

'He liked you too…despite your Lancastrian colours.' His eyes went to the dress Hawise had hung on a peg to air before retiring to her room. 'Was your red gown a deliberate, if silent, affront?'

She nodded. 'Perhaps.'

'Why did you do it, Isobel?'

'Wear the red gown?'

His head shook. 'Meet Edward so courteously when you said you would not meet him at all?'

Isobel paused a moment. 'I thought long and hard before I relented but…after what you told me about Mariette… how she humiliated you, well, I knew I couldn't add to that burden, even if the shame would not have been the same.'

'It is odd, but since I spoke to you of her that burden doesn't seem so heavy.'

'What has altered?'

'I'm not sure.'

Isobel wasn't sure either what had altered in *her* after that conversation. But she knew that putting aside her pride and greeting the Yorkist earl was the least of that alteration. There were other reasons—other feelings—that had made it impossible for her to humiliate her husband as his first wife had done. And foremost among those reasons was that attraction to Edmund had become affection for him too.

'I thought…' she began, that realisation now quivering in her voice, 'when I danced with Edward…that you seemed angry.'

'I wasn't angry…' Lifting a hand, he touched her hair,

still in its braid and hanging over one shoulder. 'I was jealous.'

Her heart skipped a beat. 'Jealous?'

'Husbands do become jealous, you know, when they see their wives in the arms of another man.'

'The dance was modest enough, and I could hardly refuse him,' Isobel countered, her breath quickening as his hand brushed her breast. 'Were you jealous of Mariette's lovers?'

His brows knitted. 'That was not the same.'

'Why not?'

'Because when you danced with Edward, it was not to make a cuckold of me.'

'No, it wasn't,' she said. 'Even if I possessed the art of coquetry, I would not do that.' A lightness possessed her, or perhaps it was light-headedness, as his gaze bored down into hers. 'Though he is very pretty—for a Yorkist,' she teased.

'Am *I* pretty?' His eyes twinkled. 'For a Yorkist, I mean?'

'No.' Isobel shook her head. 'Pretty is not the word I would use.'

'Would you dance with me all the same?'

'Now? But there is no music!'

A smile touched his mouth. 'We don't need any.'

Before she could say more, he took her hand and stepped slowly around her in a circle, so she had no choice but to turn with him. Another slow, almost stately circle, and Isobel began to giggle, entering into the spirit of it, going up on her stockinged tiptoes and holding her free arm outstretched, elegantly, as she'd seen great ladies dance on occasion.

The hounds at the hearth lifted their heads and watched,

then Sirius jumped up with a bark, his ears cocked and his tail on end.

'Shhh!' Isobel admonished him, laughing as she did so, however, realising how long it had been since she *had* laughed. 'Lord Edward is trying to sleep next door.'

'There is a good wall between us and March is a sound sleeper.' Edmund looked as if he wanted to laugh too. 'We could summon the minstrels and dance a lively saltarello and still not wake him!'

He turned her the other way, then back again, their feet not following any specific dance—or at least none that she knew. And, as they danced, with no accompaniment other than their own pleasure, Isobel felt…happy. Happier than she'd been for—how long? She hadn't felt this joy in her heart since before her father had died…before Tom went away to war…

Before Edmund came, an enemy at her door, to steal her home and change her life irrevocably. And now here she was, dancing with him, laughing too, her life indeed changed but in a way she could never have imagined.

'You dance well, Isobel.'

She inclined her head in mock response, but speaking truthfully. 'But you dance better.'

'In France and Burgundy people live to dance. Perhaps we here in England will learn to dance more too, one day.'

Even though the movements they made were leisurely, Isobel's head began to spin in a way it hadn't in the hall when she'd danced with Edward of March. That was duty… this was—what? Fun, companionship, sharing…more than that?

She didn't try to look for an answer. Instead she let Edmund lead her, turn her, draw her close then hold her away again, in formal but fluid dance steps that were unfamiliar. Yet she seemed to know them instinctively. Her feet knew how to follow his, her body swaying and dipping exactly as his did, as if they were joined together by an invisible thread.

The way they'd been on their wedding night.

Once again, like then, Isobel felt as if she'd entered a world of magic and harmony, a world in which only she and Edmund existed. And when, in unspoken unison, their feet stopped and their eyes locked, it was as if the time in between, the weeks apart, the distance that had grown and separated them, hadn't even existed.

'I have missed you these last weeks, Isobel.'

'I missed you too,' she admitted. 'Very much.'

He drew her nearer and she arched into him then, feeling the hardness of his body, his warmth that drove away the cold winter night and filled her with fire.

'Did the stars not console you?'

Isobel shook her head. 'I have not consulted them of late, not since…'

'Since the night you cast my horoscope?'

Her heart began to beat fast. 'In fact, I have begun to doubt some of the things they tell me.'

His gaze darkened. 'If *I* tell you something, would you believe it?'

'I might. What is it?'

Edmund's arms tightened about her. 'It is not just to get an heir that I married you, you *do* know that, don't you?'

'W-was it not?'

'No. The truth was I could not suffer to see you wedded to any other man, nor to think of you imprisoned in a nunnery, suppressed and muted for ever, as my mother was.'

'Oh.' But she *was* mute, made speechless at his startling words, for a moment at least. 'C-could you not?'

He shook his head. 'And neither it is just to get an heir that I want to lie with you tonight…and every night.'

Isobel felt a heavy sensation pull low in her belly, an ache begin there and rush into her breasts. 'I too want that…' she breathed, unable to deny it any longer, not to him and not to herself. 'But Edward sleeps next door…'

'What of it?' His eyes were burning down into hers, waiting, hungry, brilliant with a hunger she felt glitter in her own eyes. 'We are man and wife, Isobel. We can join when and where we wish…'

His hands smoothed downward over her back, making her spine tingle, her limbs go weak with desire. 'I know what *my* wish is, Isobel. What is yours?'

'The same, Edmund.' Isobel said, hearing her voice tremble with the truth of it. 'And as for the when and the where…let it be here and let it be now.'

Chapter Fourteen

His heart pounding, Edmund kissed her waiting lips, lightly at first, then deeper as they parted, welcomed him, demanded more. Her breasts were heaving against his chest, her fingers burying themselves in his hair, pulling him ever closer, and he could restrain himself no longer.

With none of the care with which he'd disrobed Isobel on their wedding night, he turned her and pulled apart the lacing on her kirtle, taking it, and the shift below, off over her head. Then he picked her up and carried her to the bed.

Dispensing just as swiftly with his own clothing, Edmund dropped down at her side. Tonight there would be no hesitant lead-up, no careful holding back, no asking what she wanted, what pleased her and what did not. He knew she sensed that too, as her arms closed about his neck and her legs about his hips, entrapping him, inviting him.

Their coupling, unlike that first time, was swift, hungry, passionate and impatient, as if each of them had wanted it for too long. Yet their joining, although it took only moments in the satisfying, and spanned only a few thundering heartbeats, still seemed to last an eternity. Their release came at the same time, Isobel's body arching beneath him, her cry loud and keen, his own cry muffled as he buried his face in her hair.

And afterwards he gathered her to him and they lay in silence for a long while, their skin cooling, their hearts and breaths slowing into a drowsy, blissful sense of peace.

The manor slumbered and the night passed into morning, and Edmund's eyelids began to droop. Then, just when he thought Isobel was asleep, she shifted in his arms and lifted her head from where it had lain against his shoulder.

Although the candles were nearly out and the glow from the fire dull, he knew the moment her eyes found his, because his whole body felt the connection and his heart kicked into life again.

'That night of our wedding…when we lay together… and you told me you were as afraid as I was…was that true, Edmund?'

It was such an unexpected question for her to ask, especially now. 'It was true,' he replied, stroking his fingertips down her bare arm where it lay over his chest. 'Did you think it a lie?'

'Not a lie, exactly, but I thought you only said it to ease my fear.'

'I tried to reassure you that you weren't alone in your fear, yes, but it wasn't just that.'

'What else was it?'

'Simply this…' Edmund laced his fingers between hers and from somewhere deep inside him dragged up the words he'd never admitted to anyone before. 'After Mariette, I shunned female company for a long time.'

'Because you were afraid?'

He nodded. 'Afraid of being hurt again but also I was afraid of failing someone as I'd failed her.'

'Why do you say you failed her? It doesn't seem that way to me.'

'I didn't give her what she wanted, what she needed.'

'But what did she want that you'd not already given her?' Isobel was up on her elbow now, staring down at him in the dark. 'A home, a life, love.'

'I don't know what she wanted, Isobel, not even now.'

'How could you, unless she had told you?'

Edmund was silent for a moment. 'If I'd asked her the right questions, perhaps she would have told me. At the time, I thought that if she loved me as I loved her there would be no need to ask. We would know what the other needed without having to ask.'

This time it was Isobel who was silent, her head lowering to lie in the hollow of his shoulder again. 'Perhaps love is not so simple as that.'

'Perhaps not,' he said, lacing his fingers more snugly in hers. 'At least not that kind of love.'

'What kind?'

'The kind that consumes a person until they cannot think, cannot separate truth from lies, fact from fantasy. The kind that cannot really last because it is not real.'

'Then perhaps a marriage is better without love…as ours is.'

Glad of the dark, Edmund grimaced, astonished that she did not know he loved her with all his heart, not just his body.

'When two people join,' he said, 'things can change, *they* can change as closeness grows. Sometimes physical loving leads to hearts loving, even if we think it will not… even if we *wish* it will not.'

She shifted, settled again. 'Then we must guard against that changing, and guard our hearts too, since *neither* of us wishes for that kind of love…do we.'

It wasn't a question, yet neither was it a statement. Edmund shook his head anyway. 'No, we don't.' But even as he agreed, he knew it was already too late for his heart. 'So now you know the reason for my reluctance to wed, what was yours? Why did you not marry before? I know you chose not to so as to look after your brother, but when he didn't need looking after any longer, why not then?'

'It *was* true that I preferred to remain unwed to care for my father and brother. They *both* needed me, not just Tom.' There was a little pause before she went on. 'But when you asked me…that day we were out riding… I realised, for the first time, there was more besides.'

'What was it?'

'Fear. The truth was I was afraid of the unknown.'

'Of the bedding?'

'Not really of that…no.'

She twisted away suddenly, turning onto her back and letting out a sigh, as if she couldn't find the words she wanted to say. Edmund turned too, onto his side, facing her, leaning up on his elbow.

'You are the bravest woman I have ever known, Isobel.'

'Am I? I always thought I feared nothing, but I discovered I wasn't as brave as I thought I was.' She was looking not at him, but up at the ceiling. 'It is hard to explain it… and perhaps you won't understand.'

'I will try.'

'It was the *surrender* that frightened me, the relinquishing of my freedom, my future, my very self.' Her head turned and her eyes found his. 'You see, I'd never had to give myself to anyone before, in any way, not just in the carnal sense. Since I was twelve years old, I'd answered to myself alone, never to anyone else, not even my father, who let me do as I pleased anyway.'

'Go on,' Edmund said when she paused.

'I thought that if I married I would have to answer to a

husband, as most women must. I feared marriage might be a trap that, once in it, I couldn't escape. So instead, I devoted myself to looking after my family, running the household. I didn't need anything else. I didn't know there *was* anything else, for me anyway, and if there was, I didn't want it.'

'Why not?'

'Because my life was certain, just as it was.' She turned fully on her side to face him. 'I felt…safe, free, comfortable. Everything was in my control. I made my own decisions. I knew what each day would bring and how I would meet it.'

'By reading the stars?'

'That was why I studied them in the beginning, yes.'

Edmund reached out, touched his fingertips to her temple, trailed them down her cheek. 'And are you still afraid of the unknown, Isobel?'

She nodded. 'A little. After my father was killed at Blore Heath last year, and then Tom didn't return from Northampton… I felt the world change, but I tried to cling on, pretend everything could still be as it had been before, that I could control it all.'

'Then I came.'

'Then you came…'

The exchange hung in the air between them, thicker than the frost that coated the outside of the windowpane, brighter than the stars that filled the night sky beyond.

'Now I realise it wasn't safety at all. I feared the things I didn't understand. I didn't know what marriage was, and I didn't know what *men* were, not really.'

Edmund held his breath and waited for Isobel to tell him how he'd come and turned her life upside down, destroyed her safe haven, shattered her happiness. But long moments passed and she didn't speak again, so he spoke for her.

'And you hated having to surrender not just Mistlecote,

and your sense of security, but also your fears—to *me*, of all men? A Yorkist enemy come to take everything from you?'

Isobel held his gaze, the depths of his eyes reflecting dimly the light of the moon through the window. The answer to his question eluded her, and she didn't know why it should, since he had hit on the truth—and yet...

'At first, yes, although it would have been even harder to go into a nunnery or marry Lord Ledwyche. Either of those would have been a surrender too, but at least this way I kept my home.'

'Then you are not sorry, in one respect at least, that you wedded me and not him?'

'No, I'm not sorry, Edmund, not any longer. It was just as well I did not marry before, for if I had I wouldn't have married *you* and in doing so been able to keep Mistlecote.'

It had come without hesitation, without even thinking, and yet it was true. Isobel dropped her gaze, to hide the surprise of that, even though he could hardly see it in the dark, of course. Yes, she had kept her home, but was she glad she'd married Edmund for other reasons too?

'That night I cast your horoscope,' she went on, 'and told you we must abstain... I knew then that I was not sorry that we were wed—but I *was* sorry the stars told me what they did.'

That was true too, and yet her feelings for Edmund had begun to change even before they'd been wed. Before she'd lain with him and been awakened to pleasure and intimacy and more. Because something else had come along with that awakening, a sort of invisible mist of things that had swirled unseen yet been felt all the same.

It had been there that day she'd fallen off Luna. It had rustled in the grass beneath her as she'd opened her eyes and met his, dark with concern. It had been there that night in the chapel, hovering in the musty, mote-thick air, when she'd asked him to marry her. And it had been there too the day he'd told her about Mariette and bared his broken heart to her.

What was it? Affection, as she'd already discovered? Or much more than that?

'And do you think you can be content in this marriage, Isobel, even though it has changed everything for you, as it has for me?'

Isobel stared at him. Content? *Could* she be? *Was* she even now? But, as she examined the word, she knew it wasn't the right one. It was too…inadequate, and yet she was not happy, not quite. How could she be? Happiness and carnal pleasure were not the same thing—she wasn't that naïve!

'Could *you* be content?' she turned the question back to him. 'And, even if we might be, is contentment enough for always?'

His fingers lifted, touched her hair, her cheek, trailed down her throat to the valley between her breasts, and Isobel felt her senses spark into life as she realised the time for talking was over.

'We will find that out over the years, Isobel.' His head dipped and his eyes burned into hers. 'Even though we are married unto death, you are still free, not trapped. You are not answerable to me, only to yourself, as you have always been.' His lips brushed hers gently, seeking, promising. 'I am your husband, not your master, and you are my wife. And, because of that, we have this…'

And as they joined again, rather more languidly this time, that word *content* blurred into waves and throes of ecstasy. It hovered still when, a long time later, her body aching and bathed in bliss, Isobel slipped finally into sleep. And as it vanished into dreams, it almost seemed as if war and betrayal—the enemies of contentment, and of love— might vanish too as if they'd never been.

Ned had been right when he'd predicted a harsh winter. As Christmas arrived, Mistlecote stood out stark and remote amid a sea of snow. It was colder than Isobel had ever known it and the sky was a constant blanket of grey through which the sun never peeped.

Days of inactivity, of not being able to ride, of walking about with frozen toes and numb fingers, were forgotten when the hour grew late, however. They lay with each other every night, either in his bed or in hers, warm and heedless of the weather without, their hunger growing each time rather than lessening.

Perhaps it was the winter that made thinking and doing impossible, futile in fact, since nothing could be done except to endure snow and hail and ice and cold. But when the time for pleasure came and Isobel melted into Edmund's arms, enduring ended and living began again. Sensing, feeling, touching, tasting, knowing—all of it brought her to life as if spring surged back during those blissful nights with all its hope and vitality.

On the morning of Christmas Eve, Ned died suddenly, after a convulsion gripped and contorted his old body until it crumpled to the floor. Isobel cried bitterly as they'd laid him in the chapel, his ghost accompanying the mass held before supper, his death making the occasion solemn rather than joyous.

All the household and villagers dined in the hall afterwards, as was customary, and the joy of the season returned, life going on in the midst of death, as it always did. The food was plentiful and made even richer by a gift of three fat swans sent from Edward of March. The fire roared, the walls gleamed bright with holly and ivy, and the music and mummers were diverting.

The atmosphere was as it had always been at Mistlecote in previous seasons—and yet it was not. The revelry in the hall grew to raucous levels and even the Yorkist soldiers who had once ridiculed her and chased her from the hall bade her a happy Christmas. And Isobel discovered that a feeling of contentment did indeed abound, without and within.

It was at the time of gift-giving when she felt it most keenly. Having dispensed small favours to everyone in the household, which she and Edmund did together, they sat down again and he pressed a small object wrapped in linen into her hand.

Isobel gasped in delight. 'A gift? For me?'

His brows rose. 'Did you think I would forget to give you one?'

He was handsomer than ever tonight, in the same blue surcoat that he'd worn for their wedding. His hair, slightly longer now, glinted like gold, and she thought there was an ease about him that the wine and good food could not totally account for.

With excited fingers, Isobel unwrapped the gift to find a silver clasp set with a small but brilliant emerald. All the jewellery she possessed, and that was little enough, had belonged to her mother, and no one had ever given her a jewel of such beauty before.

'Th-thank you,' she stammered. 'But I did not think to get anything for you.'

'I did not expect you to. May I pin it on you?'

He fastened the clasp to the neckline of the murrey-coloured gown, which Isobel wore often now, even though—or perhaps because—it was not as modest as her others. She felt liberated inside its velvet folds, even beautiful when Edmund told her its colour made her hair glint like dark fire, and her face fashionably pale, her waist even more slender, her breasts higher.

And sometimes, when she sat at her mirror, she examined herself to find out if he spoke the truth or whether he merely flattered her. Femininity, womanhood, fashion, things of the flesh had not interested her before and, at the same time, unsettled her because they were unfamiliar.

Well, they weren't unfamiliar any more, and now, as Edmund's fingers brushed her neckline then hovered just above her breasts, she leaned in a little, delighting in the quiver of her flesh, the response his touch evoked, the longing...

'The jewel has almost the brilliance of your eyes, Isobel...almost, but not quite.'

He'd leaned in too and his breath caressed her face a moment before his lips met hers. It was a soft, almost chaste kiss, yet one laden with the promise of the hours ahead, after the feast had ended, and they were alone.

'Ho, Edmund!'

Alain's voice broke them apart. The Frenchman had partaken of more than his usual amount of wine tonight, as had everyone, including herself, and now his flushed face appeared between them. His arms went about them both and a devilish glint lit his dark eyes.

'Has he told you, Isobel, of our little tradition on this night?'

Isobel smiled, shook her head, a little annoyed at being so rudely interrupted but bemused too. 'No,' she said. 'What is it?'

'A wrestling bout between us to show who is the better man!'

'A wrestling bout!' She gasped, though rough and tumble games were all part of the festivities. After the frugality and fasting of Advent, everyone embraced the opportunity to eat, drink and be merry. There had been an archery competition that afternoon, the children of the two villages that belonged to Mistlecote had played at Hoodman Blind, and, more raucous, a pig's bladder had been kicked about the outer bailey, in a foteballe mêlée between the Yorkist soldiers and the manor farmers—which the farmers had won, much to her delight.

Edmund shook his head. 'I think this year we could be excused, Alain.'

'Mais non!' Alain hauled Edmund to his feet. 'This year it is more than ever fitting, if only to show your prowess to your beautiful new wife, *mon cher ami!'*

Isobel smiled, the atmosphere, the wine, the food, Edmund's thoughtful gift suddenly making her feel freer than she had in years. And yes, not just content, but happy too. Perhaps she'd consumed a little *too* much wine, but it was good to see everyone else so happy as well.

'By all means,' she said. 'I would find the outcome very interesting!'

Edmund shrugged and grinned. 'Very well, Alain, on your own head be it. But, for the sake of the ladies present, I will be gentle with you this year.'

Then, with a wink at her, he followed his sergeant out into the middle of the room. Both men stripped off their over-clothing, rolled up their shirtsleeves, and engaged. Isobel saw at once that Edmund was the more agile, though the heavier Frenchman was stronger—and the worse for drink.

The contest—although it started earnestly enough—

soon deteriorated into a bout of fun, with the two entertaining the onlookers as well as testing their prowess. Laughter and encouraging shouts shook the hall, and bets were avidly placed on who would win.

Isobel laughed too, pride in Edmund's skill, his generosity of character, warming her heart as he visibly let the other man throw him time and again. She was applauding a particularly skilful though harmless throw, by her husband this time, when a voice came from just behind her.

'Mistress Calvert.'

Startled, she turned her head. Used to being called madam or Lady Deverell now, for a moment she couldn't think who could be addressing her. Then she saw Robin of Talgarth's cunning face as, under the guise of filling her winecup, he leaned close.

'Word has come that the Earl of Wiltshire will land in Wales within weeks.'

Isobel blinked and tried to drag her mind to what her ears had heard. 'The Earl of Wiltshire?' she asked, the name sounding alien on her tongue. Was she supposed to know it?

Robin offered her a plate of gingerbread, putting it in front of her, where it sat ignored. 'And, when he does, Tudor will march for the border.'

The laughter died on her lips as an icy realisation dawned and reality hurtled back. Of course, the Earl of Wiltshire was in Holland, recruiting troops for Lancaster. Tudor only awaited his arrival before he would march, her brother with him.

'Wh-what are we to do when that time comes?' Isobel asked, her blood chilling as if she'd taken no wine at all that night. 'What *can* we do?'

'When Edward of March hears that Tudor is on the move, your husband will surely receive a call to arms.'

'Yes,' she replied absently, her hand reaching for a piece of gingerbread, only to crumble it to pieces on the plate. 'And when it comes?'

'Then you must get information from him as to where the Yorkists plan to intercept Tudor's army, the strength of their forces. Forewarned, we will be forearmed and, with God's will, victorious.'

Isobel said nothing in reply as a cheer went up from the hall, bringing her attention back to the wrestlers. Alain was on the floor now, laughing in mock submission, while Edmund's foot rested, lightly enough, on his chest.

'*Je cède ! Je cède, messire!* I yield!'

Laughing too, her husband pulled the Frenchmen up and, arms around each other's shoulders, they returned to the table. Isobel sensed Robin had melted away into the shadows long before they sat themselves down, breathless from their exertions.

'Well…!' Edmund turned to her, his hand on the back of her chair, where Robin's hand had rested only moments before. 'I trust that spectacle was not too offensive to your eyes, sweeting.'

Isobel met his merry gaze, aware of the emptiness of her own. She'd never seen Edmund so filled with joy, nor heard him address her with an endearment before, at least not outside of the bedsheets.

'No, not at all.' She forced a smile, knew its falseness, as surely he must too. 'I am glad you won even though I suspect Alain was not too difficult an opponent.'

His gaze sobered a little, as if he did indeed sense the tension that had settled at the table between his leaving it and returning. 'I hope we were not too rough, nor the language of the men too coarse?'

She shook her head. 'No, I am just a bit tired now. May we retire soon?'

'We can retire now this minute, if you wish?' His gaze darkened again, but differently now as desire shone. 'The feast will continue just as merrily without our presence.'

Rising, they bade the company goodnight, to a host of thanks for such a generous feast and wishes expressed warmly for the year ahead. As they passed through into the solar, and reached her door, Isobel's feet faltered.

She had intended to make some excuse that they sleep apart, claim she was *too* tired, or had overindulged in wine, anything. It would be unbearable to lie with Edmund tonight, after Robin's instructions that she betray him. But when his mouth descended on hers and his arms came about her and he drew her close, she went instinctively, immediately.

He'd not replaced his surcoat after the wrestling bout, but had left it forgotten in the hall, and the warmth of him struck her through his linen shirt and set her senses aflame. She saw him again, nimble and lithe on his feet as, laughing, he engaged and evaded Alain. The bunching of his shoulders, the ripple of the muscles in forearm and thigh, the high colour on his cheekbones, the golden fall of his hair under the coronet of candles that hung from the ceiling.

So when he picked her up, and shoved her door open with his foot, Isobel made no excuses at all. Not tonight. Let tonight at least end with joy, with pleasure, with merriment greater even that that continuing in the hall.

Tonight let her forget that tomorrow, with the cold light of day, her betrayal would begin.

Chapter Fifteen

'Richard of York is dead?'

Edmund stared at the messenger who had ridden from the north to Shrewsbury to inform Edward of March of the death of his father, and then travelled from there to Mistlecote and other Yorkist houses in the area with the news.

'Slain in battle on the thirtieth day of December, His son Rutland was killed fleeing the battleground, they say defenceless, by the knife of Lord Clifford.'

'And Salisbury? His son, Neville?'

'Lord Neville died in the battle.' The man continued the grim toll. 'The Earl of Salisbury was taken and executed the following day. Their heads, all four of them, now hang on Micklegate Bar in the town of York, the Duke's bearing a paper crown in insult!'

Edmund had not known any of the dead men personally but he knew his overlord, Warwick, well enough to imagine the extent of his grief and of his rage, for Salisbury was his father, Neville his brother.

'Is my lord Warwick still in London?'

The man nodded. 'Where word of the defeat will doubtless have reached him by now.'

Edmund drew a sigh and gestured to Alain, sitting at his side, who had taken Ned's place as steward. 'My steward here will see to a bed for you tonight and something to eat, since supper is some hours yet.'

Then, going through into the solar, he knocked on Isobel's door and opened it without waiting for an invitation. She was sitting in the window seat, some sewing in her lap, her hounds as always lying at her feet. For the first time in weeks a thin sun had penetrated the clouds and now its beam, weak as it was, brought some warmth into the room, falling over her slender figure, glinting on the hair that hung, as it usually did, in a long plait over her shoulder.

And, as it always did too, his heart leaped in his breast and his stomach fluttered in awe…and desire. He could swear Isobel grew more beautiful every day—and every night, when she was so warm, so open, so transparent, so *his* that he could almost forget that she was plotting against York, plotting against him.

She looked up at his entrance, a smile of greeting on her mouth, her eyes glad to see him. The same way she'd looked at him at the Christmas feast when, after his wrestling bout with Alain, he'd returned to the table and seen Robin of Talgarth slinking from her side like a weasel into a hole.

The next day, Adam Ewyas had told him what doubtless Robin had told his wife. It hadn't made any difference to their lovemaking that night, nor on any of the nights that had followed since then, but by day he'd sensed the change in her. The deception. The cunning. The betrayal.

Closing the door, Edmund announced the news that was even now doubtless flying around the manor walls. 'The Duke of York is dead.'

Putting her sewing aside, she got to her feet. 'Dead? B-but how? When?'

'Three days ago. Killed in battle at Wakefield, in the north of England, his son Rutland too.'

'I…don't know what to say.'

'But does the news not gladden you, Isobel?' Edmund heard the bitterness in his words but he couldn't help it. 'I imagine that Lancastrians everywhere are rejoicing, so why should you not?'

'I am sorry for their deaths, because they were living beings, and have left bereft those who doubtless loved them,' she said. 'But I *am* glad that this fighting will be over now, as you must be too.'

'Over?' He dropped down onto the window seat and, leaning forward out of the sunbeam, let his hands hang between his knees. 'You are forgetting Edward of March, or rather the Duke of York as he is now and, in his father's place, heir to the throne.'

'But…surely…all that is changed now?'

'Changed, yes, but only in that Edward and not Richard will wear the crown.'

Isobel sat down again at his side and at once Edmund felt his senses react to her warmth, the contact of her arm and thigh with his as she leaned forward and sought his eyes.

'What is going to happen now, Edmund?'

'Margaret of Anjou and her forces will come south, if they are not already en route. Warwick will try and prevent her reaching London but, even if he fails to stop her, the people will not allow her to enter the city.'

'Will you have to go to help defend London?'

Edmund looked down as Orion's head came to rest on his knee. The younger hound was sitting up, staring at him intently, as if it could read the conflict in his heart. How strange it was that these creatures, so ready to tear him limb from limb when he'd first arrived, were now more predictable, more trustworthy, than their mistress. 'No,' he replied, 'my duty will lie here, to meet the forces from Wales when they come.'

'And will they come…soon?'

He shrugged but the movement felt like trying to throw a boulder off his shoulders. The heavy, unbearable weight of knowledge. 'I know not, Isobel.'

There was a little silence and Sirius whined, lay flat, his head on his paws. Edmund suppressed a sigh. If he were a hound, he might whine too! As it was, all he could do was as he'd done the last time. Accept the folly of his heart and pay the price of it, however high.

Mariette had paid a price too. She'd died, which, as cruel as that had been, had saved him from a life tied to her, since he could never have put her aside, or annulled their marriage. He'd been prepared to support her, despite everything, with money, a roof over her head should she need it, anything—except he himself, not ever again.

And yet, here he was once more. And Isobel lived, breathed, her vitality untainted by the ills that had taken his first wife. Perhaps the salvation this time would be his own death on the battlefield.

Lifting his head again, Edmund met her eyes at last, saw them darken, soften, then grow hungry. It was so ironic that, even while she betrayed him, she desired him. Not even Mariette had stooped to that!

But at least Isobel's betrayal was a clean one, an admirable one, even, as she placed her loyalty to Lancaster above her vows. He'd always known that right from the start. Knew it as he'd loved her, night after night, with not just his body but also with his whole soul.

'It is rumoured,' he said, his heart reaching out to her, even now, 'that your brother is among Tudor's forces.'

One thing was clear—she was nowhere near as good at

deception as Mariette had been. Her lashes flickered and the sharp intake of breath told him she knew that as well as he did.

'How…how do you know?'

Edmund almost smiled. 'From Edward's spies in Wales,' he said. 'The subterfuge in this war is almost deadlier than its battles. At least the fighting, out in the open, man to man, is honest, and more or less clean.'

Isobel searched Edmund's face, the strange tone of his voice sending a chill down her spine. This news of York's death should be a victory and yet it wasn't. Some time, somehow, over the last weeks neither York nor Lancaster had seemed to matter and yet matter more so than ever before. Her life had become split into two, like her heart, like she herself.

Since Christmas, and Robin's message, she'd acted a part, playing a careful role between Edmund's wife and Tom's sister, clinging on to her enmity and her loyalty like the ends of two ropes that pulled her asunder across a raging river and feeling herself sinking into the water bit by bit all the while.

'It feels like nothing will ever be clean or honest ever again,' she said. 'Not even when this war is over.'

His eyes remained on hers, strangely impassive. Could he see her battle with the currents? The loyalties that were tearing her to pieces? Could he see into her heart? Did he know of her love? Isobel doubted that he did, since she'd only just discovered it herself, and cruelly the discovery had come the night of the wrestling match.

In Edmund's arms, in Edmund's bed, she'd realised she loved him and had known also the terrible fact that her love would make no difference. She would betray him even though she loved him. She had no choice.

Edmund was nodding now, his expression solemn. 'Once I lived for war,' he said. 'I made my living from it, though I fought—and still fight—for causes I believe in, not just for coin.'

'Do you wish sometimes that you were *not* a soldier? Nor even a Yorkist?' Isobel asked, the question as foolish and as impossible as her love was. 'Do you wish you were just a common man?'

'With a common wife?' He gave a wry smile. 'I think you most *uncommon*, Isobel.'

'That isn't what I meant.'

'No.' He shook his head. 'I know you did not. But if we were just commonfolk, Mistlecote would not belong to you, nor to me either.'

Isobel dropped her gaze and laced her fingers in her lap, misery eating away at her soul. 'Now, in this war, even Mistlecote doesn't seem to matter any longer.'

His hands came over hers, bringing warmth and so much more. 'You would not have said that once, so why do you say it now?'

'Because it is true.'

'Why? What has changed in you, Isobel?'

Isobel lifted her shoulders, dropped them again, and searched her heart. She *had* changed, just as he'd said could happen when two people joined. Physical love for her *had* become heart love, but how could such a love live in a heart such as hers? How could she betray him—for the sake of Tom, the rightful King, for Lancaster—and yet how could she not?

His fingers tightened, a silent prompt asking again for an explanation of something he could never understand, never condone, never forgive. Taking a deep breath, Isobel removed her hands from within his, wrapped them about her midriff, ignoring the surprise, then the confusion, on his face. And, unable to tell him the truth, told him instead a long-forgotten story.

'When I was sixteen, my father bought Luna for my birthday. She was only three years old, not fully broken to the bit, wild and spirited. One day I rode her right to the top of Clee Hill, far to the north of here. It was windy, and as I turned her for home she bolted.'

Pausing, Isobel felt again the thrill, the panic, the fear, saw again the greenery flying past, the trees looming up and away, each and every one like an ogre trying to snatch her out of the saddle.

Edmund was leaning forward again, his hands once more hanging down between his knees. Long, well-shaped hands that had explored every part of her and, in the process, stolen her heart, her whole self.

'Did you manage to stop her?'

She shook her head. 'We were in the thick of the trees. I couldn't see where we were going. The branches were scratching my face, tearing at my hair. The more I pulled on the reins, the faster Luna went. So in the end I just flattened myself on her neck, closed my eyes, and let her gallop.'

'And the stars brought you home safely?'

'Yes.' She shrugged. 'But I don't know if it was the stars, or luck, or even Luna cleverly avoiding the trees and bringing us both out of the forest relatively unscathed.'

He turned his head to look at her. 'Whichever it was, it must have been frightening while it lasted.'

'It was.' Isobel met his eyes. 'And now I feel that fear again, as if I'm galloping headlong once more, with no power to stop or change direction, or even to hurl myself out of the saddle to safety. All I can do is ride it out to the very end—whatever that end proves to be.'

'Perhaps that is all that any of us can do.'

The sun began to sink outside the window, bringing a slow darkness into the room. A coolness settled as the fire burned low. The hounds lay down to sleep as, gradually, twilight came and the manor fell silent.

When Edmund stood, an eternity later, it seemed, and held out his hand, Isobel took it and let him lead her to the bed. The one place where rivalry and enmity, conflict and fear, even betrayal ceased to exist. The place where bonding and trusting and knowing were possible, where pleasure reigned and even love seemed possible, if only on her part.

Before he drew her down under the covers, he took her face in his hands, kissed her lightly, without words, but with a question in his eyes. A question she longed to answer, but she wasn't really sure what her answer would be.

And so, as they came together, their bodies joining until there seemed no edges at all between them, Isobel gave him her heart and said nothing.

January proved even bleaker than December had been. The world outside the walls remained white and life itself seemed to grind to a halt, and stand waiting, watching. Edmund had set in motion the preparations for the battle to come, making his men train daily on the flat meadow outside the walls, keeping their weapons and wits sharp, their horses fit.

As the weeks passed, rumours flew hither and thither, crisscrossing the land like pulsing, jerking nerves. The first was that the Lancastrian forces from the north, having crossed the River Trent, were plundering towns and villages as they marched southwards, turning the people in those parts against them, and making the folk of London even more resolved to bar the city gates against them.

The second rumour was that Edward of March had left Shrewsbury and based himself further south, in his castle at Wigmore. The third was not a rumour at all but a message from Edward himself, ordering the men of Mistlecote to muster and be with him before the last day of the month.

After reading it, Edmund went out and, despite the falling snow, trained with his men. They were disgruntled to go out in such weather and he couldn't blame them, but they didn't know that it wasn't a battle with Lancaster he was fighting but one with his own self.

He wielded his waster sword harder than he'd ever done before. He put himself against the strongest and the quickest of his men. He welcomed every thud that hit his body, or his helmet, grateful for every bruise.

It was his policy to pit all his men in turn against different opponents, so that they learned to adapt quickly to varying sword skills and strengths. He and Alain paired with those that needed to improve the most and, inevitably, and at last, he found himself face to face with Adam Ewyas.

At once, Edmund's mind and vision sharpened to so keen a point that he seemed to see every pore in the other man's face, every drop of sweat that pooled on lip and brow, every particle of the breath that turned to mist as he breathed.

Hardly before Adam was ready he struck, hate lending his arm inhuman strength, his waster slamming violently on the other man's shield. His opponent blinked and immediately stepped back but Edmund struck again, harder and harder. And he went on striking until Adam's parries became flailing and useless attempts to protect himself, rather than blows in exchange.

Finally his hated opponent fell backwards, shield and

waster outflung, an arm over his eyes, shrieking for mercy. Edmund stood over him, wishing the wooden sword he held aloft was instead his sharp and heavy broadsword. Imagining himself bringing it down in a gleaming, curving arc to split the man's skull in two.

'*Pour l'amour de Dieu*, Edmund, desist!'

The voice penetrated through the rage in Edmund's head and he spun around to see Alain coming towards him. Behind his sergeant, all the rest of the men were standing and watching with gaping mouths. He lowered his sword arm, the urge to kill dissipating from his chest, as if a wall of rocks had been lifted off him. Then, drawing a deep breath, he helped Adam to his feet, forcing himself to meet the bewildered gaze.

'You are not hurt?'

The man shook his head, scowled as he snatched himself free, and stumbled away. Edmund turned to Alain. 'That is enough for today. Tomorrow we will rest.'

Then, leaving his sergeant and the whole company staring after him in astonishment, he headed for his chamber. Once there, he hurled the waster into a corner and dropped down into a chair, leaning his head back against its rest and closing his eyes.

What in God's name had he been thinking? An unanswerable question, since he hadn't been thinking at all. He'd been feeling…and acting on that feeling. It wasn't just that Adam was a despicable cur, a greedy traitor, though he was that and worse. It wasn't just that he did his job of listening and watching and reporting, but that he did it with relish, as he was paid to do.

A born deceiver, Adam Ewyas excelled at his role and was well paid for his duplicity. But every time Adam came to him in secret and relayed whatever news had come from the enemy to Robin of Talgarth's ears—and also, he suspected, to Isobel's ears—Edmund hated hearing it, hated the man who spoke it. And that hate had built up inside him until today it had turned to violence.

He might not like the man but it shouldn't make sense—it *didn't* make sense—to blame Adam for carrying out his orders. It was *himself* he should blame, *himself* he should hate, for deceiving his wife even as she deceived him.

Cursing, Edmund got to his feet and woke up the slumbering logs in the hearth. Then he stripped and, pouring water from a pitcher into a basin, began to scrub the residue of the exercise field from his body, as if with all the sweat and the grime he could wash himself clean of the vileness of it all too.

But he couldn't. He couldn't change anything and he couldn't stop anything. Just like Isobel, when her mare had bolted with her down Clee Hill, he had to ride it out to the end, whatever the outcome proved to be.

Chapter Sixteen

The next days were taut with expectation. Everyone knew that the call to arms had come, but Edmund kept their destination to himself until the last moment. And he waited for Isobel to ask where the Yorkist army would make their stand, how many men Edward had at his command. He sensed *her* waiting too, for an opportune moment, a way to get that information from him, to ask without it seeming obvious. But the days passed and she didn't ask.

At night, when they lay in each other's arms, he thought that would be the time she would choose to betray him. But, strangely, that was the one time, the one place, he knew she would not. It was as if, when they'd closed the door and slipped beneath the bedcovers, the world outside ceased to exist.

On the twenty-first day of January, word reached him that Jasper Tudor had set forth from Pembroke and was heading north-east towards Brecon, gathering recruits along the way among the Welshmen of Carmarthenshire and Powys. Edward, calm, confident and determined to avenge his father's death, sat and waited at Wigmore.

And the next night, when their lovemaking had been more intense, more pleasurable than ever before, when she lay in his arms, her cheek resting in the hollow of his shoulder, it finally came.

'When will you ride out?'

Edmund stiffened and stared up at the ceiling. 'In three days' time.'

'So soon?'

'With Tudor on the march, we cannot delay much longer.'

There was a silence and, although her hand remained on his chest, her hair splayed out like silk upon his skin, her heart beating with his, Edmund sensed this one precious and unassailable bond between them begin to unravel at last.

'How many men will you take with you?'

'As many as I can,' he said. 'Alain will remain here with a small force to defend Mistlecote, should it be necessary.'

'Do you think it *will* be necessary?'

He shook his head. 'No.'

Another silence, and then she drew a breath. 'Where will you muster?'

Edmund felt his heart go cold. If it were just his own fate that lay in her hands he would tell her, but it was the fate of all his men, of the house of York itself. 'It will be somewhere between Hereford and Shrewsbury, since Tudor must cross the border between those two points, for sure.'

'How will you know where he is to cross until he actually crosses?'

'An army on the move cannot move unnoticed.'

'But if Tudor knows Edward has based himself at Wigmore, will he not cross as far away as possible from there?'

'He will seek battle, not avoid it, I'm certain of that,' he said. 'And if he is victorious, his glory will know no bounds.'

'Why?'

'Because if Edward perishes, York's cause is lost forever. There is no one of age left to effectively claim the crown, since his brothers are only aged ten and eleven.'

'Just children.' She lifted her head, worry in her eyes. 'If Lancaster prevails…what will happen to them? To their mother?'

'I doubt Margaret of Anjou will be merciful even if her husband would be. She will destroy the house of York once and for all.'

Her head lowered again, her cheek resting over his heart. 'I wish I hadn't asked. I wish you hadn't told me. Perhaps it is better not to know!'

Edmund closed his arm tighter about her. 'But you *did* ask and it is futile to wish otherwise, Isobel.'

Yes, Isobel knew it was futile and at the same time all-important. Everything seemed to hang on this moment. A moment when she could ask further still, try to get everything she needed to know out of him, relay that information to Robin. A moment to do nothing at all.

The moment passed, and then another, then another. Beneath her ear, Edmund's heart beat strong and solid. His naked belly rose and fell as he breathed. His hand began to stroke her arm, almost absently, sending little tingles of response all over her skin.

Isobel lay still, emptying her mind, thinking only on those things, the sounds, movement, responses of their two bodies, so attuned now that they might have been just one being, one soul, one heart.

But her mind wouldn't empty and from the depths of where'd she'd pushed it the awful truth rose, like an ogre from a black cave. If she betrayed Edmund, it wouldn't just be York that might be destroyed, or its dazzling young hope who even now sat at Wigmore, doubtless dreaming of the crown that might soon adorn his golden head.

This would be destroyed too, this closeness, this peace, this bliss, like an accident of war, a regrettable minor consequence. For what other result could there be, no matter which side won the battle?

'You are very quiet, Isobel.' Edmund spoke again, his voice soft, his breath stirring her hair. 'What are you thinking?'

'I am thinking of the battle that is coming and what it will mean. Not for Lancaster or York but…for you and me.'

Suddenly Isobel needed to find some sense in it all, to piece all the opposing bits together, like a disjointed puzzle that would never quite fit perfectly.

'I am Tom's sister and I am also your wife,' she went on, lifting herself up again so that she could look into his eyes. 'Does that mean I must be for both Lancaster and for York? Or against both? Or apart from both, even though that is impossible?'

'You must decide for yourself.' Edmund's body beneath her seemed to go still a moment and then he breathed again. 'I will not force you into my camp. You can be for Lancaster until eternity if you choose, as I will be for York.'

'Some choices sound simple and yet they are the ones that are hardest to make. One can only ignore them, put them off, pretend they need never be made.'

'But the day comes when one eventually has to make them?'

She nodded. 'Yes.'

He gazed at her in silence for a long time, his eyes unreadable, his face so familiar to her now that she couldn't remember a time when she didn't see it, nor imagine a time when perhaps she might never look upon it again. And yet that time might well be here.

He took a lock of her hair between his fingers, teased it, as she'd learned he liked to do. 'Will it ease you, Isobel, if I tell you that I have come to care for you, very much?'

Tears rushed up into Isobel's throat, tears she blinked back before they reached her eyes. 'I have come to care for you too, Edmund, very much.'

His expression didn't alter at all but colour flooded his face then seeped slowly away. That word hung there, bitter-sweet because—precious though it was—it wasn't enough, wasn't the whole truth.

She waited, her heart thundering, his thundering too, in unison, but the other word—love—didn't come. Perhaps it never could, for to tell him she loved him and then be-tray him would be abominable, and even more unforgiv-able than it already was.

With her fingers she traced the beautiful line of his mouth, as if by touching she could express the word any-way. Breathe it silently into a kiss as he cupped the back of her head and drew her mouth down to his. Will it to pass from her flesh into his as he gathered her into his arms.

But that night they didn't join as they'd joined all the other nights. They lay, not carnally but tenderly, in each other's arms, with their unspoken thoughts and words keep-ing sleep at bay. The night dragged and yet Isobel felt time speed up. Moments crawled and at the same time galloped towards the dawn. And when the new day came, the tan-gle of loyalties she'd tried so hard to unravel were twisted tighter than ever around her heart.

At mid-morning Isobel left the solar and entered the hall, empty since everyone was about their duties, though the fire blazed warmly, as it was a bitterly cold day. She went over to put on an extra log or two and suddenly Robin drifted out of a dark corner, startling her.

'We need to speak.'

She turned, a sick feeling thudding into her stomach. For days she'd avoided the Welshman, just as she avoided the choice she had to make. She'd begun to believe it wouldn't need to be made after all, until now.

'What about?'

'Not so openly.' He took her elbow and drew her into the same corner he'd emerged from, like a ghost out of the grave. 'Come this way.'

Annoyed, Isobel shook his hand away, silently cursing him for appearing now when she'd begun to glimpse the bright fringes of a reprieve after the dark storm of turmoil. 'What do you want, Robin?'

'Time is running out, Mistress Calvert. Has your husband revealed anything to you of the Yorkist plans?'

'No, he has not,' she replied, her annoyance turning to irritation, and panic, as a sense of being trapped in that corner in more ways than one assailed her. 'And my name is Lady Deverell. Please remember it when you address me.'

The sharp eyes narrowed. 'It is like that, is it?'

'Like what?' Isobel snapped, digging her nails into her palms to curb the urge to lash out at him. 'I don't like your question or your tone!'

An insolent grin marred his mouth. 'Now you are wedded to the enemy, it seems you have forgotten who your friends are, and your loyalty to Lancaster too.'

'That is not true,' she retorted. 'I have forgotten nothing.'

'Then prove it… Lady Deverell.'

Isobel shivered. There was an edge, a menace almost, to the way he used her title. 'How?' she asked, her feet itching to step back out into the light, but the banging of a door somewhere sending her deeper into the corner. 'What can I hope to do at this late hour?'

'We suspect the muster will be at Wigmore, since that is Edward's base, but we would have a great advantage if we knew how many of the Yorkist noblemen hereabouts will be fighting at his side.'

'My husband has told me nothing of that, and I doubt if he knows Edward's every thought!'

Robin shrugged but his reply was ominous. 'I don't think that will be any comfort to the King, nor to the cause of Lancaster when battle comes, nor to your brother either. Would you desert him too, let him go blindly to his death, as you have deserted our cause?'

Oh, that was cruel, and most cunning of all, and suddenly Isobel hated this man who had been her erstwhile ally. Robin stared at her in silence, his sharp eyes raking her face, aware of course that his aim couldn't have been more accurate. How *could* she stand aside and do nothing to help Tom, however little—or however much—that might be?

'Very well,' she said, drawing a deep breath. 'I will try.'

'Good. But it must be soon, so that a message can be sent quickly to Tudor.'

'It would never reach him surely?' Isobel couldn't keep the hope out of her voice. 'Not now.'

He smiled, horribly. 'Oh, it will, mistress, for I shall take it myself. Think you that I will be fighting on the side of York when the battle begins?'

And with that, and with no reverence at all, he left her. Isobel continued her way over to the hearth, her feet heavy, her heart heavier still. Feeding the fire, she stretched out her hands to the warmth but the flames did nothing to dispel the chill of dread that had possessed her, right down to the marrow of her bones.

The chill remained the whole day long, no matter how she ordered the fire built up, no matter how warmly she dressed against the cold and the occasional flurry of snow. If only she could run far away, ride Luna right up to the top of Clee Hill and let her gallop down it again, leave everything to the stars once more.

But she couldn't. All she could do was wait, listen, watch, with nerves a-jangle and senses sharpened as the day progressed into afternoon and then into evening. As night fell, and supper ended, and folk retired to their beds, Mistlecote seemed alive with expectation. The very walls seemed to whisper with secrets that followed her like wraiths of evil as she passed from the hall into the solar.

Even her chamber seemed filled with secrets. Isobel heard them in the crackle of the logs in the hearth, the hiss of the candles, the hail that beat at the windowpane briefly. Hours passed, and the hail stopped, and her nerves stretched tighter and tighter as the sky cleared and the stars came out.

Hawise had retired long since, Orion and Sirius slept, the manor was quiet, the night ominous. Edmund didn't come, and his footsteps hadn't passed her door to his own room, so she knew he was still abroad.

Outside, an owl shrieked, so close and so loud it seemed to be in the very room, and Isobel jumped to her feet, her heart beginning to pound. She paced to the window, looked out, saw the bailey below, white with frost beneath a full moon. But here, within, darkness—just like the screech of the owl—seemed to ooze through the walls and hang in menace from the rafters.

Finally, she went barefoot out into the passageway. Tiptoeing to the door that separated solar from hall, she heard the murmur of voices beyond. The door was shut but she eased it open, as quietly as she could, inch by inch.

Edmund and Alain were sat at table, illuminated in a pool of candlelight from the corona overhead. They were speaking in French, and she knew, from that fact alone, that they were discussing the impending battle. She understood French, though spoke it only badly, but the names of the noblemen that they listed were the same in any language.

Herbert, Deveraux, Lingen, Croft, Vaughan, Grey, Audley, FitzWalter, Dwnn, Stafford, and many others she knew by reputation. All powerful nobles and good Yorkists, some of them even former Lancastrians who had gone over to York.

Alain Vachier laughed then and spoke in English. 'The rabble that Tudor and Wiltshire bring with them will not stand a chance, Edmund! Between their Irish and Welsh and Breton and French, they can't even communicate effectively, let alone fight cohesively, and they will be wearied from a long winter march as well. Victory is already ours!'

Isobel's blood turned to ice. Edmund made no reply but she saw him nodding gravely, confident too of certain victory for York. Defeat for Tudor, for Lancaster—and for Tom, who would ride as part of that rabble from Wales. Over cold mountains, through deep snow perhaps, ill-equipped, ill-fed, fatigued—doomed.

A scraping of chairs sounded, and, in her chamber, Sirius began to bark. Whirling, she raced quickly back the way she'd come, only just closing the door behind her as Edmund's footsteps echoed in the corridor.

Hushing her hound, Isobel pulled off her kirtle and, dropping it to the floor, flung herself beneath the bedcovers, squeezing her eyes shut as Edmund entered. He never knocked these days—why should he when her chamber and her bed and her body were his? She never knocked at his door either, so familiar, so intimate, had they become. Such a part of each other, by night at least, that everything was understood.

Holding her breath, Isobel listened to him undress, place the fireguard over the slumbering logs in the hearth, wash his face and hands in the basin. She heard him stoop and pick up her kirtle, folding it over the back of a chair, and then the bed dipped and his murmur came in a warm breath at her ear.

'Isobel? Are you asleep?'

Oh, how she wished she were! But at the featherlight caress of his lips as they brushed her cheek, her whole body came to wakefulness. Eagerly she turned into his arms, her mouth hungry for the taste of his, her blood stirring in her veins.

'You are late coming to bed,' she said. 'Where have you been?'

'Talking with Alain.'

He kissed her throat, his hand smoothing down over her hip, slipping under the hem of her shift, and up again over the bare skin of her thigh. She knew his signs now because they mirrored her own. He was hungry for her too, his arousal already hard against her belly, his knee sliding between her legs and his body angling over hers as he rolled her onto her back.

'But I am weary of talking now, sweeting.'

Isobel wrapped her arms and her legs about him, pulling him closer, opening for him, craving him. She didn't want to talk either, nor to listen, nor to think, nor scheme, nor plot. She wanted Edmund deep inside her, fulfilling her, the delicious melting of her flesh into his until they became one burning bond of love.

She wanted to forget about everything else, pretend for a few hours at least that nothing else existed. As they joined, body, heart and soul, she almost succeeded.

The day before departure, while Edmund was busy with the checking of arms, and horses, and victuals, and the men rested for the march on the morrow, Isobel finally consulted the stars. Perhaps whatever she did or did not do would make no difference in the end. Perhaps the outcome of the battle, the death or survival of those she loved, was all already written anyway.

Perhaps the man who would sit on the throne when it was all over was after all destined for that role and had been since the moment of his birth.

Isobel didn't know what was right or wrong any longer, and thinking, thinking, thinking only embroiled her even deeper in confusion and helplessness. And today, as if to make her misery even more painful, the stars shed no light on the darkness whatsoever.

The sun had passed through Sagittarius—Edmund's sign—and had entered Capricornus. At this time of transit, it was good to sow and plant seeds but bad to quarrel. Nothing of the outcome of battles, or the deaths of men, or their survival, of defeat or victory.

Isobel put her charts and her astrolabe away, when once she would have checked and double checked, looked for a meaning, for a relevance, however slight. Now she did not. Instead, she sat down at the fireside and stared into the flames, with nothing but her love to guide her, to cling on to, to believe in.

Love for Edmund, who had her heart, now and forever.

Love for Tom, who was in her heart, always had been, always would be. But her brother didn't possess it in the way her husband did. And as she sat, the afternoon slipping into evening, Isobel knew that her belief needed to transcend even the stars.

The belief that her love for Edmund and for Tom would prevail against sword and fire, arrow and mace, from the charging hooves of warhorses and from the shot of guns. That her love would be like a shield big enough to protect both of them, even from each other should they meet in face-to-face combat. Keep them safe, keep them alive, bring them home.

Isobel sat and tried to harness that love, bind it tightly together, to believe as she'd never believed before. And then, as the daylight began to fade, she left her chamber and sought out Robin of Talgarth. It was a cruel irony that she found him where she'd first encountered him, ages before it seemed, sitting and fletching in the doorway of the armoury.

On the morning of departure, Edmund walked hand in hand with Isobel to where his horse awaited him in the inner courtyard. She was wrapped warmly against the weather, her cloak and hood and gloves lined with fur, but even so he felt the chill that emanated from her. He was also dressed warmly, for the cold was bitter, but there was a chill in his blood too.

Their parting in the bedroom earlier had been rather warmer. Then she'd clung to him as if she'd never let him go, and he to her, as they'd loved each other with a violent passion. They'd been so close, both in the moments of ecstasy as they'd reached fulfilment together, and in the quiet moments afterwards, as they lay in each other's arms.

But now, as he looked for perhaps the last time upon his wife, Edmund wondered if he knew Isobel any better than he'd known Mariette. For Adam Ewyas had told him she'd been speaking in secret to Robin of Talgarth the day before, but whatever words had passed between them had not come to his spy's ears.

In truth, Edmund had ceased to care. Since the day he'd knocked Adam to the ground on the training field, the man might well have been invisible, so little did he matter. And his duplicity, so useful in the beginning, had become an abomination to him now. The hour of battle had come and there was nothing left to do but wage it.

'Alain will guard you well in my absence,' he told Isobel, touching a hand to her face. 'Mistlecote is well-stocked with food and water. Keep the drawbridge up and the gates shut at all times.'

Her breath was a mist as she answered him, her gaze cloudier than the sky overhead. 'I will.'

A sudden fearful vision passed before his eyes, of her ignoring his advice, riding out on that mare of hers, oblivious to danger. 'Promise me.'

'I promise.'

On impulse, despite the damp in the air, Edmund pushed her hood down, needing to see her face clearly, the glint of her hair, the shine of her eyes, bright now with apprehension.

'I don't know when we will return, Isobel.'

'Mistlecote—and I—will be here when you do.'

They were words all men wanted to hear from their wives as they rode out to do battle. The very words that made men resolve to return, or not to go at all. He thought back to the day he'd first arrived, when she'd told him to ride away again, only hate burning then in her eyes.

It wasn't hate he saw there now but it wasn't love either. It was fear. He didn't know whether Isobel had betrayed him or not, though he'd been aware of her presence in the passageway of the solar the night he and Alain had talked battle strategy. Even if Sirius hadn't barked, Edmund had scented the fragrance of her in the air, almost seen the imprint of her feet on the floorboards.

But he'd said nothing because it made no difference. He loved Isobel no matter what she did or did not do.

'Whatever happens,' he said, 'you will be safe here.'

She nodded, even though they both knew she might well not be safe at all, or not for long, should he perish in this battle, or the next one, or those to come in the future. York would not lose, that was almost certain, but even in victory men would die.

And if he should die, would it be better to know or not to know whether betrayal had led to his death?

She gripped his arm suddenly, as if she'd read his mind. 'There is something I need to say,' she said. 'That night I read your horoscope… I didn't reveal all that I saw.'

Edmund smiled down at her, but a swift dread gripped him. 'Because it was bad?'

She shook her head. 'It said that in your sign, there is a lot of goodness. That one may make friendship among enemies, that it is good to get married. The same prediction of marriage was in my stars too.'

'Are you telling me this now in case I don't return?'

'No…' Her voice broke and she flung herself into his arms. 'I'm telling you because I…because it is true.'

Edmund crushed her to him, wishing he could tell her he *would* return, but that might not be true, so he said nothing. Alain appeared then in the archway to the outer bailey, an impatient expression on his face, and the first flakes of snow began to fall.

'Perhaps there is some hope in the stars after all,' he said, lightly enough, for he would not leave her with the sorrow he himself struggled to hide as he kissed her goodbye. 'God keep you, my Isobel, always.'

Then, tearing himself away, since the time for departure could not be put off any longer, Edmund swung himself up into the saddle. Spurring his horse forward, he galloped out through the gateway without looking back.

Chapter Seventeen

It was a week after Edmund and his men had ridden out that the phenomenon was seen in the sky. The snow had stopped, but outside the walls the land was silent, cold, and bleak, as if all living things had retreated into burrows and lairs, huts and hovels, to wait out the winter.

But on the morning of Candlemas, they all came out again to stare up at the sky in a mixture of wonder and awe, horror and fear.

Isobel too stood on the battlements with the rest of her household and looked up at the strange sight. The sky was so thin it seemed like glass, the air so cold she felt it freeze in her nose. But it was the three shining orbs low on the eastern horizon that chilled her to the bone.

At her side, Hawise spoke in a trembling whisper, her breath turning to clouds in the icy air. 'Three suns! Wh-what does it mean, madam?'

Isobel's voice trembled too, her breath a cloud as well. 'I don't know.'

'Is it an omen?'

She shrugged. 'Perhaps it is an illusion of some sort.'

'But we all see it, so it must be there!'

Hawise was right, of course, it was there—or rather they

were there: three suns in a line, blazing brightly in a sky that was strangely dark though it was just ten of the clock.

Alain Vachier approached. 'They are sun dogs.'

Isobel turned to him. 'Sun dogs?'

'At certain times, they appear and follow the sun, like hounds.'

'You have seen them before?'

The Frenchman nodded. 'Once, in France.'

'What brings them?'

'No one knows but they always occur in the coldest of winters.'

Isobel stared upwards again. Was it an omen, as Hawise believed? A sign of worsening weather? Or did it signify a disaster of some sort? Everyone watched transfixed as the sun dogs changed colour, from a reddish hue to orange, then yellow, then white, before disappearing altogether, leaving the real sun all alone to rise higher in the sky.

Oddly, their disappearance left Isobel even more unsettled, and a terrible thought possessed her. What if those suns represented the souls of those closest to her—her father, her brother, and her husband? What if Tom and Edmund had been killed in the battle? What if no news had come because there was no one left alive to bring any?

The sun dogs didn't appear again, but two days later a rumour arrived in the village and from there to the manor that a great battle had been fought at a place called Mortimer's Cross, and that Edward of York had won it.

On the third day after the phenomenon Isobel stood shivering while Hawise dressed her after a bath, her mind far away, searching the landscape in her imagination for this place she'd not heard of before.

'It is a full two months now since your last flewsa came, madam.'

Isobel started at the sound of her maid's voice and placed her palm on her belly, flat as it had always been. 'Is it two months really?'

'It is indeed.' Hawise pursed her lips. 'You must be with child.'

She looked at her maid. 'Think you it is so?'

''Tis certain.'

Pushing her arms into the surcoat Hawise held up, Isobel walked over to the window and looked out. The snow was thawing now, though a thin sheen of ice laced the pane, dripping at intervals as it slowly melted.

A babe? Edmund's babe. Edmund's heir. A choke filled her throat and she pressed her hand to her stomach again. Could it be so? A sense of joy, of wonder, vied with an angry resentment. It would be cruel indeed if fate had sought and gained Edmund's death even as it had given birth to his child!

How was it she'd not remembered the absence of her flewsa? How was it there were no changes in her body to tell her? The answer was simple. She'd been thinking only of the battle, of Edmund, of Tom, of love and loss and betrayal, for as long as she could recall. And when thinking had been impossible, she'd been waiting, waiting…

And now she could wait no more.

'Bid Alain Vachier to come to me,' she ordered Hawise. 'I wish to speak with him.'

The Frenchman appeared almost at once, granting her a reverent bow, his demeanour jubilant in Lancaster's defeat. 'You wish to speak to me, Isobel?'

'Where exactly is Mortimer's Cross?' Isobel asked him without preamble, without even bridling at his too-familiar use of her name. The Christmas feast, when he'd wrestled with Edmund and won her affection, if only fleetingly, seemed very long ago now. 'Is it far from here?'

'I believe it is somewhere on the River Lugg, near the town of Leominster, which itself is a little southward of Wigmore Castle.'

'And which is the quickest route to Wigmore Castle?'

His brows rose. 'Why are you asking?'

Isobel held his challenging stare. 'Because, since no further news has come from the battle, I am going to find out for myself what has happened.'

'Is that wise?'

'The quickest route, if you please?'

'To Leominster, which is an easy enough road from here, then follow the river north-west. It will take you directly to Wigmore.' His head tilted. 'But I advise you not to attempt it.'

'Do you expect me to sit and wait here, uselessly, for news that might never come?'

'You will do as you wish, naturally, but you will have to traverse harsh terrain, in cold weather, perhaps encountering Lancastrian soldiery fleeing the field.' He frowned. 'And if Edmund returns and finds you gone…'

'I will take one of the stable lads with me.'

The Frenchman spread his hands. 'Then if you wish to go, I cannot prevent you. But neither will I be responsible for your safety.'

Isobel sent him a withering look. 'I did not ask you to.'

An hour later, accompanied by the eldest of the stable boys and her hounds, Isobel rode out of Mistlecote's gates and headed west. The terrain was indeed harsh as Alain had warned and, though she was dressed warmly, the wind still bit through her clothing. At least there was no rain or snow to contend with, and the land was eerily empty, devoid of birdsong, and no one passed her on the road.

She was in Leominster before midday and there she located an inn and bought some cheese and ale for herself and Nicholas, the stable lad, who treated the whole thing as an adventure. For her, there was nothing of adventure in it but a nagging dread at what she would discover at the end of her journey.

After Leominster, Isobel found the river and turned to follow it north-west, her body stiff with cold and her head aching with uncertainty. She thought, with increasing concern, about the babe in her womb, and if the weather and the ride would harm it, but Hawise had said it was but the size of a fingernail as yet.

Suddenly, a league or so beyond the town, the hounds trotting at her side threw their heads up and sniffed the air. As one, they halted, their ears pricked and their tails high. Isobel drew Luna to a halt too and waited, her fingers trembling on the reins, not with cold now but with hope.

Then, around a bend in the river, a body of men came into sight. Orion gave a bark and bounded ahead, followed closely by Sirius, the two racing to meet the travellers. And Isobel's heart leapt too and a cry rose into her mouth as a banner, stained yet still bright, revealed Edmund's colours.

Kicking Luna into a canter, she went forward to meet him.

Edmund saw the rider the moment they'd rounded the bend and, even too far away to distinguish the features, even if the two hounds hadn't told him, even if that fiery chestnut mare were not unmistakable, he'd known at once it was Isobel.

His whole body jolted and he urged his horse forward even as she did the same. Then they were out of their saddles and in each other's arms, their mouths locked in a kiss, both heedless of his men, who watched and waited.

Isobel felt so fragile, so small, against his armour that Edmund was afraid of hurting her, yet he couldn't slacken his hold. While the battle had raged, bitter and bloody, he'd feared he wouldn't survive it and would never hold her again. Now he couldn't seem to let her go, even though she might have plotted so that he would *not* survive the battle!

Breaking the kiss at last, when both of them needed to breathe, he looked down into her eyes. They were awash with tears, and her face, though pinched and white with cold, was all smiles. If she had betrayed him, would she look so glad?

'Why have you ridden out, Isobel, when you must know it is not safe?'

She was shivering now in his arms, though whether it was with cold or some great emotion he couldn't tell. 'I came to meet you.'

'How did you know where to come?'

'We heard of the battle place near Wigmore two days ago.' Her hands lifted to his face and he felt them like ice even through her gloves. 'Thank God you are alive, Edmund. I could not have waited another day, another hour... I've been so worried since the day you rode out, and no news came. But what of...?' Her eyes clouded, went beyond him to the men, and the question he'd expected sooner came at last. 'What news of my brother?'

'None.' Edmund shook his head, taking her hands, drawing them downwards, enclosing them in his. Her gaze was searching his avidly, as if she steeled herself for the worst.

At least he didn't have to give her that—yet. 'I saw nothing of him, Isobel, and have not heard if he lives or if he died.'

'I see.' Slowly, she nodded. 'And what of Tudor?'

'Jasper Tudor escaped but his uncle Owen is taken to Hereford in chains, John Throckmorton and other leading Lancastrians with him. Your brother was not among them.'

There was a moment of silence and the gladness of their reunion began to dissipate like a mist when the sun came out. Except the sun didn't come out. The sky turned greyer still and the cold bit deeper. And Edmund knew that one battle might be over but another one was still being waged—the silent but insidious one between Isobel and him that had started the day he'd first ridden through the gates of her manor.

It had abated since then, and there had even been truces, moments of peace and passion, when night had fallen and the world outside had receded. But the battle had always recommenced when daylight had come, when a barrier—albeit a thin and invisible one—had separated them.

A barrier of secrets and divided loyalties that neither of them had ever been able to totally surmount, nor really confront, as if it was too indelible for them to even contemplate overcoming it. But now, if there was to be any future for them when the war between York and Lancaster was over, that barrier needed to be broken down, and soon.

'Come,' Edmund said. 'Let us go home.'

He helped her into her saddle again and mounted his own horse. They rode in silence for a few moments and then her head turned towards him.

'I did not see Robin or Adam Ewyas among your men. Are they…?'

'Adam was killed at the start of the battle. Robin defected to the other camp as soon as we set our battle lines, where it appears he'd been all along. But perhaps you knew he would do so, Isobel?'

Her eyes held his for a moment and then she looked away. 'He always was a loyal Lancastrian…as was I.'

Edmund turned his eyes to the front too. 'Three of my men were killed,' he said, 'aside from Adam. Six are wounded but the victory was easy.'

'Then Lancaster truly is vanquished?'

'I believe so. And Edward will become king,' he answered what she had not asked. 'That is almost ordained now.'

'Did you see the three suns in the sky?'

'The sun dogs?' Edmund nodded. 'The men were frightened, naturally, but Edward turned the sight to his advantage, claiming it was a sign from God of York's victory.'

'And so it proved to be.'

'Perhaps, or else his conviction won the day,' he said. 'It doesn't really matter which. This battle has changed the whole fortune of the war in York's favour.'

When they arrived at Mistlecote, those that had remained rushed out to welcome them home. Spiced ale warmed cold bellies and tubs were filled for hot baths. Supper was a lively meal as, spirits rejuvenated now by the very fact of having cheated death, men sang and drank and danced until the whole hall shook.

Fatigue soon crept in, however, and one by one they retreated to their beds, to ease aching bodies and numbed minds—the inevitable state of a soldier after battle. Edmund's body ached too as he went around the sleeping quarters, checking every man had what he needed, thanking them for their courage and loyalty, wishing them a speedy return to health if they nursed wounds.

Only when he'd spoken to each and every one did he turn and make his way to the solar, and to Isobel's arms.

Their lovemaking that night, and the nights that followed, was different. No less passionate, no less pleasurable, but to Isobel it felt as though there was something else in the bed with them, between them, since the battle. And she knew what that something else was.

Secrets.

Time and again on those nights she tried to speak, to reveal what thus far she'd kept from him, but every time she failed. And instead, as if in compensation, spoke of anything and everything else. Fears and hopes, likes and dislikes, sometimes just idle chatter that meant nothing, while the secrets remained, bubbling like broth in a pot.

'It is strange,' she said now, three mornings later, as they walked hand in hand along the river path that skirted Mistlecote's walls. The water flowed fast, as heavy rain had replaced the snow of the last few weeks, though today the sun shone, albeit weakly. 'But I've never walked with a man like this before, holding hands I mean.'

Edmund stopped and drew her against the trunk of one of the oak trees that lined the path, its bare branches a latticed canopy over their heads. 'Why is that strange, since I am your husband?'

Leaning back against the rough bark, the smell of wintry earth and sharp, clean air filling her nose, Isobel felt her senses spark into life. 'That fact makes it even more strange,' she said. 'How can things change so quickly that you don't even know they are changing until you realise you are changed too?'

He stared down at her, one hand lifting to the braid that

hung over her shoulder, his fingers tracing its plaiting. 'And *are* you changed, Isobel?'

Isobel nodded, relishing the brush of his knuckles at her breast, the tingle of her flesh beneath her thick clothes. Her body grew warm, a delicious heavy sensation pulling low in her belly, and she arched closer, longing for his hand to turn, the fingers to open, close over her breast, cup it in his palm.

'Can you not tell?' she asked.

His fingers did open then but not to close over her breast but to lift to her cheek. Even so, she had to fight not to lean into that too, almost curling her toes into the earth in order to resist.

'I think I can…' His gaze was bright in the sunlight that glanced off the surface of the river, like a light that searched for her innermost secrets. 'Because I have changed too.'

Now was the time to tell him. Now when he'd invited it, or invited something at least. Now when, on the hearing of it, he might understand. But what if he *didn't* understand, or forgive? What then for her love, their marriage, the babe that he still didn't know of?

Isobel longed to tell him until it clawed at her heart to keep it untold. But how could she reveal something so wonderful until she'd confessed to her plotting with Robin?

'You told me before…that with carnal love sometimes comes heart love,' she said, instead. 'Can other things come too? Things like trust, belief, faith, understanding?'

'Perhaps,' he nodded, his hand leaving her face to flatten on the tree trunk next to her ear, 'though that depends on the two people involved, and whether they can come to trust, to believe, to be truthful always.'

Looking away, Isobel stared at a thrush beating a snail on a rock at the riverside, to break its shell and get at the flesh inside. And that was exactly what she felt like now. As if her shell was being slowly but surely battered to pieces, leaving her exposed, vulnerable, naked.

'I have always thought of myself as being truthful,' she said, 'but what if the truth is unwelcome, hurtful even? Might it not be better to keep it inside and unsaid?'

He shrugged but there was nothing careless about it, nor about his tone. 'I can't answer that.'

'Did you ever wish Mariette had kept her truths inside? Hidden them from you instead of speaking them and causing you pain?'

'There are some truths that will come out in the end, Isobel, whether spoken or not.'

Isobel looked back at him, the words rushing to the tip of her tongue, but she bit back on them at the last moment. She couldn't risk it. She didn't trust enough. She didn't believe enough. And she was afraid. Afraid of destroying this fragile union that had bound them anew since his return from Mortimer's Cross, of crushing this love that she felt blossoming inside her, like an early flower too eager to wait for spring.

A love too delicate, too weak to withstand a harsh frost, liable to wither at the first drift of snow, the thinnest layer of ice. As if the elements agreed, a fine sleet began to fall, dripping down upon them from the leafless branches above, running down the bark of the tree to soak into the back of her cloak.

Isobel turned her eyes skyward, tears blurring her vision. 'It is starting to snow again. We should go back.'

They returned, hand in hand still, to the house, Orion and Sirius bounding ahead, their coats glistening with snowflakes. The snow was so light it would not fall long, nor stick to cover the ground, but it seemed to cover her secrets even deeper than before.

Two days later, and still Isobel hadn't spoken to him of what was on her mind, in her heart—on *his* mind, and in *his* heart too. Edmund knew he could not let this go on and yet fear stopped him from asking her. Fear of hearing what she would say. Fear of the truth and fear of lies, for in the end they both amounted to the same thing.

Betrayal.

He was crossing the courtyard to the armoury, a week after his return, when the gates opened and the guards admitted a travelling mendicant friar, doubtless come begging for alms. Changing direction, Edmund went over, his hand going to his purse to draw out some coin, but an instant later his feet stopped dead.

The man limping towards him was the same one who'd been at their wedding feast, who'd accosted Isobel in the street in Tewkesbury, then hurried away on his approach. Edmund hadn't seen his face clearly then but he did now, as he found himself staring into eyes that bore the same colour, the same expression, as Isobel's.

'Sir Edmund Deverell?'

Edmund nodded, said nothing, waited for Thomas Calvert—for doubtless it was he—to go on. He was a bold, or perhaps reckless man to walk in here, alone and apparently unarmed, disguise or no.

'I have come to speak with Lady Deverell. I have something for her.'

'What is it?'

'Your lady gave me alms in Tewkesbury, where I happened to meet her. For her kindness, I have brought her a vial of holy water from the well of St Non in Wales, where I have been on pilgrimage.'

Edmund stared into the man's face, noting the same symmetry as Isobel's face. The broad brow, wide-apart eyes, straight nose, firm chin, but all set in a more masculine bone structure. He was younger than she, taller by a good two hands, and spare rather than slender. But there was no mistaking that the two were brother and sister.

Curiosity, mixed with disbelief, and an edge of outrage all vied for position within him. Was she still plotting, even now? With her brother and with even more audacity than she'd ever had when she'd conspired with Robin of Talgarth? Or did they both consider him too witless to notice and that they could plot here in his home, right under his very nose?

'You may give the vial to me,' Edmund said coldly, torn between throwing the man into the strongroom or turfing him straight out through the gates. 'I will see my wife gets it.'

'I would rather give it to her myself, so I can thank her for her kindness that day.'

'You are brave indeed, brother, to travel these parts on such a trivial errand, and a battleground not yet washed clean of the blood of the slain,' Edmund challenged. 'Or have you not heard of the recent battle at Mortimer's Cross?'

'I have heard, yes, but a holy man may pass freely— most of the time—even through a land gripped by war.'

'And are you for York, brother…or for Lancaster?'

'I am for neither…now…though once I was.' The tone changed and the green eyes sparked. 'Even loyalties fade when the leaders of men flee the battlefield almost before a blow is struck, saving their own hides and leaving their comrades to perish in their thousands.'

'You speak of the Earl of Wiltshire?'

The mendicant—Tom Calvert—nodded. 'If any man's actions show how vile this conflict is, how self-serving for some while others are seen as expendable, then Wiltshire is that man.'

Edmund wavered. He should capture the knave now without further delay and hand him over to Warwick to deal with. But then, was such action necessary? Lancaster was vanquished, with luck forever, and this man, for all his noble title, had no land, no wealth, no home and no inheritance because he himself had taken all that from him.

No, he could no more capture and detain Isobel's brother any more than he could throw *her* into the strongroom for betraying him—if she had. 'It is said that Wiltshire fled the battle of Northampton also, in the guise of a monk,' he said, with meaning, dispensing with pretence at last. 'Was that *your* disguise then too, Lord Calvert?'

Thomas Calvert started, his hand moving to a fold in his habit, where doubtless a knife was concealed, but Edmund was quicker. Gripping the other's wrist, he spoke low and urgently.

'For Isobel's sake, I will not unfrock you, *brother*,' he said, 'but you must pledge me something in return for that mercy.'

'What can I pledge you that you have not already taken from me, Yorkist?'

The venom was worthy of any Isobel had ever spat at him, in those first days of his occupation here. Edmund felt a grudging respect surface within him. 'That is done and can't be undone, but you might still keep your freedom.'

'How?'

'Swear to me, here and now and on your oath, that you

will never take up arms against York on English soil ever again. Then you may speak with Isobel and be on your way.'

There was a long, taut silence and Edmund began to curse himself for what could well be a double folly. Turning a blind eye to Isobel's plotting and now promising her equally devious brother his freedom—what was he thinking?

'But make your mind up quickly,' he said. 'I will not offer twice.'

Another beat of silence. 'Why would you offer at all, Deverell?'

Edmund shrugged, wishing he knew that for certain. 'Because I care very much for your sister and, since she is my wife, you are my kin—whichever side you fight on.'

'I have vowed not to fight at all after this defeat, since even the King himself must know now that the cause of Lancaster is lost.' Calvert shook his wrist free but made no other move. 'My leg, broken at Northampton, is not yet fully mended, and at the battle near Wigmore I was placed, with those too young or too old for combat, to guard the baggage wagons. They fell to York, of course, when we fled, along with the rest of Tudor's forces, what was left of them.'

'Isobel tells me, nevertheless, that you are a brave man.'

'She *would* say that.' The green eyes flared with pride and unmistakable affection. 'Never was a sister more loving or loyal. Is she as loyal and loving a wife, Deverell?'

Was she? Edmund wished he knew and made no reply.

Calvert misread his silence. 'I have no right to pry into the business of a man and his wife, forgive me.' His gaze narrowed pensively. 'I never thought to call a Yorkist my kin, but if you care for Isobel as you say you do, and she for you, then it seems that I must at least try.'

'When this war is finally over, my lord, we might even become friends.'

'Mayhap.' The other man looked past him, towards the house, and a shadow darkened his eyes for a moment. 'That does not alter the fact you have stolen my inheritance, Deverell. If killing you here and now would restore it, I might be tempted, but it would not, and I would not do so for my sister's sake.'

'I am relieved to hear it,' Edmund said drily. 'But you know it would be folly to attempt it.'

Thomas Calvert nodded. 'So I will give you my pledge and go on my way—once I've spoken with Isobel—and take consolation that she at least can still call Mistlecote her home. But, if fortune turns against York, I might well return to reclaim it one day.'

'I will be here, Lord Calvert, and so will Isobel, for this *is* her home as long as she wishes it.' As he said it, Edmund recognised a way to find out if his wife *did* care for him as much as he did for her. If she loved him even as he did her. 'Or else…if she wishes to leave here now, with you, I will not prevent it.'

Surprise flared in the other's eyes. 'Isobel loves Mistlecote even more than I do. If she wanted to leave, she would have found a way to do so long before now.' Calvert's feet moved restlessly, and he was clearly eager to get on with his business. 'But I will ask her. Where is she?'

Edmund jerked his head behind him. 'You will find her in the gardens. Once you have spoken with her, I advise you to go quickly. Have you a horse?'

'No.'

'Then you will find one saddled and waiting at the gates for you.'

Their eyes held a moment longer, a host of thoughts

behind them, then with a nod Thomas Calvert passed by him. The limp at least was real, if the habit was not, and Edmund prayed that if and when their paths crossed again it would indeed be in friendship, and not in war. For he liked the man!

He watched as Calvert entered through the door of the walled garden, saw Isobel framed beyond. Shock and then joy transformed her features before the two ran towards each other and into a tight embrace.

Turning away, Edmund strolled into the hall, and from thence to the solar to await Isobel's coming. As come she must now. Through her brother, he'd issued her an option that he should perhaps have given her months ago—escape from a marriage she'd never wanted and the freedom to go wherever she liked, to live her life as she wished.

Chapter Eighteen

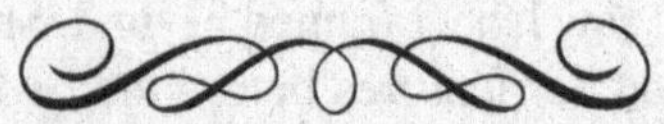

Isobel hugged Tom to her so tightly that her arms ached. Then, fear clutching at her heart, she dragged him into the shadow of the wall, where a bench occupied an alcove. They sat, her two hounds coming to lie at their feet, and gladness and worry and words and tears tumbled out of her all at the same time.

'What are you doing here, Tom? My husband will surely question your presence, even if he does not know your face. You must go quickly…it's too dangerous for you to stay.'

Her brother took her hands in his. 'I am quite safe, Isobel. Your husband has already recognised me and has allowed me to come and speak with you.'

'But why…why would he do that? Tom, what has happened? Were you at the battle? Are you a prisoner? Are you hurt? Your leg—'

'Hush, chatter-bug!'

Tom grinned and suddenly he seemed like his old self, before the war, the deaths, the deceit. If only *she* could be like her old self too, but try as she might, she couldn't.

'Isobel…' His eyes filled suddenly. 'Oh, I have missed you, sister, but you need to listen now. I haven't much time. Your husband, for reasons I don't quite understand, has chosen not to detain me, but there are other Yorkists here who might have other opinions.'

Isobel's eyes filled too. 'I have missed you too, more than I can ever tell you.'

'I didn't fight at the battle, nor am I likely to fight ever again. I have pledged to your husband not to take up arms against York in England, and I will keep that pledge. That will be no hardship, since I will be returning to Wales immediately.'

'To Mirain?'

He nodded. 'If she will have a lame dog like me, and if her stubborn fool of a father consents to let her marry a cursed Englishman instead of a good Welshman.'

Isobel squeezed his hands. 'If she loves you she will have you, regardless of her father's wishes.'

His shoulders lifted in a sigh. 'My love for her is certain, though of hers I am not yet so sure. But I have no time to talk of that now, it is *you* I want to hear about. Are you well? Are you happy?'

She tried to nod but failed. 'As happy as I have a right to be, I suppose.'

'Your husband is a good man, even though he be a Yorkist?'

'Yes.' This time there was no hesitation. 'He is a good man, Tom.'

'I think he cares for you a great deal. Do you care for him?'

Isobel nodded, and almost without thinking the words came out. 'I love him.'

'I think I can tell that from the way you speak of him. I don't know why, but he has given me permission to take you with me to Wales, if you choose to leave here.'

Her heart shuddered to a halt. 'Leave Mistlecote? Leave Edmund?'

'You do not wish it?'

Slowly, a realisation dawned on Isobel. Leaving Mistlecote, even to go with Tom, would be hard, but leaving Edmund would be impossible. 'No.'

'I told him as much. It is clear you love him very much, Isobel, in which case all will surely be well between you.'

Isobel searched her brother's eyes, saw her own reflected in them. Why was he so sure when she was full of doubts? 'Perhaps… I hope so.'

'You have doubts?'

'Did you see Robin of Talgarth? Or Adam Ewyas at Mortimer's Cross?'

He shook his head. 'No, though I heard Robin defected to our ranks before the fighting commenced. Have you any news of Adam?'

'He was killed at the start of the battle,' she informed him. 'I was supposed to send word to you through them of the Yorkist strength, but I couldn't do it.'

'I'm glad you did not. It was wrong of Robin to ask you to spy for Lancaster, Isobel. It put you in a perilous position, and I don't blame you for being reluctant to do so.'

'It wasn't that, Tom. When the time came, I couldn't betray Edmund, any more than I could have betrayed you.' Isobel swallowed as a choke distorted her words. 'So I did nothing. I just prayed that you would both come out safe, whichever side won. Can you ever forgive me?'

'There is nothing to forgive.'

They sat in silence for a moment, even though there was so much to be said, and so little time to say it. Isobel was the first to break the silence.

'I am with child, Tom.'

He smiled. 'Then I am to be an uncle!'

'Edmund doesn't know yet.'

'Why have you not told him?'

'Because I can't. I don't know why but I must tell him of my deceit first.'

'But there is no deceit to speak of, surely?'

'There is! I *thought* about betraying him, Tom. I agonised over it, even consulted the stars as to what I should do. That is deceit enough, even if in the end I left it undone.'

Her brother gazed at her for a long moment. 'If your heart cannot be at peace with it, then tell him the truth, Isobel, all of it, as you've just told me.'

'But…what if it makes him hate me?'

'He will not. Didn't you just state, with absolute faith, that Mirain would not hate me for my lameness?'

Isobel shook her head. 'It is not the same…'

'It is *exactly* the same. If he loves you, it will not matter what you do or do not do.'

Her brother sounded so sure, much more sure than she was. 'But I don't know if he loves me.'

'Then ask him. Tell him of your love and demand his in return.'

'And if he does not give it?'

'Then there will be a home for you in Wales, whenever you need it. But you won't.' Tom's eyes twinkled. 'A man in love, as I am, has a special sort of vision, Isobel. He can recognise love in another even when they do their utmost to hide it. I saw that love in your husband's face, heard it in the way he spoke about you.'

His hands squeezed briefly, tightly, on hers and Isobel felt the time for parting had come all too soon. 'You have never lacked courage, Isobel, so don't let fear deny you what you deserve now. Promise me you will speak to him.'

Isobel nodded. 'I will, I promise. I must anyway, sooner or later, with the child coming…' She broke off. 'But Tom, what about Mistlecote? Your inheritance? Now Edmund will have an heir…'

'Mistlecote was always more yours than mine, Isobel. My heart, my life, my future, belong elsewhere now.'

Quick panic seized her as she felt that future already pulling him away from her. 'But you will come back sometimes? Often? When this war is over?'

'You can depend on it.' He drew in a sigh. 'I must go but I will return, with Mirain, I hope, when your babe is born.'

'It will come at harvest time.'

'Then until harvest time, God keep you, my dear sister, and your child, and your Yorkist husband as well.'

Isobel remembered something. 'I have your ring, that Robin gave me—I will fetch it.'

He shook his head. 'Give it to my nephew—or niece—with my blessing!' A smile beamed. 'I have a blessing for you too, Isobel.'

He took something out of the leather pouch attached to his belt and pressed it into her palm. 'This vial contains water from Non's holy well. She gave birth during a storm, clinging to a cliff edge, and bore a great saint of Wales, called David. I know you will survive too, Isobel, no matter how fierce the storm you must weather. Have faith, my beloved sister.'

The words were grave but there was a smile in his voice and, as he drew her to her feet and embraced her, Isobel knew her brother had also changed these last months. The world around her seemed to shift and then settle. Sadness at parting was lessened by the knowledge that Tom lived and loved and had purpose. Could she not too find the same?

'Farewell, Tom. God keep you.'

But even as she gave him the blessing, a quick resurgence of fear closed around Isobel's heart. 'Take Sirius with you,' she urged, 'to guard you.'

He smiled. 'As you have always guarded me, even from the time when you weren't old enough to guard yourself? No, Sirius was always your hound really, and I think he would rather remain here.'

He bent and stroked the hound's head, and when he straightened again his gaze was solemn. 'Thank you for the care you gave me while I was growing up, Isobel. Oftentimes, I have wondered why you sacrificed your life so that mine would be filled with love. Was it to combat our father's indifference towards me?'

'In part, yes. But that was not his fault, just his lack, his sorrow.' Isobel smiled too, though tears burned hotly behind her eyes. 'And I sacrificed nothing, Tom. I would not have chosen differently and besides, if I'd married then and left Mistlecote, I would not now be married to Edmund.'

'Your Yorkist?' Her brother's expression became bright again. 'I'm sorry for what I said at Tewkesbury that day. I didn't understand but I do now.'

He hugged her tightly once more, then they walked from the garden arm in arm. They parted and Isobel watched him cross the bailey to the horse that awaited him at the gates. Sirius watched too but, just as she did, the hound seemed to know that Tom didn't need either of them any longer.

Pausing before mounting, Tom cast a long, lingering look around the manor, and she saw on his face that relinquishing his home was not as lightly done as he had made it seem. Then, with a lift of his hand in farewell, he sprang into the saddle as if wings had sprouted at his heels. Isobel smiled, joy flooding through her, easing the sorrow of parting. Lame or not, nothing would stop her brother obtaining his heart's desire, she was certain of that.

Wings at her heels too, Isobel mounted the steps of the hall and ran through into the solar. Pushing open the door to Edmund's chamber, she found him sitting in the window seat, his form so still he might have become part of the stone beneath him. Dressed in a loose surcoat of meadow green, one booted foot on the floor, the other resting on the seat opposite, he looked deep in thought.

The sun beamed in through the leaded glass, turning his hair to gold as it always did, but he didn't greet her as she entered. And, as she closed the door behind her, her joy faltered for a moment. He seemed more remote than she'd ever known him as she sat down opposite and sought his eyes.

'Thank you for letting Tom go free.'

His gaze met hers, as remote as the rest of him. 'Did he give you your gift?'

She nodded and, uncurling her hand, held out the little vial of water. 'It comes from a holy well dedicated to a lady called Non, the mother of a saint. She gave birth on a perilous rock as a tempest raged all about her.'

He smiled. 'A colourful story—but your brother strikes me as a colourful character himself. Where is he bound?'

'Wales, to a woman there whom he loves. He says he has turned his back on fighting, and I am glad of that.'

'If he can find peace in such an age, then I envy him. Does she love him, this woman?'

'I don't know. I hope so. I will miss him sorely, but he deserves to be where he longs to be, and be happy—as I am.'

His eyes narrowed. '*Are* you happy, Isobel?'

Isobel put the little glass vial on the window ledge where the light shone though it and splintered into myriad beautiful colours. 'I am but I will be happier still when I have spoken things to you that need to be said.'

'I have been waiting to hear them.'

'I know.' She took a breath. 'I have been searching for the right moment but, now it has come, I'm not sure where to begin.'

'With the fletching of arrows? Or apple trees that have no disease?'

His quiet questions weren't questions at all. 'I *did* plot with Robin and Adam, I admit it,' Oh, how easy it was to say it now, surrounded by light, after so long being in the dark. Now she knew that Tom was safe, that Edmund had spared him, that the war might be over. 'You were the enemy at my door, as I was yours. Would you not have done the same?'

He inclined his head. 'Doubtless.'

Why wasn't he angry? Why did she sense no emotion at all from him? Unless… 'Did you know of my conspiring, right from the beginning?'

He nodded. 'Unbeknown to you, and Robin, Adam was a double spy, pretending at loyalty to Lancaster, but everything that came to your ears came to mine.'

'Then I was not the only one in conspiracy.' Isobel gasped. 'You were too!'

A smile flitted over his lips briefly. 'Does that surprise you?'

She shook her head. 'No, not really, but does that not make us quits?'

'Perhaps. But I would not have betrayed you, Isobel, not for any cause.'

'You believe, then, that I *did* betray you?'

'You have not told me yet whether you did or did not.'

'Then I will tell you now, everything.' Drawing a breath,

Isobel laced her fingers together in her lap, steadying herself. 'I think I can now that I have begun to understand them myself.'

'I am listening.'

A little chill passed over her skin despite the warmth in the window embrasure. He was not going to make this easy for her, but why should he?

'I opposed you at first,' she began. 'I hated you then, as you well knew. But when we married, and the war encroached, everything became complicated. I had feelings that confused me, and my hate began to turn to something else. Even when Edward came here, and I was so determined to hate him too, I found myself liking him.'

'And he you.'

The comment was dry and Isobel remembered Edmund's jealousy, the way they'd danced together afterwards, his lovemaking that had possessed her in a way no other man—not even a king-to-be—could.

'Then, when we began to grow closer, physically, I realised that I was not the person I'd always thought I was. Instead of being afraid of intimacy, surrender, I embraced it, enjoyed our nights together, craved the closeness we had found.'

'I too, Isobel.'

His voice was softer this time, tender almost, and it gave Isobel the courage to finish what she had started. 'I even began to think everything would be all right between us, even between Lancaster and York. That the thing I dreaded would not happen. But at the Christmas feast, Robin asked me to find out how many men York would be likely to field at the battle. And then, two nights before you rode out, I heard you and Alain talking in the hall. I heard the names of the lords who would be there, at the battle.'

'So you told Robin?'

She shook her head. 'No, I said nothing. I did go and speak with him, not to betray you but to tell him that I would not, not then, nor ever.'

His expression didn't alter but there was a movement deep within his eyes, like a current shifting sand at the bottom of the ocean. 'Why?'

'Because… I love you.' The words bubbled up excitedly in her throat, so she said them again. 'I love you, Edmund! How *could* I betray you?'

There was no reaction whatsoever to either the word *love* or the word *betray* and Isobel felt fear grip her anew. Had faith and courage proved insufficient? Had her confession done exactly as she'd feared it would and driven them irrevocably apart?

Swallowing hard, she went on, trusting, as she had before the battle, as she had to do now, that her love would prevail. 'I prayed, day and night, that because I loved you, and loved Tom too, you would both come safely out of the battle.'

He looked away from her, at the vial of holy water, the light coming through it the same blue-grey as his eyes as a cloud passed over the sun. 'Battles are not won with love, Isobel, nor does love preserve the lives of men.'

'Perhaps not,' Isobel said, looking at the vial too. 'But you survived, did you not? And so did Tom. Mayhap that *was* luck, or skill, or chance, but I don't think so. And besides, hasn't what has occurred since proved there is more at work here?'

His eyes returned to hers. 'Such as?'

'Such as Tom relinquishing this manor to you.'

A smile touched his mouth. 'It is already mine, Isobel, so he had little choice in the matter.'

'I know that,' she acknowledged. 'But now he has surrendered it, and willingly, there will be no more fighting over it ever again.'

'Because your brother intends to remain in Wales? To make his life there?'

Isobel nodded. 'Yes. And because he knows I wish to live my life here with you.'

There was a flicker of his eyelashes. 'Is that truly what you want, Isobel?'

'Yes, it is. Do you doubt it? Is that why you told Tom I was free to go with him if I wished?'

He nodded. 'I want you to be happy.'

Isobel felt her heart heave with love but there was still more to ask. 'Why did you offer me my freedom now and not before?'

His shoulders lifted, dropped again, and she felt a little quiver of trepidation. Did he *want* her to go? Even though she'd not betrayed him, had the knowledge that she *could* have done destroyed everything between them? After all, she might love him, but he'd never said he loved her. Perhaps, after Mariette, he could *never* love, nor trust, any woman.

'Before, you only had two choices—Lord Ledwyche or a nunnery—and neither of them appealing to you. Through desperation you created a third choice—marriage to me— but it wasn't any more appealing, was it, Isobel?'

'At the time…no, it wasn't,' she confessed. 'Now it is different.'

His head turned and he looked out of the window again. 'Because the stars tell you so?'

Isobel heard the accusation, the hurt, and knew which stars he was referring to, something she also needed to explain, to erase. 'That night I cast your horoscope, insisted on abstinence…it wasn't because I wanted us to keep apart but I'd seen Tom…in Tewkesbury. I didn't know what to do and our being so close on our wedding night…confused me, so it seemed wiser, safer, to abstain.'

Edmund still stared out of the window, as if he'd not heard any of that, but she saw a clenching and unclenching of his jaw, which told her he'd both heard and understood. But did he believe?

'I missed you so much when you went away, more than I let you know, and not just in our bed. I missed you all the time, Edmund, until I thought I would die with wanting your return.'

There was a long silence. Isobel waited, almost bursting at the seams to tell him of their child, but sensing there were things *he* needed to say too, things she needed to hear. And after a long time, they came.

'When Mariette betrayed me, I didn't understand why. I thought it must be my fault. That I'd failed her in some way, driven her to do what she did, although I'd given her everything she could ever want—a home, money, safety, love.'

'But they weren't enough.'

'No, they weren't. And I know now that whatever I'd done or not done, it would never have been enough, for she didn't really want any of it. We were too different, too far apart to ever understand each other.'

'But we do not have to be far apart, Edmund, if we want to be close.'

'No,' he said, with a shake of his head. 'We don't. I understand why you barred me from your bed, Isobel. But even though, in the end, you didn't betray me, I can understand equally why you *might* have done. We were—still are—enemies.'

'But can you understand too why I never *could* have betrayed you?'

His eyes came back to hers. 'No, I cannot. Why would you *not*, Isobel?'

Isobel blinked as suddenly the sun brightened and little rays of light beamed through the vial on the window ledge. And, in those rays, she saw something she'd never seen before. Even though Edmund had been open with her about Mariette, and his shame, and his pain, she'd never really seen what now she saw in complete illumination.

'You were *waiting* for me to betray you, weren't you? You were *expecting* me to betray you. *Wanting* it, even, so that you could be proved right and that all women were like Mariette.'

The words—waiting—expecting—wanting—crashed like thunder in Edmund's ears and, as they faded, realisation came. So swiftly, and with such violence of clarity, he wondered why he'd never realised it before. He *had* been waiting, expecting, wanting, willing Isobel to confirm his fears were well-founded.

Now, as he stared into her eyes, he felt his fears surge up and swell large before splintering into a thousand pieces. Then they began to fall and dissipate, like a shower of hail turning to sundrops all around him.

Dare he believe? In her and in himself? Dare he believe that love, and trust, and honesty were possible after all? Even as Edmund asked himself that, he knew love was possible, for it already existed. It was present within him, an indelible part of him now, like the beating of his heart, the air in his lungs, the blood in his veins that kept him alive.

But was Isobel's love the same? He'd been dazzled by

love before, trusted in its honesty and strength, for that was how it had existed for him. But not for Mariette.

'Before Mortimer's Cross,' he said, 'I told you I cared for you, and you replied that you cared for me too.'

'I know.' She nodded, the light through the window catching the autumn darkness of her hair. 'But it wasn't the whole truth. I was afraid to tell you of my love in case you didn't return it.'

'And now you are not afraid?'

'No. I have told you everything now. Nothing is hidden, so how can I hide my love? Even if you cannot return it… I believe that you do care for me. I *feel* it.'

Edmund's heart twisted. Why could he not voice it? Why was he afraid to reveal all, as she had, honestly and with courage and the beauty that was inherent in her? As if she read his thoughts, her head tilted and her eyes delved into his, greener than he'd ever seen them.

'What more do you want of me, Edmund, than my love?'

He sought the answers from deep inside him and they came, forming slowly into words, like stones making up a wall, one by one, with careful attention. 'I want to be sure of you. Of this love you confess to feel. I want to know that, no matter what comes to challenge it, it will withstand everything. I want to believe—I *need* to believe—that it is founded on truth so solid that nothing, not even falsehood, will shake it.'

'As your love for Mariette was shaken?'

He nodded. 'Perhaps it is selfish of me, or perhaps it is mere cowardice, but it is a devastating thing to have one's love treated like that. To suffer and survive it once is a miracle, and I'm not sure miracles happen a second time.'

'Yet you married me when you swore never to marry again. Was that not miraculous?'

'Marriage is not necessarily love, Isobel. If a marriage falls apart, a man's heart can still be whole.'

'And so can a woman's.'

He held her gaze. 'Yours, for instance?'

'I am willing to find out…if you are?' She reached out and touched his hand where it lay on his knee, and just that light touch began to seep into his blood. 'Before you… I was anything *but* willing to risk my heart on such an uncertain thing as love. And now…'

'Now?' he prompted, his hand warming beneath hers, his heart beginning to warm too. 'To say you are willing is one thing, Isobel. It is like a man saying he will march into battle but when that battle comes, he may turn and run.'

'Like the Earl of Wiltshire?'

It was said with a smile and, for a moment, it lightened everything. 'Even so,' Edmund smiled back.

'But *you* don't run, do you, Edmund? When you say you will march, you march. When you say you will fight, you fight. You do not flee from uncertainty, from danger, even from death. So why run from love?'

'Because love is far more dangerous than any foe I've ever faced on the battlefield.'

She nodded her head slowly. 'I can believe that, now I know how powerful and precious love is. I also faced foes when we married, when I chose to surrender myself— not just my body but my whole self—to you. In vows in Tewkesbury Abbey, in deed on our wedding night, and at every moment since then. Every time we have touched, or looked, or kissed, I have surrendered, and willingly, a little part of myself. Now I find myself wholly and forever yours.'

Taking her hand, he lifted it and enclosed it in both of his. 'Do you mean that, Isobel?'

'Yes, I do.' Her fingers curled tightly around his. 'I didn't betray you, Edmund, you must believe that, even if you cannot believe anything else. I never will betray you in any way. My love for you is unshakable, and you can be sure of it, always, I promise. Now…it is up to you to accept it.'

Edmund's heart rose up into his throat. His breath stopped for a moment, and then something settled within him. A sense of comfort, of certainty, of joy and belief. And fear vanished, this time for ever.

'I can—and will—do more than accept it, Isobel,' he said. 'I will return it.'

Her lips parted in a gasp. 'Will you truly?'

'I have loved you since the moment I rode up to your gates and you came out to see me off again, those accursed hounds at your heels.'

She smiled, the sheen of tears making her eyes sparkle like stars. 'You hid it very well!'

'Why do you think I accepted your marriage proposal? If you hadn't proposed it, I would have done so myself, eventually—though then, of course, I was sure you would throw any such proposal back in my face.'

'I might well have done,' she said. 'I did not love you at first sight, Edmund, quite the opposite. But I grew to love you with every day that passed even though I tried not to. And now I love you with all my heart.'

Edmund lifted her hand to his mouth, kissed it. 'A heart that belongs to Lancaster?' he teased.

She shook her head. 'A heart that belongs to you, and you alone, as your Yorkist heart belongs to me.'

He bent his head towards hers, pausing an instant before capturing her lips. 'To you alone, Isobel. To you, always.'

And, as they kissed, the light coming through the little glass vial on the windowsill was not red for Lancaster, or white for York, but all the hues of the rainbow as it spilled over them and bathed them in colour.

'There is something else…'

It was Isobel who drew back first, her gaze dancing, full of a love that dazzled him but, unlike before, did not blind him now. Because now he knew it was as true as his own love was.

'What is it?'

'Your reason for marrying me—the one you gave me in the chapel that day, the one I used to persuade you to wed me—will soon be realised.'

Edmund didn't understand for a moment and then it hit him. 'You are with child?'

She nodded. 'We will have a babe in the autumn.'

He drew her into his arms, held her close, his heart so full he thought its walls would break, but in the best of ways. 'I love you, Isobel,' he said. 'Not even the stars can part us now.'

She giggled, her breath tickling his neck, the sound bubbling like a sunlit stream into his ears. 'I don't believe only in the stars any longer, Edmund. I believe also, and most firmly, in us and in our love.'

'As do I, my love,' he murmured, kissing her hair, her cheek, and finally her lips. 'As do I.'

Epilogue

March 1461

It was the twelfth day of March and Isobel was walking with Edmund in the garden, the two hounds at their heels. The day was warm, the sun bright in a cloudless sky, the world hopeful once more, even though York looked set to triumph once and for all.

Many things had happened this last month, since the battle at Mortimer's Cross. Edmund was now Lord Deverell, his family's ancient title restored at last as reward for his loyalty to York. Owen Tudor and John Throckmorton had been executed at Hereford. A Yorkist force under the Earl of Warwick had been defeated by Lancaster at the second battle at St Albans. Margaret of Anjou's intention to enter London had been thwarted by the people themselves, forcing her to retreat north again.

And a week ago, Edward of York had been proclaimed king. His coronation would not take place yet, however, as he was shortly to set out in pursuit of the Lancastrian army and seal his control over the north of the country as well as the south, whose people were already his adoring and loyal subjects.

Thankfully, Edmund would not be riding north but was

tasked with the duty of guarding the western borderlands. Old Owen Tudor was dead but his son, Jasper, was alive and still at liberty, his ambitions unquenched. The deposed king Henry, and his young heir, were at liberty too, urged on by the ambitious former Queen Margaret to regain the throne, and so the war still went on.

But not at Mistlecote. Here peace reigned in every corner, and no matter what happened outside the walls, Isobel knew that peace would never be broken.

As they passed beneath the apple trees where'd she'd plotted once with Robin and Adam, she took Edmund's hand and laid his palm on her stomach. The sun dappled through the branches, now green and alive again in this verdant and hopeful spring.

'Do you think I am a little bigger today than yesterday?'

His eyes twinkled. 'Indubitably.'

Isobel knew that she wasn't really any bigger than the day before, but she loved him all the more for wanting to please her. 'I think he—or she—must have been conceived the night Edward—King Edward now—slept under our roof,' she said a little mischievously, remembering how resistant she was to the heir of York stepping a foot inside the manor gate.

'A momentous night in that case,' he said, smiling and reading her mind. 'In more ways than one.'

Hand in hand they walked on again, accompanied by the singing of birds and the colours of the flowers that had already begun to sprout with renewed growth. She'd grown as well, not just in her belly, but in other ways too.

Since the day they'd confessed their love for each other, the day she'd told him everything, they'd become so close that now neither of them had to speak to know what was in the other's mind and heart. From once being strangers and enemies, they were now the closest of friends as well as ardent lovers, with much more than a marriage binding them together for always.

And now, sensing what was on his mind, she spoke. 'Have you received a reply from your mother yet to your invitation to visit us?'

He shook his head. 'No…perhaps there will *be* no reply.'

She squeezed his arm. 'I think there will be. She must be as eager to meet me as I am to meet her, and surely she will want to see her first grandchild when the time comes.'

'I hope so.'

'I *know* so. Since I am soon to be a mother, I'm convinced that *your* mother has missed you more than you believe and wishes to be a part of your life again, even though she be a nun.'

A brow arched. 'Have the stars told you as much?'

Isobel shook her head. 'No, they don't need to. I *know* she will come, Edmund.'

'In that case, my love,' he kissed her lips, 'it will be so. As Prioress, she has the means and the liberty to travel outside the convent walls when occasion demands. And we can visit her too, from time to time. Brewood is not so far from Mistlecote, after all.'

They walked on, the new grass that glistened beneath their feet the colour of the emerald Edmund had given her for Christmas, which gem she wore now to clasp her cloak.

'Do you think we will always be so content, Edmund?' Isobel asked. 'Even when we are old?'

He stopped and turned to her. 'Yes.'

She smiled, teasing him. 'You sound very certain of it!'

'I am.' Cupping her face, he looked deeply into her eyes. 'And I'm certain of *you*, Isobel, as certain as I am of myself. We have both waited a long time for this happiness, for this love, and now we have found it we must never doubt it, not even for an instant.'

'As if it were written in the stars?'

A smile spread across his face. 'Of course. And, since we are talking of the stars, have they told you anything interesting lately?'

Isobel wrapped her arms about his neck. 'Well, the sun has just entered Pisces and that bodes good for the sowing and planting of crops, building dykes and windmills and for selling horses, but one must not take medicine for the feet!'

His eyes darkened with desire. 'I don't care about crops or windmills or medicine for the feet, my sweet. What do the stars say about *love*?'

She drew his head down and murmured the prediction through a kiss. 'They say it is good to have intercourse, which is a part of love. Do you believe in the stars *now*, Edmund?'

Isobel predicted his answer even before it came.

'With all my heart.'

* * * * *

*If you enjoyed this story, be sure to read one of
Lissa Morgan's other captivating reads?*

Alliance with Her Renegade Knight
An Alliance with His Enemy Princess
The Welsh Lord's Convenient Bride

*And why not pick up Lissa Morgan's
The Warriors of Wales duet?*

The Warrior's Reluctant Wife
The Warrior's Forbidden Maiden

Historical Note

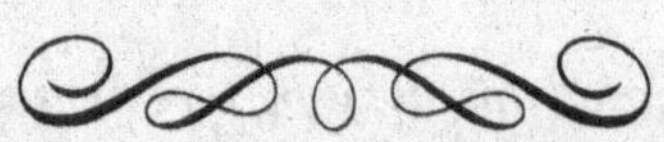

The Wars of the Roses was a long, though sporadic, conflict that began with the deposition of King Richard II in 1399. The man who usurped the throne was Henry Bolingbroke, the son of John of Gaunt, Duke of Lancaster, who was himself the third son of King Edward III. Fifty years later, in the 1450s, with a weak and possibly mentally ill king on the throne, the Lancastrian Henry VI, and the unpopularity of his queen, Margaret of Anjou, the time was ripe for the house of York to stake a claim to the throne.

This claim was led by Richard, Duke of York. Descended from Edward III's second son on his mother's side and from his fourth son on his father's side, he was one of the most powerful magnates in England. After victories over Lancaster at the first battle at St Albans in 1455 and at Blore Heath in 1459, he fled the realm following the rout at Ludford Bridge in the autumn of that same year. With him were exiled his two eldest sons and the Earl of Warwick, the Kingmaker.

Their exile was short. In the summer of 1460, Richard York returned and, although he was killed at Wakefield ther that year, along with his second son, Edmund elder son, Edward of March, came to the st striking of ways. His victory at Mortimer's Cross, and even more decisively at Towton in March 1461, won the throne for the house of York, with Edward himself as king.

In mark of the three suns—a phenomenon known as a parhelion—which appeared the day before the battle at Mortimer's Cross, Edward IV took as his emblem the Sunne in Splendour. He was a charismatic, able and popular king but he soon fell afoul of the Earl of Warwick over policy and particularly over his marriage to the Lancastrian widow, Elizabeth Woodville.

Between 1469 and early 1471, Warwick, having defected to Lancaster and in league with Edward's slippery brother George, Duke of Clarence, aided the former Queen Margaret in a rebellion against Edward. The King, and his brother Richard of Gloucester, were forced to flee to Flanders in October 1470 and Henry VI was reinstated on the throne—but only briefly.

In March 1471, Edward returned and defeated Warwick at the battle of Barnet in April, where the Earl was killed. On the fourth of May, Edward of Lancaster, son of the erstwhile king and queen, was killed at the battle of Tewkesbury, where Margaret of Anjou herself led the Lancastrian army. She was captured after the battle and eventually ransomed to the King of France. She died there in poverty in August 1482.

The deposed king Henry was also captured after Tewkesbury and imprisoned in the Tower of London, where he would perish in May 1471. Edward IV reigned until his early death at the age of forty-one in 1483, when his younger brother Richard of Gloucester took the throne, disinheriting his two young nephews, Edward's sons, who would also perish, mysteriously, in the Tower of London.

In 1485, Richard III was defeated and killed at the battle

of Bosworth by Henry Tudor, nephew of Jasper Tudor and a descendant of John of Gaunt by his mistress, Katherine Swynford. Henry married Edward IV's daughter, Elizabeth of York, thus uniting the two houses and founding the Tudor dynasty. But in the years that followed, those Yorkists who'd survived the Wars of the Roses and who had more legitimate claims to the throne than Henry VII—who based *his* claim on victory in battle—were eliminated.

The last of them, the aged Margaret Plantagenet, daughter of George of Clarence and niece of Edward IV, was executed in 1541 by Henry VIII.

Get up to 4 Free Books!

We'll send you 2 free books from each series you try
PLUS a free Mystery Gift.

Both the **Harlequin® Historical** and **Harlequin® Romance** series feature compelling novels filled with emotion and simmering romance.

YES! Please send me 2 FREE novels from the Harlequin Historical or Harlequin Romance series and my FREE Mystery Gift (gift is worth about $10 retail). I may cancel anytime by emailing ReaderServiceInfo@Harlequin.com or by calling 1-800-873-8635. If I don't cancel, I will receive 5 new Harlequin Historical books every month and be billed just $6.39 each in the U.S. or $7.19 each in Canada, or 4 new Harlequin Romance Larger-Print books every month and be billed just $7.19 each in the U.S. or $7.99 each in Canada, a savings of 20% off the cover price. It's quite a bargain! Shipping and handling is just 75¢ per book in the U.S. and $1.75 per book in Canada.* I understand that accepting the free books and gift places me under no obligation to buy anything—they are mine to keep for free no matter what I decide.

Choose one:

- ☐ Harlequin Historical (246/349 BPA G3CD)
- ☐ Harlequin Romance Larger-Print (119/319 BPA G3CD)
- ☐ Or Try Both! (246/349 & 119/319 BPA G3CE)

Name (please print)

Address

Apt. #

City

State/Province

Zip/Postal Code

Email: Please check this box ☐ if you would like to receive newsletters and promotional emails from Harlequin Enterprises ULC and its affiliates. You can unsubscribe anytime.

Mail to the Harlequin Reader Service:
IN U.S.A.: P.O. Box 1341, Buffalo, NY 14240-8531
IN CANADA: P.O. Box 603, Fort Erie, Ontario L2A 5X3

Want to explore our other series or interested in ebooks? Visit www.ReaderService.com or call 1-800-873-8635.

*Terms and prices subject to change without notice. Prices do not include sales taxes, which will be charged (if applicable) based on your state or country of residence. Canadian residents will be charged applicable taxes. Offer not valid in Quebec. This offer is limited to one order per household. Books received may not be as shown. Not valid for current subscribers to the Harlequin Historical or Harlequin Romance series. All orders subject to approval. Credit or debit balances in a customer's account(s) may be offset by any other outstanding balance owed by or to the customer. Please allow 4 to 6 weeks for delivery. Offer available while quantities last.

Your Privacy — Your information is being collected by Harlequin Enterprises ULC, operating as Harlequin Reader Service. For a complete summary of the information we collect, how we use this information and to whom it is disclosed, please visit our privacy notice located at https://corporate.harlequin.com/privacy-notice. Notice to California Residents—Under California law, you have specific rights to control and access your data. For more information on these rights and how to exercise them, visit https://corporate.harlequin.com/california-privacy. For additional information for residents of other U.S. states that provide their residents with certain rights with respect to personal data, visit https://corporate.harlequin.com/other-state-residents-privacy-rights.

HHHRLP2603

Get up to 4 Free Books!